WITCH'S MATE

ALSO BY ALICIA MONTGOMERY

THE TRUE MATES SERIES

Fated Mates

Blood Moon

Romancing the Alpha

Witch's Mate

Taming the Beast

Tempted by the Wolf

THE LONE WOLF DEFENDERS SERIES

Killian's Secret

Loving Quinn

All for Connor

THE TRUE MATES STANDALONE NOVELS

Holly Jolly Lycan Christmas

A Mate for Jackson: Bad Alpha Dads

TRUE MATES GENERATIONS

A Twist of Fate

Claiming the Alpha

Alpha Ascending

A Witch in Time

Highland Wolf

Daughter of the Dragon

Shadow Wolf

A Touch of Magic

Heart of the Wolf

THE BLACKSTONE MOUNTAIN SERIES

The Blackstone Dragon Heir

The Blackstone Bad Dragon

The Blackstone Bear

The Blackstone Wolf

The Blackstone Lion

The Blackstone She-Wolf

The Blackstone She-Bear

The Blackstone She-Dragon

This is a work of fiction. Names, characters, businesses, places, events, locales, and incidents are either the products of the author's imagination or used in a fictitious manner. Any resemblance to actual persons, living or dead, or actual events is purely coincidental.

WITCH'S MATE

BOOK 4 OF THE TRUE MATES SERIES

ALICIA MONTGOMERY

ABOUT THE AUTHOR

Alicia Montgomery has always dreamed of becoming a romance novel writer. She started writing down her stories in now long-forgotten diaries and notebooks, never thinking that her dream would come true. After taking the well-worn path to a stable career, she is now plunging into the world of self-publishing.

 facebook.com/aliciamontgomeryauthor

 twitter.com/amontromance

 bookbub.com/authors/alicia-montgomery

CHAPTER ONE

Lara Chatraine tapped her foot impatiently in front of the private elevators at the Fenrir Corporation headquarters in Midtown Manhattan. The numbers ticked down much too slowly for her taste. The maintenance department at Fenrir had sent out a memo that morning saying they were doing some upgrades and the elevators may experience slowdowns and even disruptions.

The delay was annoying and really put a crimp in her day. Though really, it was more that she was spoiled because she never had to wait for the public elevators like everyone else. Since joining Fenrir a few months ago, she had her own security badge and her palm print was already programmed into the system. These sets of elevators were for VIPs on the executive penthouse floor, their guests, and for those who worked on the 33rd floor, like her, which meant they were pretty much at her beck and call.

It was, of course, much different than the first time they had barged into Fenrir weeks ago, when she, her mother, and another witch from their coven had stormed through the doors, forcing their way inside. They were desperate to meet the CEO of Fenrir, Grant Anderson. Aside from being the head of a large multinational corporation, he was also the leader and Alpha of the New York Lycans, one of the largest and most powerful werewolf shifter clans in the world. Lycan and witch societies lived and thrived in secret, with humans blissfully unaware of their existence. The two factions were at odds with each other, though they had a tenuous truce. However, a group of former witches and warlocks, called mages, was trying to stir up trouble between the two. The mages had kidnapped her cousin Cady and had blamed a series of attacks against the New York Lycans on her.

Lara's mother Vivianne found out about the kidnapping and decided they needed the Lycans' help to rescue Cady and prevent the mages from destroying them all. When Grant's gatekeepers and security team had rebuffed their requests for a meeting, they took matters into their own hands, sneaking in and knocking out anyone who stood in their way. Lara herself had used her powers to control wind currents to literally blow his doors open. They eventually convinced the Lycans to help them find Cady.

Though they rescued Cady, the mages and their leader, Stefan, escaped. The New York Lycans and witches then decided to work together to try and stop the mages. Lara was now assisting the Lycans in trying to understand mage magic and find a way to stop them. Mages, after all, were former witches who had turned to blood magic to expand their limited powers.

She sighed and crossed her arms. Her hours at Fenrir were flexible, and today she had taken the morning off since she and her boss/best friend Dr. Jade Cross had worked late the night before. Now she was headed for a lunch date with her cousin Cady Vrost all the way at the top floor in the executive offices.

The fine hairs on the back of her neck prickled with the

sensation that told her someone was watching her. Whipping her head around, she saw a familiar figure.

"Ms. Chatraine." Liam Henney, Lycan Alpha to the San Francisco clan, nodded at her.

"Alpha," she acknowledged, then turned back to looking at the elevator doors.

Liam stepped up beside her. "Are the elevators running slow today?"

"Yeah," she confirmed. "Maintenance or something."

"Oh."

She stared up at the numbers again, which now seemed to be stuck just a couple of floors above them. From the corner of her eye, she regarded the Lycan beside her. She had only met Liam Henney once before, when they had made their dramatic entrance into Grant's office. Liam was helping the New York Lycans figure out who had kidnapped Cady and eventually helped them attack the mage stronghold. She remembered him clearly, with his electric blue eyes; his handsome, pensive face his broad shoulders; and his tall, lean body she'd love to climb like a ...

Whoa.

Where did that come from? Lara's cheeks turned pink. But who could blame her? Liam was sexy and ridiculously hot. He had a handsome face with a smile that made her stomach do flip-flops, and his almond-shaped eyes turned down slightly at the corners, giving him an exotic look. His wide shoulders were encased in a well-fitting and probably expensive suit, making him look powerful and sophisticated, but it wasn't just his attire or his looks that made him stand out. Liam Henney exuded a quiet, confident power that was understated, but it was definitely *there*. Just standing next to him she felt it. He could probably make her panties melt away with the right look.

Thank God, though, right now, he just looked annoyed. His

brows were knitted as he stared up at the numbers, and Lara had to clench her fists to stop herself from reaching over and smoothing them with her fingers.

Oh God, what's wrong with me? And what is that? She wrinkled her nose. A fresh, citrusy scent tickled her senses.

Mercifully, the elevator doors opened.

"After you." Liam gestured to the elevator car.

She stepped inside. "Going to the top floor? I can get us there," she said as she put her palm on the sensor. "I'm meeting Cady for lunch."

Liam was about to place his security badge on the scanner, but he stopped. "Yes ... thank you."

As the doors closed, Liam settled right beside her and they waited in awkward silence.

1 ... 2 ... 3 ... the red numbers indicating the floors counted up.

A heartbeat passed, and they both spoke at the same time.

"So, what are you-"

"How was your-"

20 ... 21 ... 22 ...

"Go ahead," she said.

"No, you go," he said.

More silence.

30 ... 31 ... 32 ...

"I was just going to ask if you had a good trip from San Francisco."

"Ah ... yeah. I mean, I actually came from Switzerland though. Lycan business."

"Oh. Uh, nice."

49 ... 50 ... 51 ...

Lara sighed inwardly. *Was this ride ever going to end?* It was also getting warmer, for some reason. Maybe they were also fixing the air conditioning. Good thing she was wearing a sundress and a light cardigan. It wasn't exactly corporate wear, but another perk of her job was the casual dress code.

66 ... 67 ... 68 ...

There was more awkward silence, and Lara could feel his eyes boring into the side of her head. Annoyed, she looked up at him. "Can I help you, Alpha?" she asked impatiently.

Liam opened his mouth, but a sound chimed, indicating they had arrived at the top floor. *Finally!* She moved forward to leave when Liam suddenly stepped in front of her, blocking the doors.

"Alpha, what's wrong?" she asked. "Hey, what do you think you're doing?!"

Liam's hand slammed on the close button and then on the emergency stop. The lights dimmed and flickered inside the elevator, and he stepped toward her, forcing her to walk backward. His electric blue eyes glowed in the dim elevator, and her heart slammed into her sternum when she saw the hunger in his eyes.

Time seemed to slow down as the Alpha backed her up against the wall. She gasped as his large hands gripped her shoulders and his dark head swooped down. His lips stopped a millimeter away from hers, but the moment they connected, time sped up again and all heck broke loose.

She should have pushed him away, asked him what his problem was. Really, all it would have taken was a wave of her hand. But the electricity and burst of power that shot through her the moment their lips touched shocked her. Plus, Liam was a damned good kisser. His mouth was warm and delicious, seeking hers out insistently. His hands latched around her hips, lifting her up against the wall. He grabbed at her thighs, parting them and pushing the skirt of her sundress up. Moving between them, he wrapped her legs around his waist. She gasped into his mouth in surprise as her hips slammed against him. Liam was sporting an honest-to-goodness boner down there, and from the size of it, it *was* true what they said about Lycan shifters. Damn, her panties were soaked in an instant.

A soft growl emanated from his chest, and a hand buried into her strawberry blonde hair. He pulled her head back, exposing her neck and then dragging his lips down the slender column, his teeth lightly grazing the soft flesh there. Lara whimpered, pushing her hips up and grinding against his erection.

His other hand crept up the back of her thighs, grabbing her ass and giving it a squeeze as he pushed himself closer to her. She shuddered as he found the perfect spot, the ridge of his pants-covered dick bumping up against her clit.

"Fuck!" she cried out before Liam's mouth captured hers again. The yummy citrusy fragrance was all him. His delicious scent wrapped around her, assaulting her senses. Her hands snaked around him, grabbing his shoulders as she pushed against him, her body winding tight as she could feel her orgasm approaching.

"Everything okay in there?" a voice crackled through the speaker. "Sir? I think we accidentally triggered the emergency button."

Lara whimpered in disappointment as Liam slid away from her. He blinked once, breathing heavily as he turned around and pressed the call button.

"Uhm, yeah ... we're ... fine in here," he managed to reply.

"Yeah, sorry about that, sir. We've been trying to run some upgrades in the background. I apologize for the delay, sir ... you'll be on the top floor in a sec."

Silence filled the small elevator car. Lara managed to stand up on her own two legs without melting into a puddle. She smoothed down her dress and fixed her hair. Checking her reflection in the mirrored surface of the doors, she saw that her lipstick was definitely gone.

Liam turned back to her, his eyes wide and his face inscrutable. "I ..." He rubbed the back of his head with his palm. "I'm sorry ... I don't know what happened ... fuck!" He sniffed the air. "You smell like ... me," he growled and began to stalk toward her.

Lara waved her hand, and a gust of wind circled the both of them, whisking away his scent into the vent above them and making Liam stop in his tracks. "Not a problem," she said, hoping her voice didn't come out as a nervous squeak.

"Uh ... thanks," he replied. "Listen, I-"

A loud ding interrupted him, and the lights flickered on. As soon as the doors opened, Lara sprinted out to the floor, getting away from him as quickly as possible.

What the heck happened? She shook her head.

"Oh, hey!" a familiar female voice called. Ignoring it, she kept walking toward Cady's office.

"Liam, sorry, er ... we had an emergency," a male voice said.

"What? Oh, yeah ... no worries, Grant."

"Lara!" Fast-paced footsteps caught up to her, and a hand grabbed her by the arm. "Hold up! Whatever you do, *do not* go into Cady's office unless you have some sort of forgetting potion handy! In which case, you're gonna have to share some with me!"

Lara whipped around to face Alynna, Grant Anderson's sister. "Don't what? Oh, hey Alynna." She greeted her with a nervous laugh. "I was ... uhm ... just going to see Cady." *Yeah. That's it. That's what I was doing. I totally wasn't making out with Liam Henney in the elevator.*

"Yeah ... uhm, about that." The pretty brunette Lycan linked her arm around Lara's. "Why don't you step into my office first. Jeez, are you okay? You seem flushed. And what happened to your lipstick?"

"I was ... er ... I got super hungry on the way here and scarfed down a bear claw," Lara said quickly. "There was something wrong with the elevator. I think they shut down the air-conditioning ... or something."

"Oh yeah, they've been doing those upgrades. Maintenance assured me they would fix it today."

"Is Cady okay?" Lara asked as they walked past Cady's office.

Alynna gave her a sheepish look. "Uh, yeah, about that ... this is really awkward, but, well, Grant and his lady friend decided to have a bit of afternoon delight in the office," she explained. "Unfortunately, they must have released some super Alpha pheromones or something and the entire floor got ... er ... carried away."

Lara's eyes went wide. "So ..."

"Yeah, *everyone* got carried away," Alynna emphasized. "Cady's door is still locked. And Nick's in there with her," she added, referring to Nick Vrost, Cady's Lycan husband and Grant's second-in-command.

"Oh," Lara said thoughtfully. She guessed that the moment the elevator doors had first opened, Liam was affected by whatever Lycan sex voodoo was going around. A part of her was glad he didn't just randomly kiss and feel up women in elevators as a habit.

Alynna opened the door to her office and led her in. "Yeah, sorry about that, but it was probably a good thing you guys didn't arrive a second earlier. Who knows what you guys might have seen."

Lara gave a nervous laugh. "Uh, yeah, true."

"So, why don't you take a seat?" Alynna motioned to the

couch. "I'll send Cady a message and tell her to come here when they're ... done."

"Thanks, Alynna," Lara said as she sat down. She looked around the plush office, trying not to notice how the other woman was picking up items that had fallen off the desk.

She sighed inwardly. *That certainly explained Liam's actions in the elevator.* Not that she thought he would suddenly be overcome with lust for her for no reason. However, there was no mistaking the burst of power she had felt when their lips touched. She had felt a similar, though weaker version of it before. It was a few months ago when Cady and Nick's first touch marked them as True Mates.

Lara's stomach clenched. *No, it couldn't be.* There must be some mistake, a glitch in the universe. She and Liam Henney couldn't possibly be True Mates. Because if they were, then she would have to do everything she could to prevent him or anyone else from finding out.

CHAPTER TWO

D*irty, filthy Lycans ... you deserve death and destruction ...*

The ominous words were written in blood on the wall of the two-story home in the Sunset District. Liam Henney shook his head and rubbed his face with his palms.

"Alpha." Takeda Matsumoto, his Beta, called his attention from across the room.

"What is it, Takeda?" Liam turned to the other man, who was descending the stairs. Takeda's face was as unmoving as stone, but Liam could smell and feel the anger and tension from his second-in-command.

"We've discovered three bodies in the bedroom. Two are confirmed to be one of ours. Alfred and Maeve Williams."

"And the third?"

"Possibly the murderer," Takeda replied, his lips pursing into a thin line. "This is bad."

"Tell me about it." Liam looked up at the bloody words again. "Let's walk through this again before the SFPD get here."

"Right." Takeda cleared his throat. "Alfred and Maeve Williams, aged 30 and 28, respectively. Both Lycans from the

Bay Area. Married four years ago. They have one daughter, two years old. Jillian."

Liam's face was a grim mask, thinking of the loss. Although San Francisco was one of the largest Lycan clans in the United States, there were only about 150 Lycans in total in the Bay Area. "Where is the pup?"

"She's safe, with Maeve's stepsister."

"And our suspect?"

The Beta shook his head. "We don't know, Alpha. He's not Lycan. He stabbed both victims in the heart while they were asleep, then carved these strange symbols on their bodies. Then he used their blood to write that message on the wall, then killed himself by slashing his neck. Based on the words, could he be a mage?"

For nearly a year now, the magic-wielding mages had been a thorn in the Lycans' side. As former witches who used blood magic, the mages had only one agenda: destroy all Lycans. Their attacks had mostly been concentrated around the New York clan, but it seems they were now expanding to include their allies.

"Possibly." Liam's brows knitted. "But something's not quite right."

"You feel it, too?"

"Yes," Liam said with a nod.

"I told you we should not have gotten involved with the New York clan's-"

"Enough, Takeda," Liam snapped. He and Takeda had butted heads over this for the last few months now. He sighed. "You know it was the right thing to do."

The other man shook his head. "Still, we would not have been a target if we did not join New York in the fight against the mages."

"Perhaps not now, but eventually we would have," Liam reasoned.

"But this ..." Takeda shook his head. "This is unacceptable, Alpha."

"I know." Liam's mouth was set in a tight line. "We will find out who did this. And they will pay."

Takeda nodded in agreement. "I'll have our men clean up the message and let Captain Wu know when his officers can come in."

"Good." Liam glanced at the bloody message one last time.

"If there's anything else ..."

"No, that will be all. I'll head back home and contact the High Council as soon as possible." Liam nodded to Takeda and headed out of the house, where his driver was waiting for him.

"Let's go back to Gracie," Liam instructed the driver. Located in Pacific Heights, Gracie Manor was his home, where the San Francisco Alphas had resided for generations.

"Yes, Mr. Henney," the driver replied as he started the engine.

Liam leaned back into the plush leather seats of the Bentley, rubbing his temples as he tried to soothe away the headache starting to form there. The car pulled away from the street, and Liam absentmindedly watched the scenery pass outside the window. As they drove through Golden Gate Park to head north, he sat in silence, thinking about the events of the morning.

Maeve Williams' stepsister Cara was dropping off her son at her sister's for the day, when she had discovered the writing on the wall and, unfortunately, the bodies in the bedroom. She rushed to check on the baby and was relieved to find Jillian safely sleeping in her crib. Knowing that it had to be Lycan-related, she called the Alpha's office and not 911.

Liam immediately rushed to the Williams' house. He was Alpha of one of the most powerful Lycan clans in the U.S., after all, and he took his role seriously. The loss of Alfred and Maeve was grave, but he knew there was more to come. The mages had laid low for a while, but now it looked like they had gathered their forces. This was the first time they had struck against another clan aside from New York and New Jersey. Two dead, one precious pup orphaned. He would have to inform the Lycan High Council and perhaps make another trip to New York sooner than expected.

The thought of New York brought memories flooding back into his brain of the last time he was there. *Lara.* The name had been on his mind for weeks, and if he was honest, thoughts of her consumed whatever free time he had.

It still seemed like a dream, what had happened between them in that elevator. He wasn't sure what took over him, but in an instant it was like something in him snapped. Liam was normally reserved and polite, but in that moment, he wanted no one else but Lara. Her delicious scent—like strawberries and champagne—suddenly filled his senses and he couldn't help it. He wanted to kiss those luscious lips and feel those curves pressed up against him. So he did. He grabbed her, kissed her, made her moan in just that one moment. But then, the spell was suddenly broken.

God, he felt awful afterwards. He had practically assaulted her, even if she was a willing participant. He wanted to talk to her, explain (or try to), but she ran away like a scared animal.

Weeks later, he still couldn't stop thinking about her, the taste of her mouth, and the softness of her body and curves. The whole encounter had left him confused, and he wasn't sure exactly how to get in contact with Lara. He couldn't ask Alynna or Cady for her number, as that would make them suspicious. He had hoped he would bump into her at some point, but with his busy schedule, taking care of clan business, working for the family business, and building up his own startup company, he hadn't had time to make another trip to New York. He didn't even make it to Grant's wedding. But since that day in the elevator, all he could think about was Lara Chatraine.

What would he do if he did see her again? He wasn't quite sure.

CHAPTER THREE

M onday mornings were usually slow on the 33rd floor lab, at least for Lara. However, today was probably not one of those Mondays. It was about 8 a.m., and according to the log by the entrance, Jade Cross had arrived an hour earlier. Another employee, a lab assistant, had clocked in thirty minutes after her. Lara sighed, scanned her ID card, and looked around the room for her friend.

The pretty brunette scientist was already in her labcoat, her glasses perched on her nose, and was standing in front of a large screen, peering at a bunch of numbers and calculations Lara could not decipher. She paused to hand some files to one of their human assistants, Milly, and to gave her some curt instructions. The young assistant, eager to please her boss, nodded excitedly and left.

As soon as the human was out of earshot, Lara spoke. "I wanted to ask you about something," Lara began, shoving a very large cardboard cup in front of the other woman.

"Is that—" The Lycan scientist reached out, making grabby hands at her, the calculations momentarily forgotten.

"Triple shot, extra hot latte," the witch declared.

"Thank God!" Jade grabbed the cup and took a sip, her eyes closing in pleasure. Properly caffeinated, she turned back to Lara. "Now, what did you want to ask me?"

"True Mates."

"What about them?"

"So ... what's that about?"

Jade paused and took another sip of coffee. "What do you want to know?"

Lara chewed her lip. "Uhm, I was just curious. Like, is that a sure thing?"

"What do you mean sure thing?" Jade put the cup down and turned back to the screen, her light green eyes darting over the display.

Lara wasn't offended by her friend's flippancy. She knew Jade well enough to be aware the scientist could multitask like the devil. The young Lycan was brilliant, a genius really, but sometimes she could be dense when it came to things that didn't involve science. "I mean, let's say you found your True Mate ..." Lara continued.

"Me? Or you mean a hypothetical Lycan?"

"Yeah. I mean, okay, let's say a hypothetical Lycan." Lara sighed. "Like, are True Mates required to marry? Would there be consequences if they didn't? Would they have seven years of bad luck or something if they or one of them decided not to be with the other?"

"No, not really," Jade began. "I mean, no one really knows the exact explanation for True Mates. Some say it's all magic and fate, and others theorize it's all science, a biological imperative that makes all living things seek out the best possible mate to produce offspring." She paused and looked back at the screen, then reached out to swipe her fingers back and forth across the table of numbers.

"Which do you believe?"

"Evidence shows that True Mates don't necessarily have to marry or be together. Take the Alpha's parents, for example. Michael Anderson and Callista Mayfair weren't True Mates, yet they had a perfectly healthy and normal Lycan child, the old-fashioned way." She wrinkled her nose delicately. "Of course, Michael met his True Mate, Amanda Chase, later on, while he was still married to Callista, and they had Alynna. So, who's to say it wasn't fate?"

"But you don't believe in fate, do you?" Lara asked hopefully.

Jade sighed. "I don't have enough evidence to believe in fate one hundred percent. But I know I believe in what evidence we do have. Alynna's DNA test proved she was 100% Lycan even if her mother was human. The biological system of True Mates guarantees offspring, a rare occurrence since ordinary Lycans have such a hard time reproducing. The first coupling between True Mates always produces a pup."

Lara's eyes grew wide. "Really?" That part she had only heard of but never confirmed.

"Yes, at least from all the evidence we have. Except for physical barriers, nothing can stop the conception."

"Super Lycan sperm!" Lara giggled.

Jade gave a rare smile. "Yeah. You can say that the Super Lycan sperm always finds its way."

"But, let's say ... if True Mates never, uhm, produced offspring, it wouldn't be the worst thing, right? Like they wouldn't be cursed or anything?"

"I don't ... think so," Jade replied. "I mean, it really would be up to both parties, right? You can't exactly force a mating between two people if neither wanted it. But then, from the anecdotal evidence we do have, True Mates seem to be naturally drawn to each other anyway."

"Right." Lara chewed her lip. "Uh, thanks for the information."

Jade shrugged and went back to her work.

For once, Lara was glad Jade was oblivious to things aside from her work and wasn't curious as to why she suddenly brought up True Mates. While Jade's answers weren't absolute, it gave her some hope. Of course, she wasn't certain that Liam and she were True Mates. It could have been the True Mate Alpha pheromones that Grant Anderson and his wife had apparently released that day she and Liam had their crazy make out session in the elevator.

She supposed the only way to confirm would be to have his baby, but that wasn't happening. Uh, no. No sir. Never. Not even if he flashed her that handsome smile. Or touched her with his sexy hands. Or kissed her with those ...

"Arghh!" She shook her head. Jade sent her strange look. "Uhm, sorry. I was thinking about ... something bad."

The scientist shrugged and went back to her data.

Dammit. What happened in the elevator shook her very core. Made her want to forget everything and find Liam Henney and jump his bones. But no. She couldn't. Not when there was so much at stake. The pit in her stomach clenched. She would not cause the death of another man.

CHAPTER FOUR

"Cheers to our success!" Victoria Chatraine declared as she raised her wine glass.

"Excellent job," Stefan declared, lifting his own glass. "Finally, our labors have proven successful. Daric," he called to the tall, Viking-like warlock across the room, "come join us and celebrate our success."

"Yes, Master." Daric nodded and strode to them. Victoria gave him a coy glance as she handed him a glass of red wine.

"Are you not happy, Daric?" Stefan asked. "We've finally had a victory over the Lycans!"

"We've won a battle, Master," Daric said and took a sip. "The war is far from over."

"Daric, darling," Victoria cooed and cozied up to him, "relax a little, enjoy this victory. After all, we couldn't have done it without you."

"Indeed, my protégé," Stefan added. "Your work and efforts have brought us far, much farther than I thought! Those Lycans will not know what hit them!"

"And what we have in store." Victoria clinked her glass with Daric's.

With one swig, Daric finished the glass and set it on the table. "I'm afraid I'm quite tired. I'm going to rest in my room." With a nod, he left the two alone.

As soon as he was out of earshot, Victoria turned to Stefan. "Master, don't you think it's time Daric began his mage training?"

"He is getting there." Stefan's eyes narrowed. "But not yet. We need him whole still."

Victoria pouted. "Surely, you're not after him to father a Fontaine witch or warlock? We've tried that before." Her voice was bitter and acrid, a reminder of her failure to bring her own daughter into the fold and Cady's betrayal.

"No, Victoria," Stefan shook his head. "But Daric is useful as a warlock for now. Don't worry," he gave her a smile, "once he's no longer of use to me, you can have him as your pet."

Victoria gave him a gleeful smile. "I have more good news, Master," she purred. "The next phase to infiltrate the Lycans has begun."

CHAPTER FIVE

L iam arrived in New York two days later and went to see Grant Anderson as soon as he could. He wasted no time in telling the other Alpha what had happened, and he brought along some photos of the crime scene.

"This is terrible news, Liam." Grant shook his head. "You have my deepest sympathies."

"Thank you, Grant," Liam replied.

"The pup?" There was also a photo of the little girl, Jillian. She looked like an angel in the picture, especially with her blonde, curly hair; smiling blue eyes; and chubby cheeks.

"Maeve's stepsister and her husband have agreed to raise her," Liam said. "She will want for nothing, of course, and when the time comes, we will teach her what she needs to know about being a Lycan."

"Good."

"What else do you know about the murders?" Nick Vrost, Grant's Beta, asked. His face was usually stoic and unreadable, but currently his brows were drawn together in a frown.

"Not much else." Liam motioned to the photograph on

Grant's desk. On top of the pile was the message written in blood.

Nick glanced at the picture. "And how did they die?"

"Stab wounds to the heart. But before that, he carved strange symbols into their bodies, then used their blood to write the message." Liam shook his head. "I don't know what this means."

"The murderer ... he was probably a mage," Grant assumed.

"Right. That's what we're thinking," Liam said. "But something about the whole thing doesn't add up."

"Like what?"

"Well, why them? There are far more powerful members of the clan, just as accessible and unprotected. Alfred and Maeve were everyday people, worked normal jobs, had a mortgage and a kid. And why would the murderer kill himself afterwards? Why wouldn't he just stop at killing the Williams?"

Grant leaned back in his chair and clasped his hands over his middle. "True. Something about it doesn't seem right."

"There are certainly more questions than answers," Nick said.

"What steps have you taken so far?" Grant asked.

"Well, I've already alerted the High Council. But it's been two days, and I haven't heard back, aside from their condolences and their assurances that they will get to the bottom of this. I've had the entire clan on alert and ordered extra security for our clan members and families."

"And the investigation into the murders?"

"We have people inside SFPD. Officially, the investigation will conclude that it was a break-in by a disturbed individual. We cleaned up the message, of course, but we couldn't cover up the symbols on the bodies."

"Good." Grant nodded.

"But it's not enough," Liam said in a grave voice. "Grant, I want to be more involved in this. I can't just stand by and watch as the mages slaughter us. We need to put a stop to them, before they do something worse. Let me help."

Grant and Nick looked at each other. The New York Alpha then turned to Liam. "Are you serious about this?"

Liam nodded. "Yes. I want to get more involved. The High Council obviously isn't putting a priority on this. I'll put my other projects on hold if necessary. I want justice for my people."

"All right, then." Grant stood up. "Follow me."

Grant led Liam out of his office and to the private elevators. Nick had excused himself, saying he had other business to attend to, but agreed to meet with them later on.

The New York Alpha paused as his palm hovered over the sensor that controlled the elevator. "I'm going to show you something, but you must swear an oath to never reveal what you see to anyone."

"Of course," Liam agreed.

"Do you swear on your father's grave?" Grant said.

"Now that's a serious oath." Liam's brow wrinkled.

"Then you know what I'm about to show you is important," Grant crossed his arms.

"Fine," Liam relented. "I swear on my father's grave."

"Good." Grant pressed his hand to the sensor and tapped the button for the 33rd floor.

"Where are we going?" Liam asked.

The other man didn't answer back as the elevator car descended quickly.

"Grant, before-"

"We're here," the other Alpha announced. "Follow me."

Liam let Grant leave the car first, then followed him into the small hallway. It was no more than six by ten feet, with a set of metal doors on one end. Grant looked into a small window, and then beeps, followed by the soft whir of electronic parts emanated from the door. A retinal scanner, Liam guessed as the metal doors slid open.

"What is this place?" Liam glanced around in wonder. It looked very much like one of his laboratories at Amata Ventures, his medical startup company back in Silicon Valley. However, he didn't recognize most of the equipment, and the few pieces he did know must have cost Fenrir Corporation a fortune.

"This," Grant motioned to the high-tech lab. "is our secret weapon against the mages. We've been conducting research, trying to learn everything we can about magic and the mages."

"Research on magic?" Liam asked incredulously. "But how are you doing it? The Witch Assembly would never let Lycans near anything magical."

"Well, the Witch Assembly might not approve, but that doesn't mean we can't get our hands on some magical help." Grant led them up a set of stairs to an inner lab on a raised platform. "We've been working with a coven, Vivianne Chatraine's to be precise, to learn what we can about mages and how to stop them. I believe you've met my head scientist, Dr. Jade Cross. Let's see what they're doing today."

As the door to the inner lab opened, music blasted at full volume. The soothing sounds of Vivaldi's Spring filled the room. In the middle of the lab, two figures were bent over a table with various bottles and herbs strewn about.

"I told you I wasn't good at this," one female voice said.

"Well, I still need to see how these potions work. Now all I need to do is take this beaker and--"

Grant coughed to catch the women's attention.

"Who the fudge—Alpha!" Jade stood up straight, pushing her glasses up the bridge of her nose. "And ... uh ... Alpha." She turned to Liam, her eyes wide with surprise. "Music, stop," she said and Vivaldi's strings immediately ceased. "Ah, the voice assistant works perfectly, Lara." She grinned at the witch. Grant coughed again, and she blushed. "Uh, so, Alphas, what brings you here?"

Beside her, Lara had gone very still. "Yeah, what are you doing here?" she huffed, her eyes trained on Liam.

"Sorry to disturb your work, Dr. Cross," Grant apologized.

"Yes, well, we were doing some work with herbs and po—" She clamped her mouth shut, then looked at Liam with a frown.

"Yes, right," Grant began. "There's something you need to know. There's been another attack, you see ..."

Grant began to explain to Dr. Cross what he was doing there, but Liam didn't hear a word. As soon as he realized who the other person in the lab was, Liam's eyes zeroed in on Lara Chatraine. *What was she doing here?* The redheaded witch was seemingly transfixed by something on the far wall, opposite where he was standing.

"... Liam here will give you more details, Dr. Cross," Grant finished. "Liam ... Liam?"

The San Francisco Alpha shook his head. "Er, yes. I mean, there's been an incident." Liam walked over to Jade and relayed to Dr. Cross what he had already told Grant earlier. He also took out the pictures from the crime scene and placed them on the table.

A soft gasp came from behind him. The scent of strawberries and champagne was unmistakable as Lara pushed forward, her eyes landing on the gruesome photos. Her pretty face twisted in sadness, and her mouth fell open as her green eyes flitted across the photos.

"Yes, it could be the work of mages," Jade said as she picked up the picture of the symbols carved onto one of the bodies. "What do you think, Lara?"

The young witch nodded. "Those symbols ... runes ... I recognize some of them."

"Lara Chatraine has been helping us with our research," Grant explained. "In exchange, we share all our data with her coven."

Liam looked over to Lara, and she stared back at him with luminous green eyes. Had he never noticed how beautiful they were before?

Mine.

Liam startled. His wolf. The animal inside him was present all the time, of course, but it was usually quiet. The wolf only warned him when there was danger. It had never made declarations before. *His? Theirs?*

"What would you need to know to determine what happened, Dr. Cross?" Grant's voice interrupted Liam's reverie.

"Well, I would have to examine the crime scene and possibly the bodies," she said matter-of-factly. "All of the bodies. And take some samples."

"I have some sway with the San Francisco Police Department, but I can't convince them to ship three bodies to New York, I'm afraid," Liam said.

Jade thought for a moment. "Then I'll need to go to San Francisco. Maybe Lara should come along, too; she might be able to sense something."

"No!" Lara protested.

Something in her voice, her objection to being in his territory, made Liam's wolf gnash and claw at him.

"Sounds like an excellent idea," Liam blurted out. "I grant you both permission to come to San Francisco. We should leave today." That calmed the wolf down somewhat.

"Alpha," Lara began, deliberately turning her body away from Liam and toward Grant. "I don't think my mother would approve. This isn't in our agreement."

"Well, ask her then," Grant began. "But I agree. You should

leave at once and examine the crime scene and the bodies before the SFPD conducts any further investigations."

"I agree, too." Jade nodded.

"But-"

"I would really appreciate any help you can give." Liam pushed at the pile of photos, the one of Jillian slipping out and falling to the floor. "We want to give our people the justice they deserve and prevent this from happening to anyone else."

Lara bent down and picked it up, her eyes going wide. "Did she ...?"

"No, she survived," he said. "But the justice would be for her, too. For her parents."

The witch straightened her shoulders and cleared her throat. "I'll speak to my mother."

"Thank you," Liam said warmly. He took the photo from her hand, and their fingers brushed together briefly. A small jolt of electricity shot through him, and he almost dropped the photo.

"Good." Grant turned to Jade. "The jet will be ready when you are."

"We can take mine," Liam offered. "It's not as luxurious as yours, but the ride isn't too long."

"Whichever works for you. I can send mine to bring them back, if you want. My admin, Jared, will work it out with your office." Grant motioned to the door indicating that they should leave.

"I'll see you later then, Dr. Cross." Liam nodded to the witch. "Lara." He turned and followed Grant out.

———

Lara let out a breath as soon as Liam left the lab. His scent, his presence, and everything about him wound her up tight like a spring. Just two days ago she had vowed to forget about him, and now she was possibly on her way straight into the wolf's den.

She let out a sigh, thinking about those poor Lycans and their orphaned daughter. Seeing the little girl, looking so innocent, brought out her natural protective instincts.

Deep down inside, all witches were nurturers and caregivers. The power Mother Nature gave them also came with a responsibility and a need to care for others. As a blessed witch with extra powers, the need was stronger than in most, and her every instinct screamed at her to make sure the child was all right. She felt guilty, too, because she had been rude to Liam when she saw him. She was embarrassed and surprised by his presence. What was he doing here? Overall, she had been unnerved by the Lycan invading her space.

But when she saw the photos and heard what happened, her heart broke, especially when she saw the brief flash of grief on his face. It must be hard being Alpha, having people depend on you to be strong. She wanted to reach out to him and soothe his pain away.

"Are you going to call Vivianne?" Jade asked, her voice hopeful. "If we leave tonight, we could maybe examine the bodies by tomorrow morning."

Lara shook her head mentally. Only Jade Cross would be excited about examining dead bodies. "I suppose." Fishing her phone out of her pocket, she dialed her mother's number.

"Lara, what is it?" Vivianne Chatraine's voice was full of concern. The blood bond between them was strong, and Vivianne knew when something was bothering her daughter.

"I'm fine, mother," Lara replied. "I'm here with Jade on speakerphone. The Alpha had a request for us." She relayed the events to Vivianne, keeping her fingers crossed and hoping she would object to her going to San Francisco or at least tell her she didn't need to be there.

"I'm afraid there aren't any witch covens near San Francisco to help you, Jade," Vivianne said. "I believe the nearest one is outside Los Angeles. Lara, you will have to go with her. You should go anyway to help protect Jade in case the mages are nearby."

"I don't think I'll be in any danger, Vivianne," Jade said. "But yes, I would feel better if Lara went with me. She might be able to see or sense something I can't."

"It's settled, then," the older witch declared.

"Mom, I need to speak with you for a moment. I'll take you off speaker phone."

Jade nodded at Lara and turned back to her computer, checking on their data. Lara went to her workstation for some privacy.

"Okay, Mother." Lara settled into a chair. She had been thinking of calling her mother since her talk with Jade the other day. Liam's visit today and her upcoming trip to San Francisco just cemented a decision she'd been struggling with. She took a deep breath. "I just wanted to let you know I've been thinking it's time."

"Time for what, darling?"

"Time for me to find a partner. A husband, I mean."

There was a short silence on the other end of the phone. "Lara, I don't know what to say. I mean, of course, if that's what you want—"

"Yes, it is," she said curtly. "I mean, it's time, right? And if I get married within the year, maybe you'll have a grandchild by next spring."

"Darling, don't do it for me. Or the coven."

"I just want what you and Dad have, Mother," she said. "Your covens matched you guys up, right?"

"Yes, but it wasn't an arranged marriage. You know that, right?"

"I do, and I'm not asking for that. I just wanted you to know I'm ready to meet eligible and suitable men—er, *warlocks*," she emphasized.

"All right darling, I'm sure you know your own mind. I have a few potential candidates you might want to consider."

She bit her lip. "Great."

"But I suppose that can all wait until after you come back from San Francisco. Just think about it, and let me know if you're still sure after your trip."

"I'm very sure, Mother," she replied, trying to sound confident. "Please, contact any candidates you think are suitable."

"It just seems like a hasty decision," Vivianne said. "I'm happy you want to finally find someone, but you don't have to do this now. Not if you're afraid, especially with what happened to Jonathan-"

"I'm not, Mother, I swear," Lara cut her off. The name brought back memories, painful ones. She hadn't even uttered his name in years, yet she could feel the vice tightening around her heart.

"Very well, darling." Her mother sighed. "I'll talk to you soon."

"Bye, Mother," she said before she hung up. *I guess I'm going to San Francisco.*

CHAPTER SIX

L ara had gone straight home to her studio apartment on 3rd Avenue and packed enough clothes for a two-day trip. She was hoping it would be less, but it didn't hurt to be prepared. As she closed her suitcase, she spied something green in her closet. She realized it was a dress she had bought some time ago—a green, vintage-style dress she had found in a thrift shop in Chelsea. The dress was quite modest and came down to her knees, with a square neckline and capped sleeves. But the color—a deep emerald green—was amazing with her skin tone. She hesitated for a moment and then grabbed the dress off the hanger and stuffed it into her suitcase. Maybe she and Jade would be able to go out one night, who knew? It would save her the trouble of having to buy a new dress.

She changed into some travel clothes, and soon a car picked up her and Jade (who actually lived a block away from her) and drove them to the private airstrip just outside New York City.

"Oh my," she gasped as they approached the luxurious private jet waiting on the tarmac. "I've never been on a private plane before," she whispered to Jade. "I've only flown coach."

Jade shrugged. "It's not too bad. There's just more room to walk around and less people."

The driver opened the door and helped them out of the car. They walked toward the stairs, where Liam was already waiting for them as he stood beside another familiar figure.

"Oh, Liam," Alynna Westbrooke said with a laugh as she swatted his arm playfully. "You're terrible, you know that?!"

Liam sent the pretty green-eyed brunette a warm smile, one that sent a stab of jealousy through Lara. "I swear, Alynna, it's true!"

"Doesn't mean you're still not terrible!" Alynna flashed her own smile. "Oh, Jade! Lara! You're here. Sorry, we were just reminiscing about old times."

"Yes, I'm sure you were," Lara replied coolly. "What are you doing here?" Alynna Westbrooke was already married to her True Mate, and with a kid to boot, yet here she was flirting with another man. *The nerve!*

Alynna raised a brow. "I missed Liam," she replied.

"Missed him?" Lara tried her best to keep her voice even.

Alynna gave her a syrupy sweet smile. "Missed him at the office, I mean. He was going to sign some papers for me, so I thought I'd run after him." She turned to Liam. "Since you guys were running a little late, we were just talking about old times. Liam here is a terrible person, watch out for him." She winked at the Alpha, which only made him smile.

"Well, we should be on our way. Say hi to Alex and Mika for me, Alynna," Lara flipped her hair and stomped over to the stairs leading up to the jet. She grabbed the railing, but missed a step, causing her to fly back. She closed her eyes, bracing herself for the fall, but instead found herself cradled in a pair of strong arms.

"Careful now." Liam's low baritone whispered in her ear. "Those steps have been known to kill people." His arms were wrapped around her middle in a tight embrace. Her heartbeat sped up as that delicious citrusy scent of his curled around her.

His voice sent shivers down her spine. "Put me down, please."

"As you wish," he said, releasing her to her feet.

"Uhm, thanks." She scrambled up the stairs, willing the blush on her face to go away. The steward waiting for her inside the jet greeted her by name.

"Ms. Chatraine? My name is Gage. I'll be your steward for the flight. Champagne?" He offered her a tray with three flutes of the bubbly liquid.

"Thanks!" She grabbed two of the glasses and made her way to a seat at the back. After placing her purse down on the floor beside her, she sat back and gulped down both glasses.

Jade followed soon after, taking the seat across from her and placing her own glass of champagne on the table between them. "Are you okay?"

"Me?" Her voice was high-pitched. "I'm fine."

Jade crossed her arms. "You didn't seem fine."

"I said I'm-" She paused, glancing outside the window as Alynna hugged Liam. Taking Jade's champagne flute, she downed the liquid in one swallow. "Fine. Dandy."

The Lycan narrowed her eyes at her and opened her mouth to speak, but Gage interrupted them.

"Ladies, the Captain says we're cleared to take off in ten minutes. I can't serve you any more drinks or food for the moment, but I'll have dinner ready right after we take off."

The girls thanked him, and as they buckled their seat belts, Liam entered the plane and took the seat diagonally across from Lara.

Ugh, I get to see his stupid head the whole flight, she thought. *And his stupid, handsome face.*

"Ladies," Liam greeted as he buckled his own seatbelt.

"Hope you're both comfortable. We should be there in about five hours. I have work to do, but please make yourselves at home."

Stupid, handsome, rich face.

———

For about the hundredth time, Liam tried to look away from Lara's gorgeous, sleeping face. And for the hundredth time, he failed. Minutes after they took off, she reclined her chair, leaned back and promptly fell asleep, leaving him to admire her creamy porcelain skin, delicate features, and long waves of golden red hair tumbling down her shoulders. It was a good thing Jade was facing the other way or she would have noticed how he couldn't keep his eyes off the witch.

It was pure torture. Lara had been in his thoughts for weeks now, and here she was, less than five feet away from him. He wanted her, dreamed of what she would be like in bed, and dirty thoughts filled his mind. Having her in his arms for just a moment on the tarmac had been the icing on the cake, sending his inner wolf into a frenzy and his body responding. God, he wanted her. Even Alynna could tell.

"So, Lara ..." Alynna flashed him a knowing smile.

"What about her?" He gave her an innocent look.

"Hmm ... nothing ... just interesting how, you know, she took off like that?"

"Like what?"

She laughed. "Oh, you dense man! She was jealous! Of me!"

"Jealous?" He sounded incredulous. While they were in the lab, Lara had treated him like nothing had happened between them, and for a moment he thought maybe it had all been a hallucination.

"Yeah, as in the green-eyed monster! Well, you are a catch, so it's only normal she'd have a crush on you," Alynna said.

"Crush? On me?" He was still reeling from the other woman's words. Lara, normally friendly and nice, did seem awfully cold to Alynna.

"Lara's a lovely girl," Alynna patted his arm, "just ... you know, don't break her heart. There's more to her than she lets on."

If you only knew, Alynna, he had thought to himself. Well actually, it was better she didn't know. At first, Liam had decided that staying away from Lara would be the best thing. But now knowing Lara possibly wanted him, too, beyond that encounter in the elevator, gave him some hope.

His wolf licked its lips in anticipation of a hunt.

CHAPTER SEVEN

The flight to San Francisco was smooth and uneventful. Lara closed her eyes and pretended to sleep. Her stomach growled furiously, and she was glad Gage was attentive, offering her dinner as soon as she "woke" up.

She glanced over at Liam once or twice as she ate, watching him as he worked on his laptop. It seemed strange. Normally, she went for everyday guys who worked with their hands, much like her father, but she couldn't help but feel some pride watching this particular man work.

So she maybe sort of, kind of, looked him up on the Internet. She knew he wasn't just responsible for his clan but also worked for his family business and his own startup company, Amata Ventures. His startup was working to find a treatment for lung cancer. With additional digging, she found out Liam's father had died from the disease. She admired how he wasn't just about making money but wanted to help people, too.

No, she told herself. *Forget about him.* Not only was he forbidden, but he was clearly in love with someone else. She saw how he had looked at Alynna, and she had heard the gossip around Fenrir. How he had pursued the Alpha's sister first, but she ended up choosing Alex Westbrooke instead. Their exchange at the tarmac confused Lara. Did the other woman have feelings for Liam still, despite being married to her True Mate and having his child? Alynna was naturally friendly, but she seemed extra flirtatious with Liam.

Of course, that didn't mean Liam didn't carry a torch. The hug they had exchanged had made her heart wrench with jealousy. Even if circumstances were different, or if he wasn't Alpha or a Lycan, she couldn't, *wouldn't*, be the second choice for any man. She might be settling for a marriage of convenience, but she would choose a man she could eventually learn to love and who would love her and be loyal to her for the rest of their lives.

As soon as they landed, Liam bid them goodnight, saying he had some business matters to attend to, but they were booked at a hotel not far from his home. An hour later, Lara settled into her room, tired and jet lagged, and slept soundly.

The next day, Lara put on her best "professional" outfit—a black blazer, pencil-cut skirt, heels, and a white blouse. After all, she and Jade were going to go in as academic experts to consult with the SFPD on their case. She swept her hair up in a neat chignon, leaving a few tendrils loose around her face, put on some light makeup and applied her favorite pale pink lipstick.

Liam was waiting for them in the lobby at precisely 8:30 a.m. "Good morning, Jade, Lara," he greeted. "Did you sleep well?"

"Yes, Alpha. The rooms here are amazing," Jade said. "I didn't know there was a Japanese-themed hotel in San Francisco."

"It reminds me of my uncle's home in Tokyo," Liam explained. "I used to spend every other summer there."

"Your mother's brother, correct?" Jade asked. "I remember my mother mentioning her a few times."

Liam nodded. "Yes. My cousin, Kengo, is the current Alpha of Tokyo. He's a few years older than me, though, and has had the position for about a decade now."

"Oh, shoot!" Jade bit her lip. "I left my tablet upstairs. I'll be just a second, okay?" The brunette didn't wait, but instead bolted toward the elevators.

"I'll come with-" Lara began, but the other woman waved her hand and was already in the elevator before Lara could protest. *Well, shit.*

"You look ... nice," Liam commented, his eyes roaming over her outfit.

"Thanks," she said nervously. The heat in his gaze was unmistakable. "I'm sorry about your loss," she began, hoping to steer his attention from her to the task at hand.

"Thank you," he said somberly.

"The child-"

"Jillian."

"Jillian. Is she okay? Who's taking care of her now?"

"Maeve Williams had a stepsister. She and her husband took Jillian in, and our clan will be providing for her."

Liam frowned, and Lara had to stop herself from trying to reach out and soothe him. Instead, she cleared her throat. "What's wrong with that?"

"Nothing, of course. But, well ... they're human, you see. Not that there's anything wrong with that," Liam assured her. "It's different, being raised by Lycan parents."

"I'm sure it is. But she has the support of your clan, and as you said, she'll be provided for, right?"

Liam looked comforted by her words, and Lara felt relief. The urge to ease his burden, make sure he was cared for, was sated for the moment. Being a natural caregiver, she was in tune with the needs of others, but with Liam it seemed like her instincts were on overdrive. It made her more resolved to stay away from him.

"Lara, about-"

"Got it!" Jade came barreling toward them, her tablet in hand.

Lara sighed in relief as she guessed what Liam was about to say. She had to forget about what had happened in the elevator, forget about Liam Henney.

"All right," Liam motioned to the door then. "Let's go."

———

The San Francisco Police Department's headquarters was located on 3rd Street in the Mission Bay district. The building was all glass and modern, fitting for a city known for its high-tech innovations. Liam drove them to the SFPD in a nondescript rental car, which he explained was more suitable for their cover. Thanks to the San Francisco clan's connections with the police department, they were able to secure an appointment to examine the bodies under the guise of visiting consultants to help on the murder case.

"Here you go." Liam handed them their credentials after he pulled into a parking spot. "You've got your real names, but Jade, you're a forensic expert from Scotland Yard and Lara, you're a consulting professor of ancient European mythology from NYU."

Lara checked her ID. "Wow, this looks legit."

"And who will you be?" Jade asked.

"Your driver," Liam said. "I'm joking. I'm just a concerned citizen with the right connections, bringing in experts to consult on a murder case. Chief of Police Williams knows about us and has pledged to keep our secret, and Captain Daniel Wu is actually a member of one of our oldest Alliance families. The

Wus have been our strongest human allies for generations. But aside from the two of them, no one on the force knows about us."

Liam stepped out of the car, walked to the other side, and opened the door for them. "Just follow my lead," he instructed.

The two women walked with him into the glass building. Liam looked around, and then strode over to the side where a tall Asian man in a police uniform stood.

"Captain Wu," Liam greeted.

"Mr. Henney," the other man said with a slight nod.

"This is Dr. Cross and Ms. Chatraine," Liam said in a low voice. "The consultants I told you about."

"Right." Wu nodded to the two women. "Thank you for your help. Now, just give me your IDs and I'll get your passes."

They handed him the credentials Liam had given them, and the captain walked over to the reception desk. A few minutes later, he came back with two red passes, which he handed to Lara and Jade. "Ladies, put these on and follow me." He turned to Liam, his voice low. "I'm afraid I can't let you come with them, for official reasons."

"No worries," Liam nodded. "I'll be right here."

Jade and Lara followed Captain Wu past the security barriers behind the reception desk and up a set of steps.

"We'll be going to the forensic labs. I've had the bodies of the two victims and the suspect prepared by our team, as well as any instruments you may need," Wu explained. "We've cleared the area as well, but there will be cameras watching you."

"Understood." Jade nodded. "I'll be taking pictures with my phone and notes on my tablet. Hopefully, we won't have to disturb the bodies."

They walked through several more security doors before reaching the lab. The room was sterile and nondescript, except for the three forms under white sheets laid out on the tables in the middle.

Captain Wu stood to the side. "Go ahead, do what you need to do."

A chill blasted through Lara, and the hair on her arms stood on end. She'd never been near any dead bodies, and she didn't know what to do. Jade, though, with the cold detachment ingrained through her medical training, went right to work. She put on one of the lab coats hanging to the side, latex gloves, and a surgical mask. She handed another mask to Lara, as well as her phone.

"Can you help me with the documentation?"

Lara put on the mask and then grabbed the phone. She would concentrate on trying to take photos, rather than the dead bodies on the slab.

Jade carefully pulled away the white sheets covering the bodies. Lara's hands shook slightly, but with a deep breath, she steadied them enough to start taking pictures. She concentrated on the symbols carved in their skin, taking as many detailed photos as she could.

The two bodies, one male and one female—the victims, Lara guessed—had strange runes carved into their arms and legs. The third body, a male in his 40s with thinning hair, also had similar markings, but only on his chest. She didn't know what they were exactly, but something about them seemed familiar.

The Lycan scientist, meanwhile, worked with efficiency, examining the bodies with clinical objectivity and making notes. When she was done, she put the white cloths back over them.

"Hmmm ... well." Jade thought for a moment. "The suspect is definitely human, as far as I can tell." She turned to Wu. "Have we identified him?"

"Yeah. His name's Marshall Aimes, from Arizona," Wu supplied. "He was a construction worker based in Phoenix, and according to his foreman, he stopped coming in to the site about two weeks ago. No one had heard from him since."

"So, Mr. Aimes disappears for two weeks, then somehow makes his way to San Francisco to kill the Williamses? What's the connection between the suspect and the victims? Or motives?"

Wu shook his head. "None that we know of. As far as we can tell, it almost seems random."

"I don't believe in coincidences," Jade declared as she took off her mask. She turned to Lara. "Can you sense anything?"

With a deep breath, Lara closed her eyes, willing her senses to open. From the moment they had stepped into the room, her instincts had been telling her something was wrong. But to know more, she would have to open herself up. Magic always left some traces, and most witches would be able to feel any residual magic when it was used. Around the bodies, Lara could feel remnants of magic. It was very faint, but definitely present.

"I can't explain it," she whispered. "But magic ... it's here, and it's not."

Jade wrinkled her brow. "What do you mean?"

"It's like ... there was definitely magic involved, but it's not coming from any of them. All types of magic leave some signature or trace, but I can definitely tell no one wielded it."

"Then where did it come from?"

A pit in Lara's stomach began to form, and her temple began to throb. She reached toward Marshall Aimes' body, drawing the sheet back. There were three symbols carved into his chest, two smaller ones on the sides and one large one in the middle. She didn't recognize the small ones, but since the first moment she had seen the middle one, something had been niggling at her mind. The image flashed in her mind—a triangle with a forked symbol inside. She had seen it before, when she had been studying runes with her mother.

"I think ... oh God!" She lurched forward, covering her mouth. She knew exactly what it was.

"Lara!" Jade exclaimed. "What's wrong?"

"I feel ..." Lara swayed, feeling her knees buckle. "I need to get out of here!"

The witch turned around, going as fast as her jelly-like legs would take her. She blasted past the security doors, retracing her steps as best she could until she reached the lobby of the SFPD headquarters. Air. Her lungs craved air. She ran for the doors.

"Lara!" a voice called behind her. Warm hands wrapped around her upper arms and spun her around. "Lara, what's wrong?"

Slowly she raised her head, her gaze colliding with electric blue eyes. "Liam ..." she whispered, her lids feeling heavy, her limbs limp.

"Jesus, you're shivering!"

Strong arms wrapped around her, and he pulled her against his chest. Weakly, she laid her head on him, the warmth of his body seeping into her own.

"It's okay. You're going to be okay," he soothed, his large hand rubbing her back.

They stood there for what seemed like an eternity, at least to Lara. His citrusy scent filled her nostrils, and she breathed in deep as it sent a comforting feeling through her.

"What's wrong? What happened?" he asked, concern in his voice.

"Liam ..." she whispered. "It's awful." She pulled away and looked up into his eyes. "I think ... I think I know what happened. To Maeve and Alfred. And to Marshall Aimes."

CHAPTER EIGHT

J
ade and Captain Wu weren't far behind Lara as they followed her down to the reception area.

"What happened?" Jade asked as she approached them.

Lara quickly disentangled herself from Liam, much to his dismay. "I can't ...," she said. "We need to talk. And get Grant and everyone back in New York on the phone. My mother, too."

"We'll go back to our headquarters. We can videoconference with New York there," Liam offered. He turned to Wu. "Thank you for your assistance, Captain."

"Anytime, Alpha," Wu replied. With a final nod to the ladies, he left.

Liam led them back to the car, and he put his assistant on speakerphone, telling her to set up the meeting with New York as soon as possible.

As he drove through the streets and hills of San Francisco, he glanced at Lara. When he saw her running across the lobby, his instincts had gone into overdrive. Seeing the look on her pale face and the tension in her body, his inner wolf had spurred him to chase after her and make sure she was all right. Fear, horror, panic. He could smell it off her in waves, masking her usual pleasant strawberries and champagne scent. He had reached out and taken her into his arms again, trying to ease her fear. She had been cold, shivering violently despite the climate-controlled atmosphere in the building. When she had looked up at him with those bright green eyes, her body relaxed against his and the ache in his gut eased, replaced by desire. He hoped she hadn't realize how aroused he was, and he was glad he was wearing loose slacks.

Now wasn't the time to think about that, and he quashed his feelings of lust. Something had genuinely scared Lara, something that had to do with the murders. The young woman remained frozen beside him in the passenger seat of the rented car. He couldn't smell the fear anymore, but the anxiety was still there.

Finally, they reached Gracie Manor. The big white gate opened up automatically, and he maneuvered the car into the garage. Getting out of the driver's side, he walked over to the other side to let the two women out.

"The entire first floor is my office," he explained as they approached the house. It was massive—three stories tall—and took up half the block.

"Gracie Manor, right?" Jade said as she looked up at the house. "Neoclassical Revival?"

"Built in 1910," he said. Instead of bringing them to the front door, he led them to the side entrance tucked away behind a wrought iron gate. It looked nondescript, and that was deliberate. This part of the house was meant to be hidden. The door looked like it was white-painted wood, but it was actually made of steel. Liam slid a small panel on the side and pressed his thumb to a sensor, and then the door slid open with a soft whoosh.

"This way." He let them go inside first as he secured the

door behind him. The main foyer seemed normal enough, like any office, with a well-appointed waiting room, chairs, and tasteful, if minimal, decorations.

An older Lycan woman appeared from behind one of the doors, dressed in a crisp white pantsuit. Her brown hair was pulled back in a severe bun, and large horn-rimmed glasses were perched over her pinched nose. "Primul," she said, greeting him with the traditional honorific for a Lycan's Alpha. "The conference room is ready. New York is on standby."

"Thank you, Brenda." He nodded as they entered the room. "Could you get us some coffee please?"

Brenda bowed her head and left them.

Liam motioned for Jade and Lara to take the seats closest to the head of the conference table. He took his jacket off, hung it in the closet, and then took his seat. After opening the laptop in front of him, he fired up the videoconferencing software.

"Grant," he greeted as the large screen on the other end of the room flickered to life. It projected the Fenrir main conference room in New York, where Grant, Nick Vrost with his wife Cady, Alynna, and her husband Alex Westbrooke, sat around a large table.

"We're patching in Vivianne," Grant said, holding up a finger to signal for them to wait. A second later, a smaller screen popped up in the corner with Vivianne Chatraine's face.

"Good, we're all here," Grant said. "Now, what's the matter?"

"We just came back from examining the bodies at the forensics lab," Liam explained. "Lara? What did you need to tell us?"

"You go first, Jade," Lara said, sucking in a breath. "Tell them what we found."

With a nod, Jade began to explain her findings and what Captain Wu had told them about Marshall Aimes. She also pulled up the pictures from her tablet. She tapped on her pad and projected the picture of Aimes' body. "He had this carved on his chest."

A gasp came from Vivianne's screen. Her green eyes went wide. "Lara," she called her daughter. "You saw that?"

Lara nodded. "Is it what I think it is, Mother?"

The older witch's face went grim, her eyes darkening. "I think so. What did you feel?"

"It was ... awful," she choked out. "I could feel the magic, seeping from him. But it didn't come from him."

"That's the second time you said that," Jade observed. "What does that mean? And what is that symbol? I've been trying to reverse image search it, but it's not online or in any academic database."

Vivianne sighed. "You won't find it in any database. It's an ancient symbol, found only in our books."

"What does it mean?" Grant asked.

"It's the symbol for control." Vivianne frowned. "And those two symbols beside it? Power and blood."

"Why does Marshall Aimes have these symbols carved on his chest?" Liam asked, dreading the answer.

"Because someone used it to control him. They carved those symbols, tied his soul to theirs, and directed him to kill Maeve and Alfred Williams," Lara finished, her voice trembling. "I could feel it. Their magic surrounded him, but it wasn't coming from him. He was ... human. A normal human, made into their puppet. Made to kill."

There was silence from both sides. Someone finally spoke up. "How could they do this?" Nick asked. Beside him, his wife Cady visibly paled and he put an arm around her.

"Blood magic, of course," Vivianne said. "Something like this could only be accomplished by blood magic. I mean, I don't know the details because such kinds of magic are forbidden to

us. A few centuries ago, witches destroyed most of the writings
and teachings that had to do with blood magic and anything that
would cause harm to other creatures. The only texts we have
now are informational, not instructional."

"But Stefan and his mages somehow managed to find out
how to do it," Grant pointed out.

"You can't totally destroy information," Vivianne replied.
"We do our best, but still, there will be pockets of knowledge
left. I suspect Stefan has been gathering what he can and
probably he and his mages were able to figure it out on their
own."

"How do we stop it?" Liam asked.

Vivianne's brows knitted. "I'll have to consult with other
witches and the Witch Assembly. I'll come to New York and
bring some of our books; maybe Dr. Cross can use them."

Jade frowned. "We should get back to the lab as soon as
possible. I need to start working on something that will counter
this."

"*We* need start working on it," Lara said, straightening up in
her chair.

"We all will," Grant said. "You'll have whatever resources
you need at your disposal."

"As well as mine," Liam stated.

"You and I will take these findings to the Lycan High
Council," Grant said to Liam. "They have to listen to us, now
that the mages are involving humans." Revealing their secret to
the world could mean disaster for the Lycans.

"I'll set up a meeting with them right away," Liam agreed.
"I'll start letting my people know."

"Mine too. We have a lot to discuss. We'll keep in touch,
Liam."

"Yes. I'll have the jet take Dr. Cross and Ms. Chatraine back
to New York first thing in the morning."

After their final goodbyes, the screen faded to black and the room filled with silence.

"Blood magic ... controlling humans." Jade shook her head. "I don't even know where to begin. How does that even happen? How can we stop it?"

"You'll find a way, Jade," Lara said reassuringly. "You're brilliant. You figured out how to suppress our powers."

"I almost did," Jade sighed. "The power suppressing bracelet still isn't perfect."

"But you'll get it working." Lara smiled, placing an arm around her shoulders. "And we'll get back to New York and work on this and stop them, right?"

Before Jade could answer, the door to the waiting room opened and Brenda came in with a tray of coffee. "Primul," she said, placing the tray on the table. "Mrs. Henney would like to know if the guests will be staying for dinner."

Liam frowned. "How did she ... never mind." Of course his mother knew everything that happened around the house. In fact, she knew everything that happened in the city. "Yes, well ..." He turned to Lara and Jade. "I know it's been a long and terrible day, but I'd love if you would come to dinner tonight. My mother would be thrilled to have you."

"Of course, Alpha," Jade said. Lara's head snapped to her friend, and gave her a strange look.

"It's settled then." Liam stood up. "My driver will bring you back to the hotel so you can rest and freshen up. He'll wait for you and be at your disposal if you need to run any errands. Then, he'll bring you back here by 6:30."

"Thank you for the invitation." Jade gave him a small nod.

———

"Why did you have to say yes to dinner?" Lara admonished Jade later when they were alone in the car. "Shouldn't we be on our way back to New York by now?"

"That wasn't a request, Lara," Jade said matter-of-factly. "You do not turn down an invitation from an Alpha and his mother when you're in their city, much less their home. Akiko Henney is still Lupa of San Francisco, at least until Liam marries. She's practically queen of this territory. Besides, my mother would have definitely found out if we had turned her down, and I'd never hear the end of it."

Lara had never met Jade's mother, but from the stories, she sounded like a big pain in the ass. "Fine," she grumbled. "One dinner. Can't hurt, right?"

The driver dropped them off at the lobby and handed his card to them, telling them to call him if they needed him. Lara went straight to her room, plopped herself down on her bed, and let out a loud groan.

Just what I need. Dinner with Liam Henney and his mother in their beautiful mansion. She hadn't meant to break down in front of him today, but she had felt sick and weak, and Liam's presence seemed to calm her. He chased away those awful images in her head and made her feel safe.

Not sure what to do, she drew a bath, filling the deep Japanese-style tub with warm water and bubbles. She took off her clothes, piled her hair on top of her head, and stepped into the tub. It was nice to relax after the events of that morning. She closed her eyes and let the warm water and fragrant scent of the bubble bath soothe her. Just one dinner and then she would leave San Francisco and avoid Liam Henney as much as possible. She had no other choice, and it was for his own good.

Though it would cause her pain, she had to remind herself why she and Liam couldn't be together. She opened her mind, willing the memories to come back.

"I love you, Lara." His voice, low and gentle, sent thrills up her spine. Soft brown eyes looked down at her. "I mean it."

Lara gasped, and then a smile spread across her lips. "I love you, too, Jonathan," she whispered back, wrapping her arms around him, pulling him down for a kiss. His beard was rough against her delicate skin, but she didn't care. After a long, deep kiss, he reluctantly pulled away.

"I should go. I'll be late for work." Jonathan worked as bricklayer for a construction company, and his shift for the day was about to begin.

"We're right across from the site," she said with a giggle. They had met a few weeks ago, when he and his buddies had stopped in the bar where she worked. Unlike most of the men in their town, he was actually polite and kind, helping her out when she dropped a whole tray of glasses while she was cleaning up. He had come back the next night and the day after that, and after a week of stopping in for after-work drinks, he had finally asked her out. She had said yes immediately, and they had gone out to dinner the next day.

Jonathan was a true gentleman, never pushy, and took his time with her. She found herself falling for the kind and patient man, and after a few weeks of dating, she had given him her virginity. That was last night, and she still felt giddy, hours after they slept together.

"Still, the foreman's gonna be on my ass if I'm even five minutes late." He huffed but pulled her closer. "I'll see you tonight?"

"Yes, of course," she replied and reluctantly let go of him. "Now go to work."

He gave her one last kiss and turned around toward the construction site. As Lara watched him retreat, a chilly gust of wind blasted over her. Strange. She shrugged and pulled her sweater around herself tighter.

"Lara!" Jonathan called as he turned around to face her. He waved at her.

She froze, seeing him. No. It couldn't be. "Jonathan!" she cried out. "No!"

It happened so fast, in the blink of an eye. The out-of-control blue and white pickup truck seemingly came from nowhere and hit Jonathan so hard his body bounced off the front and sent it flying off. Lara rushed to him, and all she remembered was that he was lying so still it was like he was sleeping.

The next few days were a blur, and later, her mother told her she had been in a catatonic state throughout the whole thing, from the time the paramedics came until the funeral a few days later. She shut down, unable to sleep or eat. Vivianne forced her to get out of bed each day. Finally, when Vivianne was at the end of her patience, Lara told her what she had been dreading to admit.

"I saw it," she said, sobbing in her mother's arms. It was the first time she had let herself cry. "Days before it happened, I saw it in a dream. Jonathan telling me he loved me. Him crossing the street and turning around to wave at me and the pickup hitting him. It happened exactly as it did in my dream! Even the color of the truck was the same! Over and over again, the dream came to me."

Vivianne embraced her tight, soothing her and rubbing her back. "Darling ... I'm sorry ... I ...."

"Why, Mother? I don't understand! Why did it happen?"

Her mother sighed and pulled away from her. "I should have ... I'm sorry Lara. There's something you should know. Something I should have shown you as soon as you discovered your powers."

Vivianne left her but came back a few minutes later. She was holding an old leather-bound book. "This belonged to your grandmother Elise. Her diary. You need to read it."

Lara took the old diary from her mother's hand, holding it against her chest. "I don't understand."

"You will," Vivianne said sadly. "And I'm sorry. So sorry for not telling you earlier."

It took Lara a day to finish reading the diary. It was filled with passages about Elise's life before she was married. Lara was puzzled, not sure what she was supposed to read. About halfway through, she found the pages that gave her the answers she needed.

Elise talked about one of her sisters, Mira, who was a blessed witch and had the power to make the ground shake. Mira met a young man named Thomas, and they fell in love. However, before they could get married, Thomas died in a fire at the factory where he worked. Mira confessed to Elise that she had seen the whole thing in a dream—how Thomas had suffered—and the details in her dream were exactly as it had happened in real life.

Elise Chatraine's words in her elegant handwriting haunted Lara, and she memorized the passage by heart: "Is being a blessed witch really more of a curse? Does the power come with a price? Is my sister and others like her doomed to cause the death of the men who love them?"

She didn't know if it was true, but magic always had a price. Mother Nature didn't give without taking in return. And she had taken Jonathan from Lara.

Lara was drowning. Water filled her lungs, and she couldn't breathe. Her arms flailed, feeling the cold porcelain and used it to hoist herself above the water. Choking and gasping, she grasped the sides of the tub, coughing water out of her lungs to let the air in.

She had fallen asleep, and the water had gone stone cold. She stood up, grabbing her towel and wrapping it around her.

"Shit!" she cursed. As she glanced at the clock in her room, she realized she had been in the tub so long that she only had an hour to get ready for dinner. It was too late to back out now. She spied the green dress hanging in the closet of her hotel room. There was no way she could go out and buy another outfit or borrow one from Jade. With a sigh, she began to brush her hair and prepare for dinner.

CHAPTER NINE

L ara met up with Jade in the lobby of the hotel. Lara saw the other woman as she was getting out of the elevator, dressed in a long-sleeved navy dress and plain black pumps. She suddenly felt overdressed in her green dress, black stockings, and stiletto heels.

"Shit, I should change," she said as Jade approached her.

"You'll be fine," the Lycan said, rolling her eyes. "I should have asked you to help me pick out something to wear." She looked down at her drab dress, which looked even more dull next to Lara's vibrant outfit.

"So, are you finally going to let me give you a makeover?" Lara joked. Since they had become friends, she'd been dying to help Jade revamp her closet, as well as her hair and makeup. Jade was beautiful, with her delicate English rose coloring, long wavy brown hair that came down to her waist, and pretty plump lips. Her green eyes were so pale they were almost yellow and had flecks of gold in the middle. Unfortunately, the Lycan scientist preferred to hide behind her glasses, didn't wear a stitch of makeup, and dressed like she was still nine years old on most days. Lara would often shake her head at her friend when she showed up to work in slacks or a skirt that fell below her knees, a long-sleeved shirt or frilly blouse, and ballerina flats or her well-worn red Converse high tops.

Jade was also painfully shy, preferring to hide behind her work and her brains. Lara could relate, though, as she was also shy as a child, but she quickly got over that when she started working as a waitress in a diner in their small town.

"Over my dead body," Jade snorted. "I don't need a makeover."

Lara observed that at least tonight, she had actually put a little bit of effort in her appearance. Her hair was in an artful French braid and her lips were shiny with her favorite pink lip gloss. "Whatever you say," the witch said with a laugh. "Someday, you might be begging me for one."

"Let's get this over with," Jade said impatiently. "I just want to get back to New York as soon as possible."

She knew how her friend was feeling, though Jade was probably eager to get back to her lab and start working. Lara, on the other hand, was anxious to put as many miles between her and Liam Henney as possible.

The driver was waiting for them outside, as promised. The traffic in San Francisco wasn't as bad as New York, and after traversing Van Ness Avenue, they arrived in the Pacific Heights district.

Lara gasped as they approached Gracie Manor. The mansion was even more beautiful at night. All the lights were on, and the famous San Francisco fog rolled over it slowly, covering it in a billowy white mist. It looked ethereal, magical almost.

"It's beautiful, isn't it?" Jade asked. "I heard rumors some tech billionaire was recently trying to buy it from the Henneys. He offered a ridiculous amount, ten times the value of the house, but they wouldn't sell."

"Well, why would they?" Lara said in a hushed tone.

The driver pulled into the front driveway beside the main entrance. He opened the door and gestured to marble steps leading up to a set of double doors. "They're expecting you, Dr. Cross, Ms. Chatraine, so go right ahead. The butler will greet you."

"Thank you." Lara nodded and followed Jade up the steps.

They were about to ring the doorbell when it opened. An older man dressed in a black suit was standing there.

"Good evening, Dr. Cross, Ms. Chatraine," the man greeted. "Dinner will be ready in-"

Loud barking and the sound of paws padding across the hardwood floors interrupted the butler. A brown and black beast came barreling down the hall, running toward Lara and Jade, tongue hanging out of its maw. Jade let out a yelp, quickly stepping away from the behemoth, and Lara stepped in front of her friend. Large paws bounded up, nearly knocking Lara down as a wet tongue scraped across her cheek.

"Hugo!" Liam's voice boomed across the hallway. "Hugo! Down!"

Hugo the beast bowed down, cowering low as Liam approached them. It let out a whine, looking up at its master with woeful eyes.

"Are you okay?" Liam asked Lara, his eyes full of concern.

"No worries." Lara bent down and patted Hugo on his head, giving him a scratch. "I think he was just excited, aren't you, boy?"

Hugo hopped up, seemingly agreeing with her. He licked her hand, rubbing his nose against her arm.

"Hmmm, he's not normally this friendly," Liam observed. He kneeled down next to her and then rubbed Hugo's head with both hands. "I think he likes you," he said, his electric blue eyes dancing in amusement.

"Uhm, yeah," she murmured, standing up.

"He's huge! What kind of dog is he?" Jade asked cautiously.

"Well, we're not really sure," Liam began. "I wanted to adopt a dog, and when I saw him at the shelter, he was just a little thing. They didn't know what he was either, since they rescued him. I thought he might have been a mixed Boxer breed, but now I'm thinking he's more a Mastiff mix."

"He's sweet," Lara observed as Hugo continued to lick her hand, as if begging for more affection. The redhead obliged, reaching down to scratch him behind the ear, much to the dog's delight.

The sound of an engine pulling up the driveway made the butler clear his throat. "I believe that is Mr. and Mrs. Matsumoto, Master Liam. Perhaps we should head into the dining room? Mrs. Henney should already be waiting for you."

"Can you take Hugo to the backyard please, Gregory?" Liam instructed the butler. "I'll show our guests to the dining room."

Hugo let out another whine, and Gregory led him away. "Will he be okay?" Lara asked, frowning.

"Don't worry, he's got a big backyard where he can play." Liam chuckled. "I'll let him back in the house after dinner."

Lara waved to Hugo. "I'll see you later, buddy!"

Liam led them into the dining room, which was just as elegantly designed as the rest of the house. A slim, petite female waited for them by the entryway. Lara couldn't guess her age as her alabaster skin was smooth and only showed small signs of wrinkles. Her midnight black hair was still thick and full, pulled up into an elegant bun.

"May I present my mother, Akiko Henney, Lupa of San Francisco," Liam said. "Mother, this is Dr. Jade Cross and Lara Chatraine."

"Thank you for allowing us into your territory, Lupa." Jade bowed her head, and Lara followed suit.

"Yes, thank you," Lara added.

"You're both welcome." Her smile was polite, but there was coolness to her voice. "Takeda and his wife have arrived." She craned her neck toward the newcomers who entered.

Liam quickly introduced them, before saying, "Shall we sit down to dinner?"

———

"How do you like San Francisco?" Akiko Henney asked as they were in the middle of the third course, her dark eyes keen and hawk-like.

"Er, we haven't had a chance to do much except work, Lupa," Jade replied as she took a sip of her wine. "But it's a beautiful city, right Lara?"

"Uhm, yeah, sure. I mean, yes, it's a lovely city," Lara murmured.

"I had my reservations when I first came to live here, but it's grown on me. In fact, I was just ..."

As Akiko droned on, Lara did a mental eye roll. Although Liam's mother had been polite and cordial toward her, it was obvious she thought of Lara as an outsider. Liam sat at the head of the table with Takeda on his right side and his wife, Kimiko, beside him. Akiko, as Lupa or female head of the clan, was on his left. Jade was seated next to her and Lara at the end. Whenever Akiko asked a question or made a comment, she looked toward both Lycan women, but her eyes never landed on Lara.

Jade seemed uncomfortable with the attention and did her best to include Lara in the conversation, but it was no use. She was practically invisible to the Lycans. All except Liam, of course. Though he never talked to her directly, Lara could feel his electric blue eyes on her, and she felt like prey being stalked. Once, she mustered enough strength to look back at him, and when their eyes clashed, she felt the blush creep up her cheeks, and she quickly looked down at her pumpkin soup.

"By the way," Akiko began. "I saw your mother and her husband last summer in Glyndenbourne. How is the Baroness?"

"She's doing well ... er ... I suppose," Jade fumbled. "I haven't seen her in a few months, actually."

"That's a shame; she's a lovely lady," Akiko said. "I asked her if you were seeing anyone, and she said you weren't. I was so happy to hear you were coming to San Francisco. I've been wanting you to meet Liam for a while now. And the Baroness felt the same way when I told her about you. I'm sure she'll be pleased to know you and my son are getting to know each other very well."

"Mother!" Liam admonished.

The older lady gave him an innocent smile. "As colleagues ... for now."

Meanwhile, Jade's eyes bulged and she started coughing, her face going red.

"Jesus, Jade, are you okay?" Lara leaned over and soothed her, rubbing her back. Jade heaved and let out a hacking sound, waving Lara away with her hand. Unfortunately, she also knocked down her wine glass, sending the red liquid splashing all over the front of Lara's dress.

Not minding her ruined dress, she gave Jade one last hard slap on the back, and a piece of chewed-up steak landed on the pristine white tablecloth.

The Lycan's light green eyes widened from behind her glasses when she saw the front of Lara's dress, now covered in a dark red stain. "I'm so sorry, Lara!"

Lara stood up, her chair scraping the hardwood floors. "I'll go get cleaned up," she murmured quietly, walking out of the dining room.

As soon as she closed the door behind her, she realized she didn't even know where the bathroom was. *Shit*. The wine was making the front of her dress stick to her chest, and she pulled at it, not that it helped. The dress was completely ruined. With a sigh, she turned right, hoping she'd find a bathroom.

As she walked through the enormous house, her thoughts turned to the disastrous dinner. Liam and Jade. It made sense. He was an Alpha, and Jade was apparently going to be a Baroness someday, a fact her supposed best friend forgot to mention. They'd be perfect together, of course, and they'd have perfect little Lycan babies with Jade's brains and Liam's good looks. The thought made her want to push Jade's pretty face into her mashed potatoes. No, scratch that, Jade was her friend. She wanted to put Akiko's upturned nose into the gravy boat instead.

"Fuck!" she cursed when a door she opened turned out to be a closet.

"The bathroom's this way."

Liam's voice made her jump. "Goddammit, someone needs to put a fucking bell on you Lycans!"

He let out a laugh, then took her hand, the touch sending little currents of electricity up her arm. Unable to protest or pull away, she let him lead her down the opposite way.

"You can get cleaned up in there. I'll get you something to wear."

"Sure," she said, turning away from him. His hand on her upper arm stopped her. She looked back at him. "I need to get out of this dress." His eyes blazed with desire at her words, and her eyes widened. "That's not what I meant!"

Liam gave her a feral smile, but the heat in his gaze was unmistakable. "What did you mean?" He leaned closer, his lips mere millimeters away from her ear and his breath tickling her delicate skin. Warmth spread through her body, and she could feel the desire pooling in her belly, the rush of wetness between her legs unmistakable.

"I mean ... you should get me out of this dress ... fuck, that's not what I meant either!" Damn her traitorous mouth and body.

Liam pushed her against the door of the bathroom. After moving her hair to one side, his fingers played with the zipper on her dress. "Are you sure?" he teased, his other hand tracing circles down her arm.

"Liam ...." She breathed, closing her eyes. His body was so close to hers she could feel the warmth radiating from him.

"You're so damn beautiful," he whispered, his lips grazing the shell of her ear.

"Liam, you can't ...," she protested weakly. It took all of her willpower, but she turned around and pushed him away. "This isn't what you think ...."

He seemed undeterred, his eyes never leaving hers. "Tell me what this is about then? Why I can't stop thinking of you?"

"You don't want me ... I mean it's Grant's fault!"

He frowned. "I don't understand what he has to do with this."

Lara sighed. "You don't just go around making out with random girls for no reason, right? That day in the elevator, Grant and Frankie were getting their freak on in his office and their Alpha pheromones set off everyone on the floor ... including you." She took a deep breath. "So you see? It's not you ... it was your Lycan instincts."

"That's not-" He stopped all of a sudden, shaking his head. His face was a mask of confusion.

"Lara!" Jade's voice rang down the hallway. "Where have you been? Are you sure you're okay?"

Lara quickly stepped away from Liam. "I'm here ... I'm fine ... I got lost, and the Alpha helped me find the bathroom."

"I'm going to get her something to wear," Liam said quickly, ducking away from the two women.

Jade shook her head when she saw Lara's dress. "I'm such a klutz! I'll replace the dress, I promise." She opened the door to the bathroom and tugged the other woman in. Searching the room, she found a towel and started wiping it down the front of Lara's ruined outfit.

"Really ... Jade, don't worry about it ... I'm fine!" she snapped, snatching the towel from Jade. The look of surprise on the Lycan's face sent a feeling of guilt to the pit of her stomach. "I mean ... it's just a dress," she said reassuringly.

"I just ...." Jade looked at her feet. "That was a big surprise. I mean, I didn't know our mothers had met and ... well, I didn't know anything about this ... just to let you know."

"I don't know what you're talking about," Lara said flippantly, turning the tap on to wash her hands.

"Well, at the police station, you and Liam seemed ...."

"Seemed what?"

"Seemed ... close," Jade finished.

"I was feeling sick, and he was there to help me," Lara explained. "Nothing else."

Jade's eyes narrowed at her friend. "Uh-huh."

"Yes. I swear."

A knock interrupted them.

"Come in!" they said at the same time.

The knob turned, and Liam's head popped in. "I couldn't find anything that would fit you, Lara, but I thought maybe you could cover up with this." He handed her a black button-down shirt.

"Thank you." Lara nodded as she took it.

"I'll head back to the dining room," Liam said as he left them.

Lara unfolded the shirt, and from the size, she guessed it was Liam's. The citrusy scent that clung to the fabric was unmistakable. With a long sigh, she put it on, folded up the sleeves, and tied the bottom around her waist. It would have to do.

"Er, that's not too bad." Jade glanced at her cover up. "And besides, we're just heading back to the hotel after this. At least the staff won't think you came from a murder scene."

Lara laughed. "Right. Okay, well, I suppose the night can't get any worse."

"Yeah. At least you didn't spit out Grade-A Wagyu beef onto the San Francisco Lupa's finest white tablecloth."

———

"Well, that was an enjoyable dinner," Akiko remarked as they watched the limo pull out of the driveway. "Ms. Cross is a lovely woman."

Liam shook head. His mother did not waste time. "She's a nice girl."

"And from a good Lycan family." Akiko gave a slight emphasis on the Lycan part, of course.

"I'm sure they're from good stock, Mother," he said wryly, resisting the urge to roll his eyes. He leaned down and gave her a kiss on the cheek. "I have some work to do. I'll see you in the morning."

"Liam, dear." She reached over and touched his cheek. "You know I only want what's best for you."

"I know, Mother."

"And well ... it's been over a year since your father died. I think it's time you finished mourning and moved on."

"And you?" he asked, his eyes concerned. "Have you moved on?"

"I probably never will." She shook her head. "I loved your father, and I always will. But I'm tired. I would like to pass on the mantle to another. Your wife should be rightful Lupa to our clan."

"I thought you enjoyed being Lupa?" he teased. "Most mothers wouldn't want to be replaced by a newer, younger woman."

"Ha! No one could replace me as your mother," she laughed. "But still, I've seen how being Alpha has taken its toll on you. A wife would help ease that burden. You would have someone to share your troubles and your life. And maybe have a pup or two."

"Oh, so that's really what this is?" he asked in a lighthearted tone. "You're angling for some grandchildren."

"Naturally I would want our line to be continued. But yes, a child to hold and spoil would be nice." She looked up at him hopefully.

"I want that, too, Mother," he confessed. "I would like to at least have what you and Dad had."

Akiko's eyes softened and teared slightly. "Your father was a rare man. He claims he fell in love with me at first sight, even though it was our parents pushing us to get together. I didn't believe him at first and thought his American ways were too brash and forward."

"But he won you over."

"He did. Eventually." She smiled. "He was kind and had a good heart. Like you."

Liam paused. "I miss him. A lot."

"Me too." Akiko embraced her son. "Every day."

He kissed the top of her head. "You should get some rest; it's been a long day."

Akiko nodded and stepped back. "I do hope you think about what I said. Not just about Ms. Cross, who's a lovely lady and would suit you well. A nice *Lycan* girl with whom you can share your life could be just what you need."

As his mother walked away, her words rang in his head. Of course, any Lycan mother would want a Lycan mate for her son. After all, only two Lycans could produce a Lycan pup, and even that was rare. Most Lycan couples couldn't produce children, and the few that did rarely had more than one child. The exception, of course, was the True Mate pairing, but that was even rarer. Three pairs were in existence, a minuscule fraction of the entire worldwide population of their kind. As Alpha, it was his duty to produce the next heir of the San Francisco clan. And he could only do that with another Lycan.

A strange feeling pulled at his chest, and Lara's name drifted into his mind, as it often did these days. He couldn't stop thinking about what she had said, about what had happened in the elevator. Perhaps she was right; it was all instincts and pheromones. It would be best, for everyone, if he just forgot about Lara Chatraine.

CHAPTER TEN

A loud crack of thunder made Lara open her eyes from her already shallow sleep. She had just barely drifted off when the sound woke her up. Outside, rain pelted the windows as a rain storm hit the city.

She padded over to the window, watching the lights of the city as the rain and fog made them blurry. Shivering slightly, she pulled the shirt tighter around her, breathing in the delicious scent. *Ugh, why did I wear his damn shirt to bed?* As soon as she had gotten into her room, she had tossed it aside. Realizing that she smelled like him, she had hopped into the shower to wash the scent away. However, she was drawn to the shirt. She couldn't stop herself from smelling it and breathing Liam's scent like some lunatic stalker. Whatever possessed her to wear it to bed, she didn't know.

Pressing her head against the cold window, she took another deep breath. A jolt of arousal shot through her, sending heat and wetness between her legs. She swallowed a gulp, her fingers playing with the hem of the shirt. Did she dare? Her hand didn't wait for an answer as it slipped between her legs. Tracing the seam of her pussy through her panties, she gasped, surprised at how damp she was. She pushed the fabric aside, exposing her damp lips to her fingers.

She moaned his name as her finger teased her wet lips. She imagined his hand down there, circling her clit and slipping inside. She continued to touch herself, when suddenly the hairs on the back of her neck prickled and she sensed someone outside her door. She went on full alert, hands at the ready to blow away any attacker. Slowly, she approached the door and peeked out of the keyhole.

Standing outside her door was Liam Henney. Well, at least he had been standing outside her door for half a second before quickly turning and walking away. He suddenly stopped, turned back, and stood in front of her door, raising his hand as if to knock, then froze. His brow wrinkled, and he put down his hand, then ran it through his hair in a frustrated manner. He turned around again and began to walk away.

Lara wasn't sure what got into her, but she quickly unlocked the door and opened it. "Liam," she called to his retreating back.

Slowly, he turned around. His eyes raked over her, as if he couldn't believe what he was seeing.

"What are you doing here?" she asked shyly, suddenly feeling the heat of his gaze.

"I was taking a walk. I do it to clear my head sometimes." He stalked back toward her. "And I suddenly found myself outside your hotel. And then outside your door, and I couldn't help myself."

"You're wet," she realized. His hair was mussed, both from the rain and his hands, and his clothes were damp.

"And you're wearing my shirt," he said with a cheeky grin.

Her mouth dropped open. "It's not what you think," she crossed her arms.

"You keep saying that, but for some reason it's always what I think," he said in a low voice.

Lara's face heated in embarrassment. "It's late; you should go." She was about to shut the door when his hand slammed on the wood, bracing against it.

"Did you want to be close to me as you slept? Have my scent all over you?" he whispered. "Because your scent mixed with mine is delicious."

His words shocked her, sending a jolt of arousal through her again. "Please, Liam." She pushed the door harder, but it didn't budge. "It's getting late, and I should get some sleep."

"Lara, I ...." His eyes glazed over, then his pupils dilated into pinpoints. "Jesus, you smell like ...." A deep growl rumbled from his chest. "Have you been touching yourself?"

Her eyes grew wide, and she tried to shut the door even harder, but he pushed against it. He barged into her room, and as the door closed with a loud thud, she jumped back with a jolt. Electric blue eyes glowed eerily in the darkness of her room, and he moved toward her. She backed up slowly, scared to give him her back, until she hit the wooden dresser. Liam braced his hands on either side of her, trapping her.

"We shouldn't, Liam," she begged. But he didn't seem to hear her. His warm hand gripped her wrist and raised it up to his face. His nose sniffed at her fingers, then his warm tongue slipped from his mouth, licking at her digits. Heat pooled in her belly as the rough pad of his tongue made contact with her skin.

"You ... taste ... delicious," he said. She let out a soft cry, and he sucked her fingers into his mouth.

"Liam," she breathed. He released her fingers, only to capture her mouth with his.

Electricity and power shot through her body the moment their lips touched. His tongue delved between her lips, seeking hers out in a powerful dance. Pushing up against him, she could feel his erection, grinding up insistently against her core, and her knees buckled. Without missing a beat, Liam scooped her up, placing her on top of the dresser. He shoved a hand between her legs, tracing up her thighs, and shoved her panties down, nearly ripping them off her.

Lara moaned against his lips and lifted her hips so he could pull the scrap of fabric down her legs. A warm hand cupped her sex, fingers teased her wet lips. He seemed to smile, and he let out a satisfied grunt when he felt her dripping pussy.

"You've been wet for me all this time?" He teased her with his finger, dipping the tip into her.

"Yes," she confessed. She couldn't hide it anyway. Liam already knew what she had been doing before he arrived.

"I can't stop thinking about you ... about your lips and what you would feel like around me. How your pussy would feel gripping me." He pushed a finger inside her, and she let out a whimper. "Hmmm ... much better than in my imagination."

She sucked in a breath, shocked by his words. Lara always had the impression he was so reserved and polite, a true gentleman. She never would have imagined such things coming out of his mouth, and she wanted more.

As if he read her mind, he nipped at her neck, sending shocks through her. "Do you like it when I talk dirty, Lara?" He slipped another finger in her and began to thrust his hand gently. "My hand is soaked, so I'm betting you do."

He continued to fuck her with his fingers, and he encouraged her, whispering dirty things into her ear. "God, you feel so good. So tight and wet. Are you wishing it was my cock inside you?"

"Liam." She seemed to have lost all words and all thoughts. Only Liam filled her head and her senses. She reached out, threading her fingers through his hair and pulling him down for a kiss. Tongue, teeth, and lips scraped and gnashed at each other, rough and wild, as his fingers continued to drive her toward orgasm.

"Fuck!" He gritted his teeth as she pulsed around his fingers. Lara let out a long moan, her hips bucking up to meet him. The heel of his hand ground down against her clit, sending her over the edge as white hot heat exploded all around her and she cried out his name one last time.

"That was so fucking sexy," he breathed against her ear as she collapsed against him.

She needed time to collect her thoughts. Time away from him. But she could barely put a coherent sentence together before he lifted her up and carried her to the bed. He laid her down gently and positioned himself on top of her, between her legs. He pressed his thick, hardened cock against her, and she could feel the heat of him through his pants.

"We shouldn't ..." she protested, finally coming to her senses. *God, this was all wrong.* "We can't."

His back stiffened, and his body tensed. "What?" he asked in a surprised tone and rocked back on his heels, staring down at her with his electric blue gaze.

"Liam ...." She pushed at him and rolled to her side, away from him. "Please ... we shouldn't have done that."

He ran his fingers through his hair. "What are you saying? Lara, c'mon. You know this feels right."

"And then what?" she asked accusingly. "You want a romp in bed, one night to scratch this itch? I told you, what you're feeling isn't real!"

"This seems pretty real to me. You can't hide behind pheromones this time," he said, his eyes narrowing. He crossed his arms over his chest. "I want you, and you just showed me how much you want me."

"This isn't going to work. You're an Alpha, and I'm a witch," she reasoned. "We both have responsibilities. You have obligations ...." She swallowed the bitterness building in her chest. The thought of Liam being with another woman was ripping her apart. But this was for the best. She couldn't risk it.

"I don't give a fuck about that!" he roared.

"What do you want from me, Liam?" She whipped around to face him.

He opened his mouth to speak but stopped suddenly. "This thing between us. It feels like something big. More than attraction or lust. Tell me you don't feel it, and I'll leave you alone."

Lara stared at him, willing the words to come out of her mouth. To tell him she didn't feel anything, just lust. But she couldn't. God help her, she couldn't lie to him.

A loud ring pierced the thick silence between them. Liam cursed softly and took his phone out of his pocket. "Yes?" he answered gruffly. He listened to the person on the other line intently and let out a sigh. "Yes, I'm fine. I'm coming back now." He turned to her.

"You should go; that sounded important." She nodded toward the door.

Liam looked conflicted, staring at the phone in his hand. "You might get the impression I'm some goody two shoes, that I'm just going to roll over," he said, his voice steely and serious. "But this is far from over."

Before she could say anything else, he stalked toward to her, gave her a soul-shattering kiss, and then left the room.

Lara sank down on the bed, her face in her hands. *What have I done?* She was supposed to push him away. She was supposed to stay away, but what did she do instead? Damn her traitorous body. Even now, she was still buzzing from the most powerful orgasm she'd ever had, and they didn't even have sex.

Liam's words haunted her. She had to resist him, to stop this madness. True Mates or not, she wouldn't risk his life. He would die if they fell in love with each other. She would lock up her heart and throw away the key before she let that happen.

———

The cold air hit him with a force as he stormed out of the hotel, but he welcomed the chill. Liam wanted to throw the damn phone away but resisted the urge. Takeda had called him, worried because the security team at Gracie Mansion said he had left the house and hadn't returned yet. He wanted to strangle his Beta for interrupting, but he didn't want Takeda (or his mother) to figure out where he was, so he had no choice but to leave.

The torrential rain had slowed to a drizzle, and he walked to the corner of the street and decided to wait for a taxi there.

Truly, when he had left the house, he was just going for a walk to clear his head. His emotions were in turmoil, and though he knew he had to stay away from Lara, he suddenly found himself at her hotel, walking into the lobby and pressing the elevator button for her floor. He was ready to walk away when she had opened the door, wearing nothing but his shirt. Her exquisite scent, mixed with his and her own arousal, had pushed him over the edge, and he had to have a taste. He wanted to do more than just touch her, and watching her explode in orgasm in his arms, her face twisted in ecstasy, almost did him in. If she hadn't stopped him, he would have buried himself deep inside her, with that sweet pussy wrapped around his cock, fucking her until she screamed his name.

"I must be losing my damn mind," he muttered to himself, raking his fingers through his hair. He had women—human and Lycan—throwing themselves at him. Yet for the past few weeks, all his body craved was that redheaded witch. Did she possess some power over him? Was Lara playing with him or was there some reason she seemed to call out to him like a siren but retreated the moment he came panting after her. Being around her was turning him into a sex-crazed maniac. He should just walk away from her, while he still had some damn dignity.

No. Mine.

He shook his head at his wolf's words. If he wasn't out of his mind, then his wolf was. The animal had practically howled in happiness when he was with Lara, then threatened to break free from his skin when he had left her. He was getting more and more vocal and out of control. He wished he could go somewhere and just shift, let the wolf take over and forget the world and his responsibilities. If he weren't Alpha, it would be different. But Lara was right. He had a duty to his clan.

Bright lights twinkled in the distance, and he raised his hands to hail the passing cab. He climbed in and gave the cabbie his address, then stared into the distance as the car took him farther away from Lara.

CHAPTER ELEVEN

"**A**re you okay?"

"For the last time, Jade," Lara said as she looked over the magazine in her hands. "I'm fine."

"Then why have you been reading an upside down magazine for the last five minutes?"

Lara let out an indignant squeak and threw the glossy journal aside. Unfortunately, there was nothing else to read in the jet. But at least they were on their way back. The car and the driver had picked them up around noon at the hotel, and by two in the afternoon they had taken off. Liam was nowhere to be seen, but Gage did relay the Alpha's apologies for not seeing them off personally, as he was stuck in meetings the whole day.

Yes, she was glad to be going back. A strange, edgy ache had formed in her stomach when she woke up that morning, but she had ignored it, figuring it was something she had eaten.

"Are you mad at me or something?" Light green eyes looked at her dolefully.

"What?" Lara exclaimed. "No!"

"Is it about last night?"

Lara's face turned red. Did Jade know? Her room was right next to hers; maybe she had heard her and Liam ... *Oh God.*

"It was something I said at dinner, right? I'm sorry about Mrs. Henney. I was trying to include you as much as I could, but she kept talking to me and-"

Lara breathed a sigh of relief. "You never told me your mother was a Baroness. That's like royalty, right?" She hoped the change of subject would distract Jade. "Are you going to be a Baroness after her?"

"Goodness, no!" She shook her head. "Her husband, my stepfather, is Baron Huxley. I'm nowhere near in line to take any title. My real dad is American, a New York Lycan, so I'm just a plain old Miss."

"Oh, I see." Lara was glad the conversation steered away from last night's dinner. *And everything else about last night.* She was also relieved they were on their way back to New York. And she told that small, small part of her that pined for Liam to shut up. "So, what are we going to start with tomorrow? Are we going to try to work on the bracelet? Or figure out how the mages are controlling the humans?"

Jade's nose wrinkled. "Actually ... I know it'll be late when we land in New York, but I need to go to the lab. I have this strange feeling."

"Feeling?"

"Yeah, I can't put my finger on it ... but I need to check something out, and it can't wait until morning. The mages ... we need to stop them."

Lara clucked her tongue. "I'm coming with you. If only to stop you from working all night."

"You don't have to-"

"I want to," Lara said. Jade's words and reminder about the mages sobered her. There were much bigger things at stake now. They had to stop the mages before they struck again.

The rest of the flight was relatively silent and they landed sometime after eleven p.m. It was nearly midnight by the time the car dropped them off at Fenrir. The lobby, usually busy and bustling with activity, was eerily quiet and empty, save for the night security guard waiting at the reception desk. They showed him their badges, and he waved them through.

"So tell me again why we're here and what couldn't wait until morning?" Lara asked. She was tired from the trip, and all she wanted to do was flop down on her bed and sleep for hours. Although the jet had been comfortable, she felt restless. Her thoughts kept drifting to last night, and that uncomfortable feeling in her middle just wouldn't go away. As the plane flew farther and farther from San Francisco, it got worse.

"It's a theory of mine, but what you said about magic seeping through ... I had this thought." Jade paused as the elevator stopped on their floor. "I'll show you when we get to my computer."

They walked into the laboratory after getting their biometrics scanned. "Illuminate, 50 percent," Jade commanded, and the lights in the lab flickered to life. As they walked toward the stairs leading to Jade's inner lab, the Lycan suddenly stopped. She put a hand on Jade's arm, her light green eyes glowing behind her glasses.

Lara immediately stopped. Jade had never displayed any Lycan abilities or qualities in the time they'd known each other. In fact, if she didn't know Jade was a shifter, she would seem like an ordinary human. For something to set off her Lycan instincts, it had to be *big*.

Jade took a delicate sniff and then cocked her head to the side, toward the large walk-in refrigerator where they kept all kinds of samples. Lara opened her mouth to speak, but Jade shushed her. Carefully, Jade fished her phone out of her purse, dialing an emergency contact pre-programmed into it.

All of a sudden, a figure dressed in black burst from the walk-in fridge, knocking down several monitors and experiment set ups. Whoever—or whatever—it was, it was fast and strong, but the presence didn't feel like a mage or witch to Lara.

The main door slid open, and three men dressed in Fenrir's security uniform burst in, surrounding the figure. Instead of surrendering, though, the figure attacked them head on. He bowed low in a defensive stance, then sprung forward as one man came at him with handcuffs. His leg struck out, striking him in the head and knocking him down. The two remaining security guards raised their weapons, but he came flying at them with blinding speed, kicking the gun away from one man and then swinging over to the other, his legs wrapping around the man's neck and bringing him down on the floor.

"Shit!" Lara cursed. The intruder got to his feet in one smooth motion, then bound toward the open door. With the wave of her hand, Lara made one of the computer monitors fly across the room, hitting the intruder on the head, knocking him down.

A soft groan came from the figure as he lay on the floor. Cautiously, Lara stalked over to him. He was dressed in a dark cat suit and a ski mask, which she promptly ripped off.

"What the?" Lara's eyes widened.

"He" was a she. Long blonde curls tumbled down her shoulders; her long, sweeping eyelashes cast delicate shadows over high cheekbones. One of the security people must have gotten one hit in, because there was a cut on her jaw, but from the looks of it, it was already healing. Lara gasped. This wasn't just an ordinary cat burglar. She was a Lycan.

———

Lara and Jade stood behind the one-way mirror, watching as the Lycan woman sat with an eerie stillness in the other room. It was like a police interrogation room, at least the ones she had seen in movies and on TV. The woman sat with her wrists in cuffs chained to the table in front of her. An empty chair stood on the other side. Lara didn't know such a place in Fenrir existed, though she shouldn't have been surprised.

As they had waited for more security personnel to come in, Jade had explained that she had scented the other Lycan when they had arrived. Since the lab was kept sterile, she knew someone was in there. She had immediately called an emergency number, which triggered the alarm and sent the security team up to the lab.

It was nearly two o'clock in the morning. She yawned and then took a sip of her coffee to stay awake. It wasn't long until reinforcements came and took the intruder away. Grant, Nick, Alynna, and Alex arrived soon after that. She was curious as to who this intruder was and what she wanted, which is why she opted to stay. The Lycans, on the other hand, were probably more interested in how she was able to bypass Fenrir's high-tech security system and make it all the way into the lab on the 33rd floor.

The single door in the interrogation room slid open, and Grant, Nick, Alex, and Alynna filed inside. Grant sat in the chair opposite the woman and folded his hands on the table, while the rest stood behind him.

"Do you know who I am?" Grant asked, his voice cold and authoritative.

The woman's eyes lifted up to meet his gaze. "I don't know, should I?"

"You don't speak to the Alpha of New York that way, Lone Wolf," Nick said through gritted teeth. He reached over and grabbed the woman's hand, exposing the mark of a wolf's head on her wrist.

Jade gasped beside Lara. "I've never met a Lone Wolf."

"What's a Lone Wolf?" Lara asked.

"They're basically Lycans without clans."

"Not all Lycans have a clan?"

Jade shook her head. "Not always. Lone Wolves are those who simply don't have one, for whatever reason. Most Lycan clans are small, and with the trouble we have reproducing, some clans are reduced to single families."

"So, if you lose your family or clan, then you become a Lone Wolf?"

"If you can't find another clan to take you in. Or some of them are actually banished from their clans."

Lara turned her attention back to the interrogation room.

"... or you can tell us your name now and save us the time and trouble of going to the Lycan High Council for your records," Grant continued.

The young woman smirked. "And why would I do that? That would take all the fun out of it."

Grant leaned back and crossed his arms. "You might think you're funny, but I'm not laughing. I can do this all night. In fact, we can take turns." He motioned to Alynna, Alex, and Nick. "I'll go back to bed and get some sleep, while Nick sits here and interrogates you for a couple of hours. Then he can go home, and Alynna and Alex can have a turn. Then, I'll be back, fresh as a daisy, in the morning. You, on the other hand, will sit there with no rest, no food, and no water. Let's see who outlasts who."

The Lycan woman grumbled. "Meredith."

Alynna guffawed. "Just Meredith? Like Cher? Or Madonna?"

Meredith gave her a venomous look. "Perhaps you need

more Lycan history lessons, Princess," she sneered. "Lone Wolves don't have last names."

"So, Meredith," Grant continued. "Why are you here? Who sent you to break into our lab, and how did you get in?"

She gave Grant a wolfish smile. "Again, why would I tell you these things? You've already caught me, why not just ship me off to the Lycan High Council for punishment?"

"We have some of the most sophisticated and top-of-the-line security systems in the world," Grant began. "Some not even available on the market, and others we developed ourselves. Yet you, a Lone Wolf, broke into our lab, one of the most secure areas in the building. Oh no, Meredith, I'm not sending you to the Lycan High Council. You're far too valuable, and you've seen too much. We'll have to silence you."

Her eyes widened. "Wait! You can't do that! I demand judgment from the High Council! It's my right!"

"Grant." Alynna put a hand on her brother's shoulder. "Can I talk to you in private for a moment?" She looked at Nick and Alex. "Everyone should hear what I have to say."

The Alpha nodded, and they all left the interrogation room, making their way to the back room where Jade and Lara had been observing them.

"What is it, Alynna?" Grant asked.

The young woman turned to Jade. "You said she had broken into the lab, right? Did she try to hurt you?"

Jade shook her head. "No, I don't think so. When we came in and I scented her, she was in the walk-in fridge. It sounded like she was rummaging through whatever we had in there."

"And when you discovered her, she tried to run away?"

Lara nodded. "She bolted toward the doors."

"What if she wasn't there to hurt anyone?" Alynna asked aloud. "It sounds like she was trying to steal something and she didn't anticipate Jade and Lara making a sudden appearance at midnight."

"What are you saying?" Nick's brow knitted.

"Well, she's probably not connected to the mages, and she's not here to hurt anyone. She wasn't carrying any weapons, just a smartphone and a few tools. I think she was here to steal stuff."

"She's still not supposed to be here," Alex said. "Doesn't matter if she wasn't trying to hurt anyone."

"But we can't kill her!" Alynna protested. "That's not right!"

"Kill her?" Grant exclaimed. "We're not going to kill her!"

"Then why did you tell her she's seen too much? That she needed to be silenced?"

"I was just trying to gauge her emotions, see if she was willing to talk," Grant said. "If we send her to the Lycan High Council now, we'll never know how she broke into our security protocols. I want her interrogated, so we can patch up any holes in our system before the High Council takes her."

Alynna thought for a moment. "I have a gut feeling, and you know I'm usually never wrong about these things. Let me try to talk to her. Please Grant? Just us. At least in the room."

The Alpha nodded. "All right, see what you can get out of her."

Alynna left the observation room and went back into the other room with Meredith. She sat on the chair Grant was previously occupying.

"I told you I want a judgment from the High Council. I demand it; it's my right."

"And you'll have it," Alynna began. "Still, we have you on surveillance footage. You broke into our headquarters, attacked our people-"

"They were attacking me!" Meredith shouted.

"Because you broke into our facilities! Besides, we don't

know what you were up to. You could have been hiding in the dark, waiting to kill Dr. Cross."

"I swear I wasn't there to kill her! Only to steal ..." Her eyes flashed in anger, but then she slumped back down, realizing she had revealed too much.

"Steal what, Meredith?" Alynna asked. "So quiet all of a sudden? Well, since you're in the mood to listen, let me tell you what's going to happen. I *have* been studying my Lycan history lessons. The High Council will rule in favor of the New York clan. It'll be your word, the word of a self-confessed thief, against the most powerful clan in the world. Do you think you're going to go to a cushy Lycan jail? Oh no, we will seek the highest punishment for you. You'll be taken to the High Security Detention Center in ... hmmm ... remind me where it is again?"

"Siberia," Meredith grumbled, crossing her arms over her chest.

"Right. Siberia. You'll probably be there a couple of years, maybe more if we decide to appeal against your parole. I hope you like the cold," Alynna said with a smirk.

"What's my alternative?" the other woman barked.

"Oh, who said I'm offering an alternative?"

Meredith jerked forward in surprise. "Then what was that speech for? You want something."

Alynna laughed. "I suppose you could call it an alternative. But it would depend on you."

"On me?"

"Yes. It would depend on how much you want to cooperate."

She slumped back in defeat. "What do you want to know?"

"Are you working for the mages? Or for anyone else?"

Meredith's eyes narrowed. "What's a mage? And no, I'm not working for anyone else."

"Then what were you doing in our lab?"

She paused and took a deep breath. "I wanted to ... I was going to steal some corporate secrets and sell them to Fenrir's competitors."

Alynna looked genuinely shocked. "Wait ... you're a corporate spy?"

"Er, not exactly ...." Meredith bit her lip. "No one hired me, but this is what I do. I steal things and sell them for money."

"So you really don't know anything about witches or mages?"

She let out an exasperated sigh. "Again, I don't know what a mage is. Look." She leaned forward, placing her hands on the table. "I hacked into your system. I found your building and security plans—old ones—but most of them were still good. The office on the 33rd floor was the most secure place in the building. I figured you'd have all the best stuff in here. I was going to steal whatever new tech Fenrir was developing, sell it to the highest bidder, and then retire on a tropical island somewhere."

"You do know Grant Anderson, our CEO, is the Alpha of New York, right?"

She shrugged. "He was the richest man in town. I figured he wouldn't miss a couple of million dollars."

"How long have you been casing us?"

"About six months. That's the longest I've ever had to wait to do a job, mind you. I didn't plan on the doctor and the witch being here tonight. In fact, I'd been following them for a couple of weeks now. I know they're the two people who log in and out of the 33rd floor the most. I followed them to that private air strip and I hacked into the security there to see where they were going. The pilot didn't log in a return flight, so I figured I would at least have a few days."

Alynna looked incredulous. "I want everything you have on us. All your computer, cloud files. Everything."

"Fine, you'll get it. If I get my deal."

"Like I said, it depends on your cooperation."

"What else do you want from me?"

Alynna smiled. "Here's the deal ..."

"Alynna, are you insane?" Grant asked.

Lara had never seen the Alpha so agitated, but then again, the circumstances were understandable. After Alynna had explained her terms to the Lycan thief, she had returned to the observation room. Everyone had started talking to her at once, except for Lara and Jade.

"Maybe I am, but c'mon, Grant, it's brilliant!" Alynna exclaimed.

"Brilliantly insane." Grant rubbed his face with his hands. "You just asked a Lone Wolf, a corporate thief trying to steal from us, to join our security team!" He looked at Nick. "Tell me this is insane."

"Actually, Grant," Nick began. "I think it's a wise move."

"You're agreeing with her?" Grant put up his hands. "You've both gone insane."

"It makes sense, Primul," Alex said. "Keep your enemies close. It took a lot of work, but she was able to break into Fenrir. Sure, she'd be secure in the Siberia detention center, but think of what she could do for us."

"And what if it turns out she is working for the mages?" Grant countered.

"I don't think she is," Alynna said. "But we'll take every precaution. She'll be housed here in Fenrir, in a secure facility, and she'll wear an ankle bracelet. Her every move will be restricted, and she'll have to earn our trust. Besides, did you see her kick our guys' asses? Imagine having her on our side in a fight. She's a badass Lycan who can fight, hack, and steal."

Grant ran his hands through his hair. "Fine. But the moment she gets out of line, we're shipping her to Siberia. I still have to talk to the Council and negotiate terms of her detention." He looked at his watch. "Dammit, Frankie will be furious if I'm not home soon."

"Go home and be with your wife," Alynna said. "I'll take responsibility for Meredith."

"Fine. We'll go over the plan tomorrow." Grant turned to Alex. "You guys go home soon, I'm sure Mika's not going to be happy if you're not there first thing when she wakes up. Nick, let's go talk to the council." Both men left, leaving the rest of them in the room.

"You know I'll always support you, baby doll," Alex said as he drew his wife into his arms. "But I have to agree with Grant on one thing: this sounds insane."

Alynna blew out a breath, causing a tendril of her dark hair to fly away from her face. "I just ... I have this gut feeling, you know? Like, there's something about her that's ... that'll be good for us, for New York. Besides, the clan took me in and I was a complete stranger before that night we met at Blood Moon."

Alex gave her a nostalgic smile, his amber eyes glowing softly. "That's different, baby; you're one of us. You're meant to be with us." He frowned. "Meredith ... she's a Lone Wolf, she's not meant for clan life. She may not want to stay."

Alynna turned to Lara and Jade. "I hope this is okay with you both. She did break into your lab after all."

"I don't think she was there to hurt us, to be honest," Lara replied. "And when you asked her about the mages, she did sound like she didn't know what you were talking about."

"She did break a few experiments," Jade frowned, "but she

didn't try to hurt us. She was surprised and scared when we discovered her. And she was just trying to get away."

"See, that's what I thought. She was probably scared, being caught red-handed. Her first instinct was to flee, not fight."

Alex's brow wrinkled. "I hope we don't regret this."

CHAPTER TWELVE

L ara didn't get home until five a.m., and when she finally did arrive at her apartment, she collapsed in her bed. She woke up around eleven a.m., showered, put on her makeup, dressed in a light lavender blouse and khaki skirt, and made her way back to Fenrir. Grant had requested everyone to be back by noon for a lunch meeting in the conference room so they could regroup and figure out what to do next.

By the time she got there, everyone was already there, including one person she did not expect to see so soon.

"Hello, Lara," Liam greeted, his blue eyes raking over her. He was sitting in one of the chairs around the conference table.

"L-L-Liam," she sputtered. "What are you doing here?"

"Liam arrived early this morning," Alynna explained. "He said with so much urgent business in New York, and with everything happening with the mages, he thought it would be best to keep a close eye on things here."

"Shouldn't you be at home, with your clan?" Lara asked, her voice pitching higher than she wanted. Alynna smiled and her hand lightly patted his. Lara tamped down the urge to rip the younger woman's arm away.

Liam gave her a wolfish smile. "Things at home are well taken care of. I thought it best to come to New York and stay close to the developments here."

"Right." Lara flipped her hair and sat next to Jade, who was staring intently at her laptop screen.

Grant cleared his throat. "Let's begin, shall we? First, Dr. Cross?"

"I'm working on a few theories," Jade began. "I need to figure out first how the mages are controlling the humans. Vivianne has sent over a couple of books, and I've started reading them."

"I'll help," Lara piped in. "I've probably read some of those books at least once."

"However, I can't guarantee I'll find out how they did it." Jade frowned. "Not unless I can actually see it happening."

"Of course." Grant nodded. "Figure out as best you can how it's being done and then a way to stop or block them. Next," he turned to Nick, "security. What are we doing on that front?"

Nick leaned forward. "We've already alerted all our allies. Jersey and San Francisco, of course, Chicago, Connecticut, Philadelphia, and D.C. But until we convince the High Council to make it a concern for all clans, there's very little else we can do."

"Frankie, Liam, and I will be taking care of that," Grant said. "Since we're the three Alphas affected by the mage attacks, they'll have to listen to us."

"I'm concerned about one thing, something I'm sure you've thought about," Liam piped up. "A dozen mages or so, we can fight, but if they're controlling humans, then that means they have an unlimited supply of people who can fight for them. How many able-bodied Lycans can fight against an army of mage-controlled human slaves? Right now I have about 150 in my clan, and I estimate only 40 percent of them are over eighteen and under 50."

The New York Alpha's brow furrowed. "What do you suggest?"

"We need to bring in the humans. Not just alliance families, but the bigger human population. Maybe start with a few who can be trusted, some people in the government," Liam suggested.

"We've kept our existence a secret for hundreds of years," Nick said. "We can't just come out and tell the rest of the world about Lycans."

"That's why we start small. A few influencers here and there. The mages aren't just attacking us—they're attacking humans, too. Marshall Aimes was a victim, he deserves justice, and his people should know what they're up against."

"It's a risk," Alynna added. "But what if there's a situation where the mages attack in public? Or someone posts a video of a human being controlled by a mage? The last thing we want is to suddenly be outed."

Grant straightened up in his chair. "Those are all good points. But telling the humans ... that's up to the High Council. Besides, it wouldn't be just us who would be outed." His green eyes turned to Lara. "You'd be exposed, too."

"Then we should plead our case," Lara suggested. "Us to the Witch Assembly and you to your Council."

"Right. We have a meeting with the Council later today and will discuss this. Meanwhile about our new guest. The Council has approved our request, and she'll be in our custody for ten years ...."

Lara didn't envy the Alphas and all the responsibilities they had on their shoulders. She sneaked a look at Liam, who seemed deep in thought, his blue eyes pensive. A lock of dark hair had fallen over his forehead, and she longed to reach out and smooth it back and make his worries go away. She suddenly felt eyes on her, and Alynna was looking straight at her. A blush crept up her neck, and she turned away. She focused on Nick Vrost instead.

"Meredith has been fitted with a tracking bracelet to monitor her every move," Nick continued. "She seems to be cooperating with us so far."

"Keep an eye on your little project, Alynna. She's your responsibility," Grant warned his sister.

"Aye-aye, Alpha." She gave him a jaunty two-fingered salute.

He rolled his eyes. "Right. Now let's break for lunch and afterwards, Liam and I will get on the call with the Council as soon as Frankie gets here."

CHAPTER THIRTEEN

After they had finished eating, everyone except Liam left the conference room. Grant had gone to his admin's desk to get a few things ready for the meeting with the High Council. Liam breathed a sigh of relief, as he wasn't sure how much longer he could control himself around Lara. She looked lovely that morning, even with her eyes flashing with anger and surprise when she saw him sitting there. Whether Alynna had been deliberately trying to needle the young witch, he wasn't sure, but he thought he might have detected a hint of jealousy.

Coming to New York had been an impulse move. His inner wolf had been scratching and biting at him, unwilling to leave him alone. It was like he had sensed that Lara was far away, and he threatened to break out unless he got on the first plane to New York. He had caught the red eye, and the moment the wheels of the plane landed in JFK, his wolf had calmed and settled.

His thoughts were interrupted by the door opening and Frankie Anderson stepping inside the office. The New Jersey

Alpha (or was she the New York Lupa now? Liam wasn't sure) smiled as soon as she saw Liam, her mismatched blue and green eyes sparkling.

"Lupa," he greeted as he stood up from his chair.

"Liam! How nice to see you again!" Frankie greeted as she came up to him and gave him a hug. "I didn't know you were coming to New York."

"It was a last-minute thing." He scratched the back of his head and grinned down at her. "I'm sorry for missing your wedding. I had to take care of an emergency in Rio."

"It was too bad you couldn't come," Frankie said as she sat down beside him.

"Yeah, I heard it was exciting," Liam said with a knowing smile. Alynna had filled him in on the appearance of Grant's crazy stalker and how his mother had thwarted the young woman with a well-placed uppercut.

Frankie let out a laugh. "It certainly was."

"You are trouble at any event, aren't you?" Liam teased, making Frankie burst into another peal of laughter.

"Are you flirting with my wife?" Grant asked as he entered the conference room. His faithful admin, Jared, was right behind him. His tone was lighthearted, but Liam could detect just a hint of seriousness.

"I wouldn't dare, at least not in your own office." Liam winked at Frankie.

"Ah, *cazzo*," she said playfully, as she stood up to greet her husband. Grant wrapped an arm around her waist possessively and pulled her up to him for a passionate kiss. Liam turned away politely, but he couldn't help but feel a pang of envy. It was obvious the two were very much in love.

"C'mon," Frankie pulled away from him, "let's not embarrass poor Liam. I'm sure he doesn't need a show."

Grant grinned at his wife. "Whatever you say, sweetheart." He placed a hand on Frankie's stomach in an affectionate manner, and the two exchanged a heated glance. The electricity between the two was so palpable, Liam began to feel uncomfortable.

As if sensing his unease, Grant cleared his throat and led his wife to the chair next to his. "Let's get this meeting started, shall we? Jared?"

The young Lycan man who was playing with the screen stood up straight. "Yes, Primul. Switzerland is online."

"Put them up on the screen."

———

The meeting with the Lycan High Council went much better than Liam had thought it would, but the three Alphas didn't get their way. All the members of the council were in attendance— Rodrigo Baeles from Brazil, Jun Park from Korea, Oded Khan from Iran, Adama Amuyaga from Ghana, and of course, their de facto leader and elder, Lljuffa Suitdottir from Sweden, who took the lead in the meeting. Grant and Frankie pled their case, and Liam reported what had happened in San Francisco. The five council members were shocked, and they promised swift action on their part. The loss of Lycan life was not a small matter, considering their dwindling numbers.

However, the Alphas didn't get anything solid from the council, no matter how much they pushed. They'd been lobbying the High Council for months to work with the Witch Assembly and have some plan of action. At the very least, a formal statement or rebuke would alert all the Lycan clans all over the world. The attacks at Fenrir and Grant's attempted murder hadn't swayed them, but now the mages were targeting humans. The mages could expose their secret, so they should have no choice but to take them seriously.

Grant and Frankie had other business to discuss with the council, so Liam excused himself from the meeting. He was glad to go, as the meeting was giving him a headache. Liam tried to pay as much attention as he could, but he couldn't wait to get out. Being so near Lara, he had to go and find her. And then what? He wasn't sure.

While taking the elevator to the lobby, he decided he would wait for Lara. It was almost 5 p.m., so she should be coming out any moment.

Time passed slowly, it seemed, at least to Liam. He checked his watch numerous times. It was almost 6:30 p.m. Where the heck was she? Was she avoiding him? Did she sneak out another exit when she saw him waiting? He cursed softly. He was about to give up when he spied a familiar figure headed toward the exit. "Jade!" he called out.

The Lycan scientist stopped in her tracks. "Alpha." She nodded at Liam. "Can I help you with anything?"

"Yes," he began but hesitated. "I mean, I was wondering ...." Shit. How was he supposed to explain why he wanted to see Lara?

Jade pushed her glasses up the bridge of her nose and then crossed her arms. "She's not here."

"I don't-" Liam stopped, forgoing the lie. "Where can I find her, then?"

She sighed. "Meet me at Rusty's in the East Village at 9 p.m. tonight."

"I don't understand."

"Listen." She looked him straight in the eye. "Do you want to see her or not? My best friend hasn't been the same since we came back from San Francisco. You obviously have something to do with it, I'm not blind. Now, show up at Rusty's or not, I don't care. But if you want to know where she is, trust me and meet me there, okay?"

Liam looked down at the scientist. Jade was about a whole foot shorter than him, and he had a hundred pounds on her, yet the piercing look she gave him made it hard to say no. "All right."

CHAPTER FOURTEEN

A t 9 p.m. on the dot, Liam was already waiting outside Rusty's, as Jade had instructed. A few seconds later, the scientist appeared, walking around the corner from the bar.

She gave him a quick once over. "Let's go." She nodded toward the entrance of the dive bar, and he followed her down the steps, going in behind her as she pushed the heavy wooden door open.

Rusty's seemed almost out of place in New York, where hipster themed bars and glittering clubs ruled the social scene. It was narrow but long, with the bar taking up space in one end and a couple of booths on the opposite side. It didn't have a particular theme, but the dark wood paneling, neon beer advertisements, and low lighting made it seem like it should have been on the roadside somewhere in middle America, not in the Big Apple.

"Why are we-" Liam stopped short as Jade jerked her head toward the bar. Or rather, the bartender.

Strawberry blonde curls were piled sexily on top of her head, her lips were painted red, and she was wearing a low-cut black T-shirt that showed off her cleavage. Liam's body instantly reacted to Lara as she stood behind the bar, mixing a drink and chatting with a customer. Said customer seemed to enjoy her company, his eyes never leaving her ample breasts.

His blood began to boil, and his wolf let out a growl, releasing a deep rumbling from his chest. Striding over to the back of the bar, he grabbed Lara by the arm and pulled her to him.

"What the hell? You can't come back here!" Luminous green eyes grew wide in shock, her painted lips formed into a perfect "O." "Liam? What are you doing here? How did you know ...?"

"What am I doing here?" he asked, his voice tinged with anger. "What are *you* doing here? Why are you working here?"

"I need this job!" She pulled her arm away from him.

"You need this job?" he roared at her. The thought of her broke and unable to pay her bills gnawed at him. His wolf growled angrily at him, and he deserved it. He should have been taking care of her. "Do you need money? I can give you money!"

"What?" she asked in an incredulous voice. "I don't need your-"

"Hey, Red," the burly older man at the other end of the bar interrupted her. "You can't have boyfriends behind the bar. Health code rules."

"Sorry, Rusty." She waved at him. "I'm taking my break now, while we're slow." She wiped her hands on a towel hanging from a rack and then removed her apron, placing it on the hook behind her.

When Liam realized she was wearing a tiny pair of denim shorts that showed off her long legs, he ripped the apron from the hook and handed it back to her. "Put it back on," he snarled, barely keeping himself in check.

Lara rolled her eyes and then put the apron back on. "Happy?" she asked, jutting her chin up in defiance.

Ignoring her, he pulled her away from the bar and sat her down in the farthest booth. "Talk," he said as he slid in next to her, spreading his arms across the back of the seat and the table, essentially trapping her against the wall.

Green eyes blazed up at him. "I don't owe you an explanation! How did you know ... wait, never mind. Jade. That traitor."

She crossed her arms over her chest, which only pushed her breasts up higher. Liam's eyes were drawn down like magnets to the ample curves, and he groaned inwardly as he imagined what her nipples would look like. Probably pale and pink, puckered like raspberries and-

"Eyes up here," she huffed, making his head snap up. "Now, what are you doing here?"

"I was waiting for you at Fenrir after work. You didn't come out, so Jade brought me here." There was also no sign of the Lycan scientist, he just realized. Did she just bring him here and then leave? "Now tell me why you're working here. Are you in trouble? Doesn't Fenrir pay you enough money?"

"Not that it's any of your business, but Fenrir pays me plenty, but most of it goes into a common fund for my coven," she explained.

Liam frowned. "You're the one working for it, shouldn't you be able to keep your money?"

"It doesn't work that way, not with witch covens. We live as a community, kind of like Lycan clans, but we share everything. I grew up never needing or wanting for anything, because the coven took care of me. Besides, Fenrir pays me a shit ton, and I've made more money than I'll ever see or need in my life. They also pay for my apartment and all my daily expenses while I'm working, so I haven't even touched my share of the salary."

The Lycan looked confused. "Then why are you here?"

"You wouldn't understand."

"Try me."

She gave an exaggerated sigh. "Witches are nurturers by nature. We have this need to take care of people. If we don't, we feel empty inside. Bartending allows me to do that in some way. People are always looking to share their troubles with anyone willing to listen. Rusty lets me pick up a shift one night a week so his regular bartender, Joy, can stay at home with her kid."

"You couldn't do anything else?"

"Well, some witches work as teachers, nurses, or even doctors. I never went to college, and I've been doing this since I was 18, though I started as a waitress at a diner when I was 16. I was a really shy kid, and it helped get me out of my shell." She shrugged. "I'm sorry you don't approve and you think this job is lowly, but-"

"That's not what I meant!" he interrupted, the look of her hurt on her face slashing at his insides. He took her hand in his, rubbing her palms with his thumbs. "I don't think less of you because you worked as a server or bartender. I just don't like what you're wearing and having all these men stare at you."

She laughed. "I've had much worse than that guy. I can take care of myself."

But I should be the one taking care of you, he thought.

"Liam, you can let go of my hand now," she said, a blush creeping up her neck.

"Red, c'mon!" Rusty barked from the bar. "You can make out with your boyfriend later; bar's starting to fill up." Sure enough, two large groups of patrons had come in at the same time, and the line at the bar was two deep.

Lara grew even redder, which he couldn't help but find cute. "I should go ...." Lara pushed at him gently. He stood up and let her pass but followed her to the bar as she resumed her shift.

"Can I get you anything?" she asked as she began taking orders.

"Just a beer," Liam said.

She nodded and grabbed a bottle from the cooler behind her. "On the house," she said as she handed him the bottle.

With a nod, he grabbed it and took a swig, letting the bitter drink cool his throat. He scooted farther away from her, taking the last seat at the bar. Rusty, who must have been the bar owner and Lara's boss, gave him a strange look but went about his business, helping Lara serve the patrons and cleaning up used glasses.

Liam sipped his beer, watching Lara work and seeing a whole different side of her. He realized he didn't know a lot about her and what she was like growing up as a witch. She intrigued him for sure, but he wanted to know everything about her. He'd never felt this way about any woman. Sure, he'd dated before and had his share of lovers, but few held his interest for more than a few weeks. The closest thing he had to actually liking or falling in love with someone was Alynna, but there was always something that stopped him, and he knew that was because she was meant for someone else.

"Can I get you another drink?" Rusty asked, eyeing his empty bottle.

"Sure. Another beer, please."

The older man grunted and got a cold bottle from the cooler, then slid it over to him. "Lara never told me she had a boyfriend." He eyed Liam suspiciously.

"I don't suppose she tells you everything," he countered.

"She's been working here for months now; I've never seen her bring a man in or even go out with any of the guys who hang around here. And they can be quite persistent."

Liam gripped the bottle of beer in his hand so hard it almost broke. The thought of all those men flirting with her and asking her out made him want to smash something—preferably one of the heads of those men flirting with her now, their eyes roving over her luscious body.

"A real heartbreaker, that one." Rusty shook his head and walked to the other end of the bar.

Liam took another bitter swig, wishing he had something stronger that could get even a Lycan drunk. The liquid felt good but didn't do anything to quench the real thirst he felt, nor calm his wolf. The damn animal was scratching at him, urging him to go and show those men who Lara belonged to.

Fucking hell. Liam considered himself a practical man, cool and collected. His parents had raised him to be polite and treat everyone, especially females, with respect. The women he'd dated in the past (except for maybe one or two very bitter ones) always told him he was a "good guy." But ever since that encounter with Lara in the elevator, he had become some sort of possessive alpha male he-man. He was itching to bleed something—or someone.

The hours ticked on, and by the time Rusty gave out the last call warning, Liam was wound tighter than a spring. A couple of the customers had bought Lara drinks, which she discreetly poured down the sink when no one was looking. The shots, though, she couldn't turn away, but she only had one or two that night. Rusty was cleaning up and shutting down the bar while Lara disappeared into the back room.

Liam's keen hearing heard a distinct crash from the other room, and the hairs on the back of his neck stood on end. He shot to his feet and ran to the back room, ignoring Rusty's protests. As he flung the door open, Lara's soft cry made his wolf snarl and growl.

"I told you, I'm not interested!"

A large figure clad in an expensive Armani suit loomed over the redhead, his hand braced on either side of her as he trapped her against the wall. She was pressed up against the concrete, her face red with anger.

"Not interested in me? A broke little waitress like you in New York? C'mon honey, don't you know who I am?" He leaned down.

Red filled Liam's vision as he marched toward them. He didn't wait another second before grabbing the man's shoulders and pulling him off Lara. A sense of satisfaction settled over him as the man's face twisted in surprise.

"What the fuck, man?!"

"Get away from her," he growled.

Mine, his wolf snarled.

The other man pulled his arm back, but Liam's inhumanly fast reflexes beat him, and his fist connected with bone, muscle, and skin. The man's eyes rolled back, and he fell in a slump as Liam released him.

"I was about to take care of him!" Lara said, raising her hand. "You do know I can call up a tornado if I wanted to, right?"

"You sure were taking your sweet time," Liam spat.

Green eyes flashed with anger. "Are you implying I wanted this creep feeling me up?"

"What? No!" *Shit.* He rubbed his face in frustration. "I mean, what were you waiting for?"

"I can't just show my power to anyone," she stated, her arms crossing over her chest. "I was trying to get him to stop first! And then you come in here with your weird Alpha vibes and knock the shit out of him!"

"He deserved it!" His wolf yipped in agreement. The animal seemed to bristle and was urging him to kill the other man. *Fuck, what was wrong with him?*

"Shit, Red, I knew you'd be trouble," Rusty said as he entered the back room. He shook his head.

"Fuck! Rusty, I'm-"

"Shush, Red." The older man bent down and checked the man's pulse. "Still alive, thank Jeebus."

"Shit, I'm so sorry, Rusty," she cried, putting her hand to her face.

"I said shush, Red," the other man barked. "You've got nothing to be sorry for, okay? Not if this sonofabitch tried anything with you. I'm gonna call the cops. Do you wanna press charges?"

"No."

"Yes," Liam answered at the same time, which earned him a scowl from Lara. "This guy could sue the bar, Lara."

"I wouldn't put it past the bastard," Rusty said with a nod. "Pressing charges could give us leverage."

She let out a breath. "Fine. Call the cops."

———

Lara rubbed her arms to keep the cold away. Despite the fact that it was summer, a chill ran through her as she thought of what happened in the back room. She had finished giving her statement to the police, and while Liam was giving his, she had snuck out to the back alley.

The guy was a regular; his name was Brad or John or something generic. He was some big-shot Wall Street type who thought he was doing her a favor by slumming it at Rusty's and paying attention to her. He tipped a twenty for every drink and laid it on thick whenever he showed up, which seemed to be almost every shift she worked. He always bragged about how much money he made and what he spent it on, whether it was a new toy or fancy vacation, making sure Lara was always around to hear the dollar amounts.

She ignored him as best she could, but he was persistent, asking her out several times. She wasn't sure what had triggered him tonight, but she wondered if he saw her talking to Liam earlier as he walked in with his friends. He had been uncharacteristically rude to her, even saying lewd comments to make his asshole buddies laugh. When she brushed him away again, she had thought that was the end of it, but apparently he had snuck into the back room and pounced on her the first chance he got. If Liam hadn't been there ....

Truth be told, she had frozen in terror. She'd had her share of persistent men, but none had ever tried to physically overpower her. She had felt afraid, unsure of how she could get him to stop without having to resort to revealing her powers. By the time she had snapped out of it, Liam had dragged her attacker away.

"Are you all right?"

Liam's low baritone voice soothed her, caressed her almost. "I'm fine."

"You're cold."

"I'm not." Before she could protest further, a pair of strong arms came around her and pulled her against a hard, warm chest. She felt warmer, his body running as hot as a furnace and his scent enveloping her.

"Rusty's taking care of everything," he said as she relaxed into him.

They stayed quiet for a few minutes until a discrete cough made Lara jump away from Liam.

Rusty's head popped out from behind the back door leading to the alley. "The police just left; they said they'd call us back about signing some papers so you can formally press charges."

"Thanks, Rusty," Lara said. "I'd like to go home now."

"Maybe your boyfriend ...." He cocked his head toward Liam.

"Liam."

"He's not my boyfriend," she said at the same time.

The older man shook his head. "Could've fooled me. Anyway, maybe he wants to be our bouncer or something. You sure got a mean right hook, son."

Liam smiled. "I'll think about it."

With a final nod, Rusty ducked back into the bar.

"I'll take you home," Liam said.

"I'm fine. I'll catch the subway or something." Lara started to walk away from him, but he grabbed her arm.

"No," he stated. "I don't have a car service, and I just took a cab here, but I'm taking you back home."

She was so bone tired, she didn't even argue as he led her out to the front of the bar. He flagged a passing cab and opened the door before helping her inside.

The door slammed behind her, and for a moment, she thought he was just going to leave her. But he stood outside the cab, staring at the door before he shook his head, then got into the front seat.

"Where are we goin'?" the cabbie asked. Liam looked back at her, and she gave the driver her address.

As the cab made its way uptown on 3rd Avenue, Lara snuck glances at Liam. His normally kempt dark hair was tousled, probably from running his hand through it with his fingers. She couldn't see his face from this angle, but the image of those glowing blue eyes as he grabbed her attacker away from her sent shivers down her spine. Despite the fact that she was raised to be a strong and independent woman/witch, she couldn't help but find the possessive and protective streak he displayed tonight sexy. When she first met Liam, she had thought him reserved and well-mannered, but now she was seeing a whole new side of him.

No. She shouldn't think of him like that. But as memories from that night in San Francisco flooded back into her brain, she couldn't help it. Heat spread through her body, starting from between her legs, and the insistent throbbing there was slowly driving her mad. Looking down the line of his broad shoulders and arms, she wondered what his bare chest looked like underneath his crisp white button-down shirt. He'd seen her half-naked and touched her in the most intimate of places, but she realized she'd never even seen him with his shirt off.

The muscle in his jaw tensed, and he turned his head to look back at her. Turning away quickly, she hoped he didn't notice her ogling him.

The cab stopped in front of her building, and Liam quickly got out and opened the door for her.

"Thanks," she murmured as she stepped out, taking his hand as he helped her. The zing of electricity with his touch made her skin tingle.

"I'll walk you to your door," he said in a low voice, his hand touching her lower back lightly, guiding her into the building and toward the elevator.

Lara bit her lip. His hand never left her lower back, and the heat seemed to brand her. God, it was like the temperature spike in the elevator, and then *that* thought reminded her of the elevator in Fenrir. *Get a hold of yourself.* She took a deep breath and waited for the elevator car to reach her floor.

The door opened, and when they reached her apartment, her heart felt heavy, knowing he was leaving soon.

"I'll see you-"

"Stay." She couldn't help but say the word. She didn't want him to leave. She wanted him to stay and hold her. Make her feel safe. Make love to her. Just for one night, she wanted to know what he looked like, naked and on top of her, inside her. Arousal burned through her body, and nothing else would slake her desire. She wanted Liam and knew he wanted her, too.

"Lara, I can't-"

"I don't feel safe." Low blow. But she could see it worked. There was hesitation in his eyes as he struggled with the decision.

He nodded, and she opened the door with her key.

Her apartment was small, but well-furnished and designed. It was a long studio apartment, and the front door opened to a kitchen/dining area, separated from the living room by a breakfast bar. A shelf further divided the space, and her queen-sized bed was at the other end, right by the large windows that had a fantastic view of the Chrysler Building.

"This is nice," he said, looking around.

"Yeah, it's small but cozy." She put her purse down on the kitchen counter.

"Lara this isn't ... what I mean is ...," he stammered, then ran his fingers through his hair. "Fuck!" He strode toward her and grabbed her arms, pulling her close. As his head lowered, her heart hammered against her chest and she closed her eyes. Expecting his lips on hers, she was surprised when it landed on her cheek instead.

"Sleep," he whispered. "Let me sleep beside you."

She sighed, the fatigue seeping into her bones. "I'm gonna get ready for bed." Without another word, she went to the bathroom.

Sleep? Was that a code word for sex? Shaking her head, she looked at herself in the mirror. *Jeeze.* No wonder Liam wasn't trying anything. Most of her hair had come undone from her updo and hung limp around her face. Her eyeliner was all smudged, making her look like a crazed raccoon, and most of her lipstick was gone. She'd have to fix that if she was going to seduce Liam.

After scrubbing her face clean, she took a deep breath. Looking around the bathroom, she realized she didn't have anything sexy to wear. *OK, improvise.* She put on a white tank top, but not the matching pajamas. Her ample breasts stretched the fabric tight, her aroused nipples poking through the white cloth. Shimmying out of her shorts, she kept her sexy lace underwear on. *It would have to do.*

"Liam?" she called as she opened the door. He was already on the bed, his feet bare but clothes still on. Lara walked closer to the bed. "Liam, I wanted to-"

She stopped when she saw his eyes were closed. "Liam?"

Silence. She gave him a gentle nudge and called his name again.

The bastard didn't even move.

"Seriously?" she huffed. Letting out a long sigh, she lay next to him, her body straight and stiff as a board. What the heck was going on? A couple days ago, he couldn't wait to get in her pants. Now, he was snoozing soundly in her bed.

The bed dipped slightly, and she held her breath. Strong arms wrapped around her, and hope sparked in her chest. He nestled his nose into her hair, his lips nearly touching her ear. And then he began to snore softly.

Well, fuck.

CHAPTER FIFTEEN

"Lara, are you listening to me?"

"Wha ... yes!"

"What did I just say then?" Jade crossed her arms over her chest and raised her brow.

"You said that I should ... put the thingy on that." She waved her hand over the first piece of equipment she could find.

"That's the coffee machine."

"Right." Lara sighed.

"Why don't you go home for the afternoon?" the Lycan scientist suggested. "Milly," she called into the intercom which linked them to the outer lab. "Can you come here for a second?

"But you need my help for the bracelet!" she protested.

"You've done what you can; I really think it's coming along well. I do have other projects you can help with."

Jade had been working on a special bracelet that could stop a witch or warlock from using his or her power, with Lara as her guinea pig. In theory, it should also work on a mage. They had had some hiccups throughout the development of the device, but as they focused their resources and time on the project, they had definitely made more progress. When they had tested it initially, Lara could still fight the special anti-biorhythm waves that the bracelet emitted to counter her own power. This latest iteration (Mark 15, according to Jade), was definitely much stronger, and it took more concentration on her part to break the device's hold.

"Of course," Jade began. "If you're busy with *other* things ..."

"No, I'd love to help. I'm fine, I swear ... I just haven't been sleeping right."

Jade guffawed and muttered what Lara thought was "That's what she said" under her breath.

"What did you say?"

"Nothing."

Before Lara could say anything else, the door opened and Milly stepped into the inner lab. Jade whipped around and started relaying instructions to the other assistant.

Yes, it was definitely lack of sleep that was making her brain go haywire, Lara thought. Not the lack of sex. Or the fact that for four days now, she'd been waking up next to a hot, gorgeous Lycan who did nothing but snore next to her. At least one of them was getting his beauty sleep.

God, was she that unattractive and unsexy? Every night, Liam would show up at her home. She didn't even ask him to stay those following nights; he simply followed her to her apartment. After the first night, she was prepared, wearing her sexiest lingerie to bed, but he simply cuddled her from behind and snoozed away. The night after that, she squirmed around, trying to face him and press her breasts against him, but he just kissed her forehead and whispered goodnight before falling asleep. And last night? Well, she gave up and closed her eyes as he nuzzled her neck and relaxed his body against hers.

For four torturous nights she slept in his arms, unable to sleep, her body aching and wanting. Each morning, she would wake up with his rock-hard erection pressed up against her ass, but he never made a move. He slept in whatever clothes he had worn during the day and never took off anything except his shoes and socks. She was so desperate to feel his naked skin on hers that she rubbed her heels against his toes. *He must think I'm some sort of foot fetishist.*

This morning, once again it seemed like his battering ram was trying to storm her castle, but no siege took place. Liam gave her a soft kiss on the cheek, rolled over, and went to the bathroom.

"Argh!" she groaned aloud. What was wrong with him? What was wrong with her? She had practically served up her body to Liam, and he wouldn't even make a move. Each morning, he'd give her a kiss goodbye and leave, only to show up at her house later that night to torture her all over again.

A shrill sound interrupted her thoughts. She grabbed the phone from her pocket and glanced at the Caller ID. "Mother," she greeted.

"Lara, how are you? I've missed you, and so has your father," Vivianne replied.

"I miss you guys, too." A heavy feeling pressed over her chest. She usually went home to the coven every weekend, but with the trip to San Francisco and so much work to be done at the lab, she simply didn't have the time.

"I have a surprise for you, darling. I'm on my way to New York now; I should be there within the hour."

"What?" she exclaimed. "That's wonderful!" Excitement fluttered in her heart. It had been too long since she'd seen her mom. In her twenty-four years, living in New York City was the first time she'd ever been away from her parents and the coven.

That was just the way it was, as witches always fared better with their kind. Oh, how she missed her mother's energy and warmth.

"Do you work tonight? Should we have dinner?"

"No, I'm free tonight," she said.

"Excellent. Let's meet at that cafe around the corner from Fenrir. I'm afraid I can't stay long. I'll probably drive back as soon as we're done."

She frowned. It was a three-hour drive back to the upstate compound, which meant Vivianne would probably have to cut dinner short. A quick glance at the clock told her it was a quarter past three. "How about I just meet you as soon as you get in?"

"Oh really darling? That would be great. Are you sure Jade won't mind?"

Lara looked over at the scientist who was busy reading through her test results. "I don't think so."

"Perfect. I'll see you when I get in."

"See you then, Mother." She put the phone down. "Jade, I'm going to go meet my mother, if that's okay?"

The brunette pushed her glasses up her nose and nodded. "Sure thing. Say hi to Vivianne for me."

"Will do!" She waved goodbye to Jade as she picked up her purse and left the lab, heading straight to the cafe. She sat down at a table near the window and a few moments later, her mother walked in. Lara shot to her feet, then ran into Vivianne's embrace.

"I've missed you, darling," her mother said, giving her a kiss on the cheek.

"Me, too." She breathed in her mom's familiar perfume, the scent filling her with comfort. Being an only child, she and her mother were very close. They looked so much alike and Vivianne had aged so well that people thought they were sisters.

"Now," Vivianne began as they sat down, "tell me what's going on with you."

Lara filled her mom in (minus everything that had been going on with Liam, of course), from the trip to San Francisco to her work in the lab.

"I've been in talks with the Witch Assembly, too," Vivianne said. "I think I've convinced them of the urgency of the mage matter." Her eyes grew sad. "I just wish it hadn't taken more deaths for them to take things seriously."

"Using blood magic to control humans shouldn't be anything but a serious matter." Lara gritted her teeth.

"The Assembly will resume talks with the Lycan High Council. That's the best we can hope for, for now. Now, darling, about the other matter."

"Other matter?"

"You know, the suitors."

"Oh, right."

The older woman frowned. "Are you sure ...."

"Yes," she said quickly. "I'm sure."

"All right. I've narrowed it down to a few candidates." Vivianne paused to take a sip of her water. "Most are interested, and one is very interested. In fact, he's eager to meet with you."

"Fine, set it up," Lara replied, her eyes scanning the paper menu in front of her.

"Don't you want to know his name?"

"Uhm, sure ...."

"Wesley Morgan."

Lara's head snapped up. "From the Massachusetts coven?" She didn't know Wesley personally but had heard of the coven. They were one of the bigger and more influential covens in the northeast United States.

"Yes." Vivianne's eyes practically glowed with happiness.

"He's very nice, a little older than you, and will probably one day be an elder of his coven. Handsome, too."

"Sounds nice," she replied. "When does he want to meet?"

"As soon as possible, darling."

"How about tomorrow?"

"Tomorrow?" Vivianne asked in a surprised voice.

"Yeah, there's no use waiting." Lara shrugged. "He's from a good family, a good position. If we're compatible, then we shouldn't waste time getting to know each other."

"Well, I'm sure I can arrange it. Do you want to drive back with me tonight?"

"Yeah, I just have to go back to the lab and tell Jade. I haven't been home in a while; I'm sure she'll understand."

"Very well, darling. Whatever you want."

Vivianne called the young waiter to their table, and they ordered their drinks and meals. Lara inwardly sighed in relief, but a knot in the middle of her stomach began to form. No, this was what she needed. Get on with her life, find a husband, produce the next Fontaine heir. Forget Liam Henney. True Mates? Sheesh, what was she thinking? It was obvious he didn't want her in that way. Maybe it was the pheromones. Or maybe he still held a torch for Alynna and couldn't bring himself to make love to her. Whatever the reason, she wasn't going to stick around to find out.

———

After their light meal, Vivianne went up to see Grant and Nick, while Lara headed back to lab.

"I need a couple days off," she said to her friend as she entered the inner lab. Jade was busy making modifications to the bracelet using 3D modeling software to try out different designs. "You said you didn't need me for a bit, right?"

"Of course you can have some time off. You've earned it. When are you leaving?"

"Tonight. I'm driving back home with my mother."

"Tonight?" Jade asked in a surprised voice. She turned away from the computer and faced her friend. "Why are you leaving so soon?"

"I have coven business to attend to," she said curtly.

"When will you be back?"

She shrugged. "I'm not sure. Depends."

Jade stood up and put her hands on her hips. "Depends on what? And what coven business?"

Lara worried her lip. "I'm ... going to meet with this guy."

"What guy?

"A warlock from another coven."

"Oh, is this about the mages?" Jade inquired.

"No. It's ...." Lara bit her lip again.

Jade's keen eyes narrowed. "What's going on here, Lara?"

"Nothing! I mean it's just a guy my mom wanted me to meet."

"Oh." Jade looked disappointed. "Like a blind date?"

"Er, sort of. I'm looking for potential ... husbands." She regretted saying that, but she didn't want to lie to her friend.

"What?" Jade's eyes grew wide. "What do you mean husband? Have you met him before?"

"No. But he's a warlock from another coven, a good one."

The Lycan scientist scratched her head. "Are you saying you're going into an arranged marriage? Does Vivianne know?"

"My mother set it up."

"Hold on!" Jade raised a hand, then paced back and forth. "I don't understand. Where did this come from? Why are you suddenly ... I mean ...."

"This is just how it's done," Lara explained.

"All witch marriages are arranged?"

"No." Lara huffed. "Look, we're all free to marry and love who we like. But if we want to, we can meet witches and warlocks from other covens and see if we're suitable."

"So why don't you wait for someone you love?" Jade asked. "You're only twenty-four."

"Yes, but I have a duty to my coven. To my bloodline." Lara crossed her arms over her chest. "I'm Charlotte Fontaine's last living witch heir. We need to up our numbers, especially with what's going on with the mages."

"So you'll be a sacrificial lamb? A broodmare to boost numbers? Lara, you're much more than that! And what about Liam?"

The name brought an uncomfortable feeling to her gut. "What about him?"

Jade rolled her eyes. "He obviously likes you, and I can tell you like him!"

"I do not! And he doesn't like me!" she protested.

"How do you know?"

What was she supposed to say? *Uh, well Jade, we've been sleeping together, but not sleeping together. He just lies there and does nothing while I lie there like a pathetic idiot, wishing he'd drill me into the mattress.*

"Lara, he's obviously in lo-"

"You don't know anything!" Lara shouted before Jade could finish the word. Maybe it was better Liam didn't want her. "It's complicated; I don't expect a Lycan like you to understand!" The moment the words came out of her mouth, she regretted them. Jade's face crumpled, the hurt obvious on her face. "Jade, that's not what I meant! I'm so sorr—"

"Go, then." Jade turned away from her, going back to her computer. "Take as much time as you need."

"Jade." She put her hand on the other woman's shoulder, but she shrugged it off.

"I said you can go." Her voice was cold as ice, and guilt slashed through Lara's belly.

"I'll ... I'll see you when I get back."

Jade let out a huff but said nothing. With a heavy heart, Lara left the lab.

CHAPTER SIXTEEN

"Are you sure?" Daric looked at the message on the phone.

"Yes," Victoria confirmed. "Our little spy has finally come through with some important intel."

"Your idea was ingenious, Victoria," Stefan commended. "And this is important news indeed. Who knew those creatures could be so clever?"

"They even hid their little laboratory from the High Council and the Assembly," Victoria sneered. "Those fools had no idea what Grant Anderson and my dear sister were cooking up."

"This could be a problem, Master," Daric said. Aside from the report of what the Lycans were doing at their facilities, there were also pictures and schematics of a bracelet that could potentially stop witches and warlocks from using their powers. "We can't let them continue."

"Indeed," Stefan said. "Looks like we'll be putting *our* new toys to the test."

CHAPTER SEVENTEEN

For the second time in a few days, Liam found himself waiting at the Fenrir lobby. He paced back and forth, running his hands through his hair. The receptionist eyed him warily but said nothing. At first the older woman had recognized him and asked if he needed to go to Grant's floor, but he declined. He considered asking her if he could access the 33rd floor, but with all the security surrounding the lab, she'd probably deny there was even such a floor. He could probably have asked Grant or Alynna, but that would raise too many suspicions.

Where the heck was she?

Liam stopped and checked the elevator again. He was antsy, and why wouldn't he be? Last night, he showed up at her apartment, knocked a couple of times and rang the bell, but there was no one home. He even went to Rusty's, but as soon as he got there, the older man informed him Lara wasn't working that night.

Anger and frustration burned through him, and his wolf couldn't be appeased; it clawed and howled at him. Where was she? Did she just disappear? He didn't even have her phone number, not even Jade's. He had gone back to his hotel and lay awake half the evening, trying to keep his wolf from taking over his body and roaming New York City to try and find Lara.

Fuck, he messed up. After that night at Rusty's, she seemed so scared and vulnerable. He knew she wanted him, could smell her arousal. But somehow it felt wrong. He couldn't take advantage of her. Liam wanted her badly, but he had to put his own needs aside. She said she didn't feel safe, and those words burned through his middle. He couldn't rest, knowing how frightened she was. He had to make sure she felt safe and secure. Then she had offered herself up like Cleopatra unrolling from the rug, and he had almost taken her right then and there. Despite his desire for her, he wanted her to want him, and not because she felt grateful or scared.

He had slept for an hour or two, but kept waking up. Unable to sleep, he showered, dressed, and then decided to wait at Fenrir for Lara to show up and arrived at 6:30 a.m. sharp.

He had been waiting for two hours, but there was no sign of her. However, as soon as Jade entered the building, he stalked toward her.

"Where is she?" he asked.

"Well, good morning to you, too," Jade replied in an irate voice.

"Good morning," he said gruffly. "Now, Lara. Where did she go?"

Jade frowned, then a sadness briefly flashed across her face. "She went home."

"I checked; she wasn't at home."

"Not her apartment," Jade bit out. "Home. To her coven."

"Oh." Fucking hell. Had he driven her away? Or come on too strong? "When will she be back?"

"I don't know." Jade shrugged and walked away.

"Wait!" Liam called. "I need to see her."

Jade turned around, peering at him with those light green eyes from behind her glasses. "I'll give you directions to the coven compound upstate, but if I do, you need to do me a favor."

"Anything."

"You need to go and see her as soon as possible, okay?"

Jade's request seemed strange, but it was his plan anyway. "I will."

———

Lara's eyes glossed over as Wesley droned on about his estate in Massachusetts during dinner. Or was it about his family history? Or his many businesses? She wasn't quite sure, but she gave him and his parents a polite smile while fantasizing about stabbing her ears with the pretty silverware that had belonged to her grandmother. This was a disaster. *What was I thinking?*

Vivianne hadn't been kidding when she said Wesley Morgan wanted to see her right away. They had come to the New York coven compound the following night for an early dinner. Wesley and his parents, James and Anna, had driven in from Western Massachusetts, eager to meet her. Vivianne and Graham, Lara's father, had prepared dinner at home for the occasion. The Morgan's had arrived on time, and even brought some wine and a few gifts.

Wesley was handsome, and his parents seemed nice enough. He was blonde, blue-eyed, tall, and built like a track star. But there was just something about him, something off that she couldn't put her finger on. From the moment they had met, Wesley's eyes looked at her greedily, not unlike the men at Rusty's. At least the customers at the bar were a little more discreet. She suddenly felt like she was under a microscope whenever Wesley's gaze came upon her.

And as the dinner progressed, she grew even less inclined to get to know him. All he wanted to talk about was politics and gossip, or himself. The Morgans were an old, aristocratic family, after all, and much older than the Fontaines. Wesley's uncle served as one of the members of the Witch Assembly.

"So Lara, your mother mentioned you've been living in the city," Anna said, when there was an actual lull in the conversation.

"Uhm, yes, Mrs. Morgan," she replied politely.

"And what have you been doing there?"

Lara looked at her mother, who answered for her. "She's actually there to spend time with her cousin, Cady Vrost."

"Cady?" James' eyebrows rose. "Isn't that ... Victoria's daughter? I thought her father was named Gray or something?"

Graham nodded. "Yes, that's right. But she's married now. To the New York Beta."

Anna's eyes bugged out, and she nearly choked on her wine. Her husband gave her a helpful pat on the back. "B-beta?" she stammered. "As in, the Lycans?"

"Of course!" James said. "I remember hearing the story from my brother. She's not a witch, though, right?"

"Nope, no powers," Vivianne supplied. "But turns out she was the fated mate to the Beta."

"Well, can't stop fate, I suppose," James said with humor. "And how do you spend your time there, Lara?"

"I've been working with Cady ... in the marketing department," she fibbed. She didn't realize she'd have to come up with some cover and that sounded much better than the real story. After all, she couldn't tell them she was helping the Lycans and showing them how her powers worked. "I was thinking of getting into marketing. And maybe going to school."

"Well, I suppose it's nice that you have a hobby," Wesley remarked. "But you know, you needn't be worried about getting a job once we're married. I'll be providing for you and our children."

Lara shot her parents a look, and Graham spoke up. "There'll be time enough for such discussions," he said in a lighthearted voice. "But why don't I go and get dessert?" He stood up and went to the kitchen.

"Oh, a man who cooks!" Anna marveled. "It must be nice." She smiled at Vivianne.

"I hope you inherited some of your father's cooking skills," Wesley said.

The sneer in his voice made Lara's blood boil, and she narrowed her eyes. Wesley had been making side glances at her father the whole night. He thought she didn't notice. Sure, her dad was unconventional, but he was more of a man than that weaselly warlock. She wondered for a second what would happen if she sent a small air current toward his wine glass and tipped it onto his expensive Italian suit.

As if hearing her thoughts, Vivianne shot her daughter a glance. "James, why don't you tell us about the party at the Henricksons'? I was so disappointed to have missed it."

James Morgan proceeded to tell them about some boring gathering, and a few minutes later Graham came in with slices of cheesecake for everyone. As he placed a plate in front of Lara, he gave her a small smile but said nothing.

Lara was glad they were already on dessert, and she scarfed down her piece quickly. As soon as they were all done, Anna declared it was getting late and they should start driving back home. Lara and her parents escorted their guests to their car.

"It was wonderful meeting you, Lara," Wesley said as he took her hand and brought it up to his lips. He looked at Vivianne. "I'll be in touch. I'm sure we'll have a lot to talk about."

Vivianne gave him a bright smile. "Of course."

As soon as everyone said their goodbyes and the Morgans' car was out of sight, Lara sighed with relief.

Graham and Vivianne looked at each other.

"What?" she asked.

"So, what did you think of Wesley?" Vivianne said.

"He's er ... interesting."

"He's an ass," Graham stated. "And if I never see him again, it'll be too soon." Lara didn't think she could love her father more than at that moment.

"Well, Lara?" Vivianne's face was inscrutable.

"I ... I'm sorry, Mother." Lara shook her head. "I can't ... I can't marry him. I'm so sorry."

"There's no need to apologize," Vivianne soothed, taking her daughter's hand. "I'm just ... I'm glad you tried. And that you're open to finding someone again."

Lara said nothing but nodded.

"Look, why don't you go in and get ready for bed? Don't worry about the Morgans; I'll take care of it, okay?"

"Thank you," she said gratefully. She was glad to be rid of Wesley Morgan.

"Of course," Graham said. "You're not—wait, did the Morgans leave something behind?" He looked around her and squinted his eyes, as if trying to make out something far away.

Lara turned around. There was a vehicle headed toward their house. It was dark, like the Morgans' chauffeur-driven Mercedes, but as it came closer, it became clear it was an SUV.

"Are you expecting anyone, Graham?" Vivianne asked.

"No, are you?"

The vehicle stopped in front of their home, and as the door of the SUV opened, Lara felt the hairs on the back of her neck prickle.

Liam.

CHAPTER EIGHTEEN

The drive to the town of Little Water in Upstate New York hadn't taken as long as Liam had thought, but the preparations to get there took much longer than anticipated. After Jade had given him precise instructions on how to get to the New York coven's compound, he had to pick up a special package at the private airstrip outside New York City. Then he had realized the package was way too big for the car he had rented so he had to wait until the rental company could find a bigger vehicle. But it had been worth it, and he couldn't wait to see Lara's face when he showed up.

After about three hours of driving, he finally reached Little Water. The witch coven compound wasn't in the charming little town, and Jade explained that he had to drive just outside it, about 15 miles out into the more remote part of town. He drove down Main Street and followed it until he reached a small country road. After about 20 minutes of driving down that road, he finally found the turnoff that led to the compound.

And so he found himself driving straight into a witch coven compound. It was actually quite … normal. Not that he was expecting anything abnormal. The compound was pretty. Small houses lined the main street, all well-maintained and their gardens immaculate. It looked like any suburban American street, except they were surrounded by enormous trees and thick forest. He continued driving until he reached the end of the cul-de-sac where he found a ranch-style home painted in white and blue, just as Jade had described.

The whole trip, he'd been wracking his brain, trying to figure out what exactly he was going to do when he knocked on Lara's door and what his first words would be once she saw him. This part of his plan he didn't figure out beforehand, but he hoped he could wing it.

As soon as he parked the car in front of the house and saw Lara standing on the front porch with her mom and an older gentleman, he knew he didn't have to worry about announcing himself and knocking on the door. And when he opened the doors to the SUV, the first words out of his mouth weren't exactly what he thought they'd be.

"Hugo! You beast, get off her!" Liam shouted as he climbed out of the driver's seat. Hugo had been going crazy as they approached the house, and Liam thought the dog just needed to relieve himself. As soon as the passenger door opened, he bounded up the porch steps and placed his huge paws on the front of Lara's dress.

"Hugo! What are you ...?" The dog's large, wet tongue licked Lara's face, making her giggle. "Oh my! How did you get here?" She gently pushed him down on all fours, and then scratched his ears. "That's a good boy ...."

"Uhm, sorry about that," Liam said sheepishly, scratching the back of his head. "He's been cooped up for the last couple of hours." He climbed up the steps and grabbed Hugo by the collar. "Calm down, boy."

"Alpha, how nice of you to ... drop by?" Vivianne Chatraine raised a brow at him.

Liam cleared his throat. "Uhm, yes. Well ... I ...." He should have known Vivianne would be here, too. "I had Hugo fly out here from San Francisco. He missed her."

"Oh, did he?" Vivianne smirked.

The older man beside them cleared his throat. "And you are ...?" He gave Liam a suspicious look and crossed his arms over his large barrel chest. Dressed in red flannel, jeans, work boots and sporting a thick white beard, he looked like a lumberjack. Or Santa Claus. A grumpy Santa Claus, anyway.

"Oh Graham, this is Liam Henney, Alpha of the San Francisco clan and Lara's, uh ...."

"Friend," Liam said quickly, extending his hand toward the older man.

"A friend, huh?" Graham eyed him. "I'm Graham, Lara's father." He took Liam's hand.

"Nice to meet you, sir." Liam returned his firm handshake.

"Alpha," Vivianne began. "Will you excuse us?" Vivianne took Graham by the arm and dragged him inside the house.

"What are you doing here?" Lara whispered to him as soon as the door closed.

"Why are you whispering?" he asked loudly.

"Because ... argh!" she exclaimed, throwing her hands in the air. Hugo nuzzled her side, nearly knocking her over.

Liam caught her before she fell, pulling her close to him. God, he missed her, missed being close to her and smelling her delicious strawberries and champagne scent.

Lara looked up at him, meeting his eyes, then quickly disentangled herself from his arms. "Answer my question. What are you doing, and how did you get here?"

"Jade gave me directions."

"Jade?" her voice raised slightly. "You didn't answer my first question."

"I went to Rusty's last night, and you weren't there. You

weren't home either, and you didn't tell me where you were," he explained. "Why did you run away from me?"

"I wasn't running away; I went home!" she said in an exasperated voice.

"You left without telling me; I think that's running away."

"I don't have to explain my whereabouts to my *friends*," she said, emphasizing the last word.

Liam opened his mouth to speak but realized he didn't have a counter. Before he could say anything, the front door opened and Lara's father came back out to the porch.

"Alpha," Graham said in his gruff voice.

"Liam, please."

He nodded. "Liam. It's getting late, son."

"Yes," Lara said in a fake cheery voice. "Thanks for bringing Hugo; it was nice to see him. Enjoy the drive back."

"Actually, it's way too late for Liam to be driving back, and that poor pooch of his shouldn't be cooped up in a car for another three hours." Graham patted Hugo's head, and the dog licked his hand. "He should stay. Both of them. Your mother's already getting the spare room ready."

"What?" Lara asked, her eyes growing wide.

"Thank you, sir. I appreciate it," Liam said. Lara shot him a dirty look.

"Well, we still have some leftover pot roast from dinner; you're welcome to have some if you're hungry." He turned to his daughter. "Your mom and I will be heading to bed. Take care of our guest, will you, Lara?"

"Fine."

With one last nod, he bid them goodnight and went back in the house.

"C'mon," Lara grumbled. "I'll show you to your room."

Liam followed Lara into the house with Hugo behind them,

his tongue wagging. Once again, Liam was struck by how normal everything inside seemed.

"Not what you expected?" Lara said as she led him down the hallway.

"Not at all," he replied with a chuckle.

"I'm afraid we just put away our cauldrons and pointy hats," she said wryly, which elicited another laugh from him.

"Well, here you go," Lara said as they stopped at the door at the end of the hallway. "The guest room's in here. There's a bathroom with towels and stuff. Feel free to root around the kitchen if you're hungry. I'm sure Hugo will enjoy the pot roast, too." She scratched Hugo on the head, earning her a happy whine from the dog. "I'm going to bed. Goodnight." She walked to the door next to his, went inside, and slammed the door.

"Well, boy," he glanced down at Hugo, "what do you think I should do?"

Hugo looked at him with doleful eyes and cocked his head.

"Yeah, that's what I thought."

CHAPTER NINETEEN

L ara woke up as the sun streamed into her bedroom. She had thought she wouldn't be able to sleep, since she was so confused and angry that Liam was here. However, strangely enough, she had slept soundly. After taking a quick shower and putting on some leggings, a shirt, and her shoes, she padded out of her room. The door to the guest room was open, and she spied the neatly made bed with sheets folded on top of the covers. Had Liam left already? Before she could think about him any further, she squashed down the disappointment and walked to the kitchen.

"Mom? Dad?" she called out. They were usually up at this time, having coffee at the kitchen table or outside on the porch. The kitchen was empty, but the scent of fresh coffee wafted through the air.

There was a note taped to the refrigerator with her name on it. Opening the piece of paper, she read the contents as she poured herself a cup of coffee.

Lara,

Your father and I are headed to the Smith farm to help them with an emergency. We'll be back tomorrow morning.

XOXO.

"What?" she exclaimed out loud. Had her parents suddenly left her alone? She shook her head. There was something not right here.

A sharp bark interrupted her thoughts. *Hugo!* That meant Liam was still here. She rushed out the back door, which lead to the rear porch and back yard. Of course, "back yard" was really their acreage behind the house. The huge dog looked like he was having the time of his life, running around and chasing squirrels.

The rhythmic thwack of metal against wood caught her attention. Turning her head toward the wood pile to the right of the porch, she half-expected her father to be standing there, chopping wood as he did in the morning. What she saw, however, was something surprising. It was Liam, chopping down log after log and wearing only a pair of sweatpants.

With the axe raised high, the muscles along Liam's bare back and shoulders rippled as he brought the heavy tool down. The piece of wood split in two in one motion. Sweat dripped down between his shoulder blades, and he took another log from the pile and positioned it on the chopping block. She couldn't help but stare at him, her eyes moving down from his wide shoulders to his strong back to his tapered, trim waist. He wasn't overly muscled, more on the lean side, but his form was phenomenal.

Liam must have sensed her watching him because he quickly turned around. A blush crept up her cheeks, realizing she'd been caught. He flashed her a smile and then stalked up to her.

Oh, dear Lord.

If the back side of him was attractive, the front was even better. Thick corded muscles stretched across his shoulders. His arms were strong and—was that a tattoo around his right arm? His perfect pecs were divided by a strong line. His six-pack was defined and led down to the deep V along his hips. A light sprinkling of hair disappeared under the low-hanging sweats, and the outline of his cock was obvious through the gray fabric. She quickly averted her eyes and took a sip of her coffee.

"Good morning," he greeted as he jogged up the steps. He grabbed a towel hanging from the bannister and wiped off the sweat.

"Good morning," she murmured, staring into the thick, dark liquid in her cup.

"I saw your parents this morning; they said they had to go to a friend's farm."

"Yeah, they left me a note." God, even four feet away he was still too close. The mixture of sweat and his citrusy smell sent heat through her body and desire straight between her legs. "What are you doing?"

"I asked your mom if there was anything I could do to repay her for her hospitality. She asked me if I could chop some wood since she and your dad were called away."

"Shirtless?" She put her hand over her mouth. "I mean, where did you get your clothes?"

"Oh, these?" He grabbed a white shirt and put it over his head, and she sighed in relief. "She said it belonged to one of your cousins or something. I think it fits okay. I brought some other clothes too, but your mom didn't want me to get them dirty."

The shirt was about a size too small and clung to his body, only puckering out where his nipples were. She wondered what they tasted like.

"Okay," she whispered. "I mean, I should go back." She turned to head back into the house, feeling dizzy all of a sudden.

"Wait," Liam said in his low baritone. "Will you show me around your compound? I'm out of wood, too. I was thinking I should get some more. Your dad said there are always fallen logs around the property I could collect once I was done." The small smile tugging at the corner of his lips made him seem even more handsome.

"Uhm, sure. I need to go ... get my boots and I'll come out in five minutes." By the time she came back, Liam was playing with Hugo in the yard, tossing him a stick, which the goofy giant dog happily fetched and brought back to his master.

"What would you like to see first?" she asked as she walked up to him.

"Well, I've seen your house and the back yard. How about showing me and Hugo the woods around your home?"

"Sure." She nodded and led them toward the thick grouping of trees at the far end of the property.

"This really isn't what I expected," Liam confessed as he followed Lara. She took them to the small foot path that led deeper into the woods. As soon as Hugo saw the path, he darted straight ahead, his happy barks echoing through the forest.

"Oh yeah?" She smirked. "Walking into a witch coven ... what did you expect? Cobwebs and bats? Pointy hats and warts?"

"Oh no, not warts," he said, stepping ahead of her. He pulled a branch out of the way so she could walk safely past. "It seems very normal."

"Well, we have to appear normal, you know," she stated. "We're one of the oldest covens on the east coast, and we lasted this long because we're careful."

"No one's ever stumbled upon your compound before?"

She sidestepped a stray branch on the path. "Yeah, about

that. This place is protected by magical wards and spells. If anyone were to come by it, they would think it's nothing special and just move along."

"Huh."

"Yeah. Huh." She gave him a strange look. "It's funny how you found us so quickly."

"I had help." Liam gave her a smile. "And I almost did miss it."

"Right."

"So, I'm curious, if you don't mind sharing witch secrets ...."

"Yes?"

"Your dad."

She let out a laugh. "You're wondering how my parents got together, right?"

"Yeah ... it just seems ... you know ... mismatched."

It wasn't the first time someone had asked her about Vivianne and Graham. They did make a strange pair, with Vivianne so elegant and worldly, while Graham was the complete opposite. Her father very down to earth, gruff, and loved to work with his hands. She decided to indulge him. "Most people assume my dad's not in the picture, since I have the same name as my mom and grandmother."

"Is he your real dad?"

"My biological dad, you mean? Yes." She was used to the look Liam gave her, so she continued. "Our culture is very different from human or Lycan culture. For example, in my family, it's always the female children who have the powers. And in witch society, the amount of magic you have determines your rank." She paused. "Now, it'll take me too long to explain the hierarchy of the witch and warlock families and why they're that way, but in the order of things, my mother outranks my father. So, when they got married, he took her name."

"Wait." Liam paused, putting a hand on her shoulder. "So your dad ... his name is Graham Chatraine?"

She nodded. "Yup. That's legal, by the way. He changed it."

"He didn't mind?"

"Well, he loves my mother, and if he wanted to marry her, that was the condition."

"Wow, I can't believe ...."

"Do you think less of him because of that?" Lara asked.

"Not at all; I really respect your dad for doing that."

Lara was surprised by his answer. "Well that's how things are done. He's originally from Tennessee; he used to live near the Smokey Mountains with his coven. Yes." She laughed when he made a face. "There are redneck witches and warlocks, just like there are redneck Lycans."

"So he moved out here?"

"Yeah. He didn't mind marrying a higher-ranking witch, but he wasn't too crazy about moving to New York. He actually thought my mother lived in New York City at first. But they fell in love, and he moved out here. Believe it or not, my dad built the house and he maintains it. He loves working with his hands, so he's a handyman for the coven."

Liam grew quiet, and they continued deeper into the woods with her in the lead.

The walked in silence, but after a while Lara couldn't take it anymore. She stopped and then turned around. "What are you doing here?" She finally asked the burning question on her mind.

He seemed surprised but narrowed his eyes at her. "Why did you run away?"

"I did *not* run!" She stepped forward, looking up at him.

"Then why didn't you tell me you were leaving?"

"I didn't know I was supposed to ask for your permission," she countered. Anger rose up in her.

"That's not what I wanted!"

"Then what do you want?" she screamed at him. She pushed at his chest in anger, the air currents around her rushing toward him. Power rushed through her body, and she struggled to control it.

"I just want to know you're okay," he said, putting his hands up in defense.

"Why? Is it because I'm your *friend*?"

"What are you talking about?"

"Argh!" She threw her hands up in frustration. She turned around, but he grabbed her and spun her back to face him.

"What did I do, Lara? To make you run away from me?" he asked softly.

"I said I-"

"Don't lie to me," he said, an edge in his voice.

She looked up into his eyes; her breath caught in her throat. What was she supposed to say? She ran away because he didn't have sex with her? Or because she was scared of falling for him?

"It's nothing!" She pulled away from him and ran down the path in the opposite direction. Liam called her name, but she ignored him, continuing toward the house and running as fast as her legs could carry her. However, even with a head start, Liam caught up with her just as she was running up the steps to the back porch.

"Stop! Lara, stop!" He reached her at the top of the steps and turned her around to face him. "Now, tell me what did I do?"

"Nothing! You didn't do anything!"

He frowned. "Is it because I didn't have sex with you?"

She took a deep breath. "Liam, it's not ... it's fine. I know you just think of me as your friend, and that's fine. You're probably still in love with Alynna and-"

"Hold on!" He grabbed her shoulders and pushed her up

against the door. "First of all, I didn't push you to have sex that night because I could tell you were still shocked and scared. It seemed to me that since San Francisco, you didn't want anything to do with me, and suddenly you were inviting me to bed? I wanted you to come to me because you wanted to, not because you were scared or because you felt grateful that I rescued you from that asshole."

"I-"

"Let me finish." His grip held her in place. "Next, I'm not in love with Alynna or anyone else. She's my friend, that's all. And as for thinking of you as a friend ... well, I have enough friends."

His lips came down fast on hers, so fast she didn't have time to protest or move away. Not that she would have. She parted her lips, letting him slip his warm tongue into her mouth.

Liam pressed up against her, his cock like steel as it pushed up against her very core. Unable to help herself, she ground up against him, moving her hips until her clit bumped against the ridge of his cock. Pleasure zinged through her, from the spot where their bodies were grinding against each other. Wetness pooled between her legs, soaking her underwear.

"Your bed or mine?" Liam managed to say as he pulled away from her.

"Yours," she cried softly as he lifted her up into his arms and wrapped her legs around him. She clung to him as they walked through the house, down the hallway, and to the guest room, where he deposited her on the bed.

As she moved to unbutton her shirt, Liam shot her a heated look. "No, don't. I want to unwrap you myself," he said with a cheeky grin and whipped off his own shirt. He shucked off his sweats in one motion, causing his thick penis to bob up against his flat stomach. Dear Lord, he was big. And how could he get so hard all of a sudden?

His eyes seemed to glow in the dim light of the room.

Crawling over to her, he grabbed her ankles and pulled her to his lap, which elicited a gasp from Lara. Nimble fingers made quick work of the buttons on her shirt, and he quickly unclasped her bra and tossed it away.

"Gorgeous," he said as his eyes devoured her naked breasts. Large, warm hands cupped them, and he bent down to put one puffy pink nipple in his mouth. "Even better than in my imagination."

Liam gently pushed her down, then reached between her legs. He pulled at her leggings, pushing them down in one motion along with her panties. "Fuck, you smell amazing." Fingers played with her clit, making her moan and buck her hip. "I can't wait, sweetheart," he whispered as her positioned himself between her legs. "I've been waiting too long to feel you around me. I promise, I'll make you scream and moan while I lick you later ... but for now ...."

"Wait," she gasped. She didn't want him to stop, but she couldn't risk it. "I'm not on any kind of birth control."

His eyes grew lucid, and he nodded. "Wait here." He disappeared for a moment into the bathroom and came out with a foil packet. Quickly, he ripped off one side with his teeth and placed the thin sheath over his cock, before climbing on top of her.

"Lara," he whispered as the tip of his cock pushed at her entrance, moving in slowly.

She cried out as he suddenly filled her in one motion. Gripping his hair, she tried to anchor herself as his cock began to slide out slowly.

"So perfect." He was so thick and long that Lara had to bite her lip to keep from crying out, as the slight sting of pain gave way to pure pleasure. His hands gripped her ass, pulling her hips up so he could fuck her deeper. "Jesus, you're tight and so wet, sweetheart."

She moaned, unable to think or breathe or cry. Liam was now picking up the pace, rocking into her fast and deep, his cock hitting just the right spot to send shockwaves through her. She felt herself tightening around him, gripping him as her body began to convulse.

"Liam!" she cried, her hands waving in the air, sending papers flying across the room and books falling off the shelves. Trying to get a hold of her power, she gripped his biceps and bit into his shoulders, which only made him let out a growl and pump into her faster, as one hand snaked up her breast to tweak and tease her nipple. That sent her over the edge and the orgasm came fast and blinding. Even as she closed her eyes, whiteness filled her vision.

Liam rumbled her name, thrust into her one last time, and then his body grew tight like a bowstring. His hand moved between them, stroking her clit and making her cum once more. As her pussy tightened around him, he let out a guttural sound that half-sounded like her name and a growl, and then collapsed on top of her.

Heavy breathing from both of them slowly evened out. Liam rolled away, his feet planting onto the hardwood floor with a heavy thud before he raced to the bathroom. He came back out quickly and slipped his sweats over his lower body and climbed back into bed with her. "Sorry," he murmured, giving her a quick kiss on the forehead. "Just needed to clean up." He pulled her back against his chest and settled his arms over her.

Right. The condom. She'd been so caught up in what they were doing she had almost lost her head. Thank God she had remembered. She couldn't risk it. Not that they were True Mates or anything. Right? No, of course not.

"You seem deep in thought for someone who's just had two orgasms," he teased.

"Oh, ha ha." She turned in his arms. "I just-"

A bark followed by a yipping sound made both of them sit up.

"Hugo!" Liam hopped off the bed and disappeared down the hallway. A few minutes later, the huge beast came bounding into the bedroom.

"Hey, down boy!" Lara tried to keep the sheet around her chest and calm the excited dog as it tried to lick her face.

"Sorry about that ... guess he doesn't like being forgotten," Liam said sheepishly as he pulled Hugo off the bed. He led the dog out of the room and shut the door behind him.

"It's okay, we should have let him in." A blush crept up her cheeks.

"Hey now," he said, sitting down next to her and caressing her cheek. Tipping her head up, he kissed her softly. "Want some lunch? I could probably whip something up."

"You cook?"

He laughed. "C'mon. I'll cook, you watch, and I'll tell you about the time I worked at a restaurant."

CHAPTER TWENTY

A s promised, Liam cooked up a massive lunch for them as he told Lara about his summers spent working at a Mexican restaurant in the Mission District. His mother wanted him to learn about hard work, so she had sent him to her friend's restaurant. He began by washing dishes, then moved up to bus boy, and eventually helped with the actual cooking. Three summers he did that, and each night, he would come home exhausted, but it was one of the best experiences of his life.

And now, watching Lara eat and enjoy the food he made, this was definitely *the* best experience in his life. *Well, not the best,* he thought with a grin. Lara was a beautiful woman, but in his arms, she was exquisite. His wolf was pleased, too, seeing how he was taking care of her. The animal seemed to settle much more when she was around.

After lunch, they got re-dressed and went outside. Lara showed him the rest of the property, the parts they hadn't gotten to earlier. The entire coven compound was much larger than he thought, and they spent most of the afternoon circling the perimeter. Hugo opted to stay behind and snooze on the porch.

"What was it like, growing up in a witch coven?" They walked hand in hand, following another foot path. Lara had explained that there were lots of foot paths in the forest because the witches got most of their wild herbs there.

"Well, I suppose it's not much different than a normal childhood. I went to the school in Little Water, had friends there, and the other kids here."

"And all the witches and warlocks grew up together?"

She nodded. "And studied together. You probably don't know, but not all children of witches and warlocks have magic. Most do, and there's a higher chance if both parents are magical. All the children learn about herbs and potions and spells, but right around puberty, the power either manifests itself, or it just doesn't."

"How does the power work, exactly?"

"Well, see, witches and warlocks use nature magic. All our potions come from ingredients taken from the earth and our spells draw power from nature. The knowledge, like, how to mix the right ingredients and say the right words has been passed down for generations. However, all these potions and spells are, in themselves, inert. Any human can mix herbs and chant spells. However, when a witch says the spell or mixes the potions, only then does it become magically active."

"Didn't the humans ever suspect what you were?"

"Not for the most part," she replied. "All training is done within the compound, and we are sworn never to reveal ourselves. I'm sure you Lycans have the same kind of laws."

"We do," Liam said. "But we try to blend in with humans as much as possible. We hide in plain sight, for the most part. But a place like your compound, and so close to a town, surely that attracts attention?"

"We explained that the compound belonged to an ancestor of ours, who had gifted the land to her children and descendants, and that we were free to live and build our homes here. Which is the truth."

"These woods are a part of that land?"

She nodded. "Yeah. I love it here, and I'm glad we have it. I used to come out here a lot to get away, and also to practice my powers. It's not like I can just practice in the house."

"No, you can't." He gave her a wink, remembering what had happened to the papers and books in the bedroom. She blushed, her delicate skin taking on color. He thought she looked even more beautiful.

"Are you the only blessed witch in your coven?" He helped her over a fallen log, lifting her up by the waist and holding her against his chest.

"Yes. Probably on the east coast, too. We're very rare. The only other one I know in America is a cousin who lives outside Tennessee. She can call rain." Lara smiled up at him as he slid her down his body. "What about you? What was it like growing up as a Lycan? And a future Alpha?"

He took her hand and kissed it, then tucked it into his arm. "Normal, too, I guess."

Lara agreed silently. Despite what she personally thought of Akiko Henney, she had to admire the Lupa for raising her son to be grounded and humble, despite his obviously privileged background.

"Normal, up until I hit puberty, at least," Liam continued. "Then, I had to learn to control my shifting. All Lycan teens have to go to a summer camp or after school program of sorts. We can't be shifting around humans or we'd risk exposing our secret."

"So you go to shifter school?"

Liam laughed. "Yeah. One of our clan members took us into Muir woods for one summer. Taught us how to shift, control ourselves, and even defend ourselves in wolf form."

She wrinkled her brow. "I think I've only ever seen you in your wolf form that time when we rescued Cady."

"Would you like to see it? My wolf, I mean?"

"Are you allowed to show me?"

"Of course. I mean, you've already seen it." He began to take off his shirt. "But I'll show you mine if you show me yours."

"What? Get naked?"

"No, silly." He leaned down and kissed her. "I mean, will you show me what you can do? With your powers?"

"You want to see?"

He nodded. "Show me what you've got."

Lara took a step back and spread her arms and closed her eyes. As she opened them, she focused on a tree branch about twenty feet away. She lifted her hand and sent the currents toward the branch, knocking it down.

"Wow," he said, impressed. "I didn't know you had that much control."

She smiled and moved her hand in a circle, sending the leaves at her feet swirling around her. "I've never really called on a tornado, at least I haven't tried."

"I'm curious about something. Since you can control wind currents, can you fly?" he asked.

"No." She shook her head. "Believe me, I've tried. And it hurt! I levitated myself once but lost control. All I got was a sprained ankle."

"Your powers are pretty cool, though." He grinned at her.

She smirked. "Now you show me yours."

With a sneaky smile, he pushed his sweats down, enjoying the blush on her cheeks as her eyes immediately zeroed in on his half-hard dick. He focused, calling the wolf from within. Then his body hunched into himself, and his wolf burst from his skin. Lara gasped.

Being in his wolf form, his senses were even more

heightened. The grass, trees, wind, Lara's delicious scent—he could smell everything. He could also hear everything, from the squirrel scrambling up the tree behind them to the raccoon rooting around the ground for a grub about 20 feet away.

"You're beautiful," Lara said as she reached for him cautiously. He knew his wolf was impressive with thick, dark fur and blue eyes. Most Lycans in their animal form were much larger than normal wolves, and he wouldn't have taken the Alpha position if his animal weren't so physically dominant. On its hind legs, his wolf was over six feet tall with massive jaws that could probably snap a human torso in half.

He could smell the fear rolling off Lara, but there was nothing for her to worry about. Neither he nor his wolf would ever harm her. In fact, his protective instincts seemed to amplify around her. Her hands touched the soft fur on his head, and he nuzzled against her.

"There's no one around here," she said, stroking his fur. "If you like, you can run around, be free."

With a last lick of her hand, Liam's wolf darted into the trees. Powerful paws beat on the ground as he ran through the woods. It had been too long since he'd had this kind of freedom. The pressures and obligations of being an Alpha, running a business, getting his startup off the ground, all those things had kept him far too busy.

The wolf ran as fast and as far as his legs could take him. The end of the property came into view, and somehow he felt a powerful pull to turn back. Probably the magical wards set up by the coven. In his wolf form, everything that was magical was amplified, too. He stopped, backed away from the invisible force and headed back toward Lara.

Air currents followed him, almost beckoning him back. The currents caressed his fur, like a lover would, and when he saw Lara sitting on the grass cross-legged, her eyes closed and arms outstretched, he knew it was her way of calling him back to her. A few feet before he reached her, he instantly changed back into his human form.

Lara's eyes flew open. Her cheeks were heated, and her heady scent mixed with arousal tickled his nose. He was rock hard instantly, his cock standing at attention. Without another word, he pulled her up to her feet and walked her backward until she was braced against one of the tall pine trees.

"Liam?" she asked.

"You smell amazing, did I ever tell you that?" He nuzzled her neck, breathing in her scent. "Especially like this, when I can smell how much you want me." Liam knelt down in front of her, his hands trailing over her breasts and belly until they reached the fly of her pants. Fingers popped off the buttons, and he tugged the jeans and her panties down in one motion.

"I didn't bring a condom," he said, sliding his hands behind her, cupping her ass cheeks. "So I'm going to have to get creative."

Lara whimpered as Liam buried his face in her wet sex and hooked one leg over his shoulder. His mouth lapped at her pussy lips, already so drenched with her own juices. Christ, she was delicious. He pulled her closer, trying to get as much of her as he could in his mouth. Sliding his tongue along her slit, he probed her, slipping inside her. She cried out and grabbed his head, moaning his name as her hips met the thrusting of his tongue. Her pussy sucked at his tongue, clenching around him.

"Liam!" she screamed. Her body tightened, and Liam switched his tongue with his fingers as his lips latched onto her hard clit. He sucked deep as his fingers fucked her harder, bringing her over the edge. Her body shook as her orgasm washed over her like a wave, and Liam urged her on, lapping and thrusting harder.

Lara collapsed against the tree, breathing heavily. Liam

could hear her heartbeat as it thudded a maddening rhythm, then slowed down. Breathing a sigh, she grabbed his shoulders and pulled him up. He leaned down and gave her a slow, sensual kiss, wanting her to taste herself on his lips.

She moaned and pressed her naked torso up against the bulge in his pants. Before he could do anything else, she turned him around and made him lean against the tree.

"Lara, what are you doing?" Really, though, that sparkle in her eyes and her kneeling down should have given him a clue.

"Getting creative." She bobbed her head down at his cock, licking the pearl of precum that had formed on the tip.

"Lara," he moaned as her soft, perfect lips wrapped around the tip of his cock. Her tongue swiped at him, swirling around him. The sensation seemed to increase tenfold, and he sank his fingers into her thick auburn locks. Slowly, she took more of him in, as much as she could.

Small, soft hands wrapped around the thick base, squeezing him. Fuck, she was gorgeous on her knees, pleasuring him. The low vibrations she made with her mouth made him jerk his hips.

"Sweetheart," he groaned. "You don't have to ...."

Lara could only get past the tip, but she used her hands to milk him. She used both hands, stroking his length up and down. He wanted to push himself into her mouth all the way but satisfied himself with short, shallow strokes. Besides, that tongue of hers ....

"Lara ... if you don't stop ... I might ...."

She released him with a soft pop. "You might what?" Her face tilted up at him; she was wearing a naughty smile.

"I won't last long if you keep that up," he said in a low, throaty voice.

"Then don't." She popped him back into her mouth, and he let out a groan. He shouldn't, but she wanted him. Wanted him to lose control. Damn if it wasn't sexy as hell.

He held back as long as he could, but her sweet mouth sucking on his cock was too much. With a roar of pleasure, he let go, spurting out hot jets of cum straight into her mouth. With eyes opened, she took him all in, looking up at him as she swallowed every last drop.

Lara stood up, wiping her mouth with the back of her hand. She flashed him the most wicked smile, and he pulled her close to him. "You are one naughty witch." He buried his nose in her hair, inhaling the pure scent of her.

"And you are delicious." She smirked, rubbing herself over his semi-hard cock, both of them still naked from the waist down.

He twisted her around and tugged her closer to him. "Careful there." Sliding his hands down her belly, he tickled the soft patch of neatly-trimmed hair over her sex. "I should punish bad little witches like you."

Her breath hitched, and she melted against him. "Let's go back to the house."

––––––––

Liam whistled happily as he flipped pancakes over the stove. The bacon was warming up in the oven and the coffee was brewing, which meant breakfast would be ready in minutes. His muscles ached, but it was well worth it as he pushed Lara to the brink of exhaustion last night. He smiled, imagining her beautiful face tucked into his side as she slept soundly afterwards.

After their romp in the woods, they had walked back to the house and Liam had carried her straight into her bedroom, wanting to bury himself in her again. He took her against the wall, teasing her and making her mewl and cry until she had begged him to make her cum. God, she was magnificent, and he had brought her onto the bed where he lay under her, watching her gorgeous tits bounce up and down as she took charge. She rode him hard and fast, taking her own pleasure. Lara came at least twice before he let go and lost himself in her.

Liam wanted to keep her in bed all day. However, they were running out of condoms, and he was pretty sure they were going to need a lot more. So they went into town for dinner and stopped by the pharmacy. Of course, he couldn't get any STDs, and there was a low possibility of getting her pregnant, since Lycans didn't reproduce as easily as humans. Still, he wanted to respect her wishes. His wolf, however, seemed to relish the thought of her belly growing large with his pup. No, of course not. Biologically, the child would be human, of course. He shook his head. Thinking of that would only lead to a place he couldn't go.

He pushed those thoughts aside and concentrated on breakfast. Yes, breakfast, he could do. He slid the fluffy pancake onto a plate and proceeded to add another cup of batter onto the hot pan.

Normally, his senses picked up everything that went around, but he was so distracted that he missed the sound of the motor cutting out in the driveway and the turning of the key in the lock as the front door opened.

"Good morning, Alpha." Vivianne Chatraine leaned against the side of the kitchen doorframe, the smile on her face bright. She looked like the cat that ate the cream.

Liam nearly dropped the pancake as he was mid-flip but caught it. "Oh, Vivianne, I didn't realize ... you and ... you're back."

Vivianne seemed unusually calm, despite the fact that Liam was wearing nothing but a bathrobe. Lara's fluffy pink floral bathrobe. He groaned inwardly, wishing he'd brought more clean clothes.

"Making breakfast, I see?" She gave him a knowing smile.

"Yes. Uhm, we ... Lara and I ... we were going to head back to New York as soon as you came back. Wanted to get a head start."

The older witch cocked her head to the side. "I'm sure you did." She turned around to leave but stopped. "My husband is unpacking the car. I suggest maybe taking this time to change into something more ... appropriate?"

Liam nodded and put the pan down, then quickly walked to the guest room. They had slept in her room last night, so at least he didn't have to worry about waking her up. He quickly showered and got dressed in his last clean outfit, a pair of dark jeans and a long-sleeved henley shirt. As he passed by Lara's room, he saw that the door was open, which meant she was up.

He walked to the kitchen, where Lara and her parents were already sitting at the table, enjoying breakfast and chatting happily.

"Sit down, son." Graham called him over, putting down the newspaper he'd been perusing. "Thank you for making us breakfast."

Liam felt guilt shoot through him but sat down next to the older man anyway. "Of course. It was the least I could do for your hospitality."

Lara's eyes went wide, and she choked on her coffee.

"Are you all right, darling?" Vivianne frowned.

"I'm fine, Mother," Lara said with a cough. "It's hot. The coffee's hot." She took a deep breath. "So, tell me about your trip. How are the Smiths?"

Vivianne told them about helping their friends with their farm. Graham added a word or two every now and then, but for the most part, he let his wife talk.

"It's always nice to see them, of course." Vivianne turned to Liam. "And you, Alpha, did you have a good visit?"

"Yes, I enjoyed it very much," Liam said without missing a beat.

"And we need to get back to New York," Lara said, shooting to her feet. She gave Liam a look and cocked her head. "Right, Liam?"

He nodded. "Of course. I'm ready when you are."

"Okay then, I'm going to get dressed and packed." With that, she left the three of them alone. Vivianne gave him a knowing smile, while Graham continued to sip his coffee and read the paper.

———

Another hour passed and soon they were ready for the drive back. Lara seemed reluctant to leave her parents, and Liam couldn't blame her. The compound was her home, after all. But last night, as they were having dinner, they came to a mutual agreement it was best if they went back to New York. It was a short, blissful getaway, but both of them had responsibilities and they didn't know when the mages would strike next. Neither, however, talked about if they were going to continue sleeping together. She didn't say no, of course, which Liam thought was a victory for him.

Vivianne and Graham saw them off, with the older witch giving Liam another one of her mysterious smiles. She was smart, and she probably knew what had gone on between him and Lara, but she said nothing. Maybe she even approved. Of course, there was also Graham. But if he suspected anything, he didn't give any indication of approval or disapproval on the matter.

An hour passed by as they drove back to New York City in comfortable silence. Hugo was happily munching away on a bone in the back seat. Glancing over to the passenger side, he saw that Lara was staring at her phone, frowning.

"What's the matter?"

She huffed out a quick breath. "It's Jade. Her phone, I mean. I've been calling her since I left New York. She hasn't been picking up, and all my calls go straight to voicemail." She frowned again. "I was hoping she'd cool down after a few days and not be mad at me anymore."

"Mad at you? Why would she be mad at you?"

Lara leaned her head against the cool glass of the window and sighed. "We ... we fought just before I left. She was voicing her concern on some ... personal matters, and I said some things that were out of line."

"Jade seems like a nice person. She'll forgive you. Maybe she just needs more time."

"Yeah, maybe ... but I can't help but feel like something's off." Lara huffed. "Or yeah, maybe she hates me." She looked down at her lap sadly.

"Sweetheart, don't be blue." He reached over and took her hand in his, keeping his other hand on the wheel. "If you've really said something horrible, then tell her you're sorry."

She looked at him, a small smile on her face. "I will."

As if on cue, Lara's phone began to ring. In her excitement, she nearly dropped it on the floor of the SUV but quickly grabbed it. "Hello? Oh, hi Cady, what's up?"

Liam kept his eyes on the road but Lara in his peripheral vision.

"No, I've been at the compound. She's not with me." Lara chewed her lip, a worried frown on her face. "Yes, try that. Give me call when you do. Bye."

"What's wrong?" Liam's voice turned serious. The look on Lara's face told him something wasn't right.

"That was Cady. She asked if Jade was with me. No one's heard from her since she left the lab last night."

"Maybe she slept in? Had a late night?" Liam offered.

"They're checking her apartment now." Lara stared at her phone, her eyes never straying from the dark screen. Then, once again, it started ringing. This time she picked it up before the second ring. "Hello?" Her brows knitted, and she grew silent as she listened to the speaker on the other end.

Liam pulled over to the side, waiting for Lara to start speaking. "Well?" he asked as soon as she put down the phone.

She looked at him, her face pale. "She's been taken."

Liam stepped on the gas

CHAPTER TWENTY-ONE

They made the drive back to New York City in record time. After dropping off Hugo at Liam's hotel, they went straight to Fenrir.

Nick, Cady, Alex, and Alynna were already there waiting for them in Grant's office. No one said a word, but the tension was palpable. A few minutes later, Grant walked in, massaging his temple, his phone glued to his ear.

"Frankie, sweetheart, please just do as I say ... yes, I know the restaurant is important, but I want you at The Enclave now, okay?" He looked at the people gathered in his office and put up a hand. "I need you there. Mika's, there too, so I want you there with her. Yes, thank you. Fine, fine. Yes, I love you. See you later." Without missing a beat, he sat down in his chair. "Where are we?"

"Jade clocked out of the lab at 7:05 p.m," Alynna began.

"You weren't with her?" Grant looked at Lara accusingly. The witch paled and shook her head.

"Watch it," Liam growled, standing in front of Lara. "It's not her fault."

"Hold on there," Alynna said. "Can we put the Alpha shit on hold here? We have more important things to worry about."

Grant sighed. "I'm not mad at you, Lara. Not at all." He gave Liam a wary glance then looked back at Lara. "I apologize for my outburst."

"No, it's fine ...." Lara looked like she was on the verge of tears. "I ... I decided I missed home and asked for a few days off. I last saw her the day I left."

"Okay, then, how do we know she was taken?" Grant turned back to Alynna.

The brunette took out her pad. "We checked everywhere, all the places she could possibly be, which isn't really a lot of places. She only goes to Fenrir, the supermarket, a few cafes and restaurants, and her apartment. Never even leaves Midtown." She gave her tablet a few taps. "Last night, as far as we could tell, she went straight home. We were able to grab footage from the security camera from her building." Alynna turned the tablet toward them.

A grainy CCTV video on the screen showed the street in front of Jade's apartment building. A few seconds into it, the young Lycan scientist could be seen crossing the street. As she stepped on the sidewalk in front of her building, two dark-colored vans pulled up behind her. The doors slid open, and about a dozen men leapt out, surrounding Jade. Two of them grabbed her, and Jade struggled, but they overpowered her. They carried her, kicking and screaming, before putting her into the van, which sped away.

Lara let out a small cry, and Cady moved beside her, putting an arm around her shoulders. Tears streamed down Lara's cheeks. "She ... she and I had a fight before I left ... I said some mean things."

"I think it's obvious who took Jade," Grant said. "But why her?"

"And how do we get her back?" Liam asked.

"I don't know." Alynna shook her head. "Did the mages know what she was doing? About her research? Or did they just pick her at random? I'm not sure. But we're working on finding her. I have my hacker friends on this."

"How about that Lone Wolf? What's her name again?" Grant asked.

"Meredith?" Alynna supplied. "What about her?"

"Well, she's your project," her brother stated. "What do you think? Can she be involved in this? She did break into Jade's lab."

"My gut tells me no," Alynna said. "She's been cooperative for the last couple of days. Gave us everything she had on us and how she broke in. Meredith sure is something, a genius and very talented, but I don't think she's evil. Besides, she's had no communication with the outside world."

"But you should still interrogate her," Grant said. "I mean it."

Alynna frowned but nodded. "Fine, I will."

"There's one more thing, Primul," Alex said as he took the tablet from his wife's hand and replayed the footage. "Look at these guys. These aren't just ordinary men. They were well-prepared and knew exactly what to do. Probably military-trained. In full Lycan form, Jade would have killed half of them. Even in her human form, with her enhanced strength, she would have given one or two men some trouble. But they knew where she was going to be, and what she was. No one sends a dozen well-trained men after one tiny scientist."

"So you think they knew she's a Lycan?"

Alex nodded. "And I think they wanted us to find this. Wanted to show us their full force."

"Shit," Nick cursed. "With the people we have right now,

we could probably take on these guys. But if they have more, we're going to need reinforcements."

Grant let out a long sigh. "I have an idea. It's a long shot, but it might be the only one we have."

They talked for a few more minutes, trying to divide the work and get the rescue operation underway. Lara offered to go with Cady, Alynna, and Alex to try and see if she could do anything to help find Jade. On the off chance that they could figure out a way to track her down, Lara also sent everyone her most recent picture of the scientist. It was a candid picture she had taken of her friend while they were in San Francisco. She was facing the camera but looking in the distance with a slight smile on her face and her brown hair tumbling over her shoulders.

Liam tried to talk to Lara before they left, but he couldn't figure out what to say. He wanted to comfort her and tell her everything was going to be all right. But he couldn't, not with everyone around. Before she left, however, the witch gave him a weak smile and a nod, which he returned. Her worry and pain left a gnawing ache in his middle, and he vowed to do whatever was necessary to find Jade.

"I was out of line, Grant," Liam said as soon as the others left. "I apologize."

Nick and Grant looked at each other. "It's all right, Liam. I was stressed out, but I shouldn't have taken it out on Lara. Jade is my responsibility. I should have insisted she live in The Enclave," he said, referring to the New York Lycan compound where most of the shifters in the city lived.

"Now, tell me what I can do to help."

The New York Alpha turned to his Beta. "Nick, do you remember that thing I asked you to look into a few weeks ago? Discreetly?"

"Of course. I have the file in my office."

"Bring it and meet us downstairs." Nick nodded and left them.

"Where are we going?" Liam asked as Grant stood up and walked toward the door.

"We're going to get some help," the other Alpha said cryptically.

———

The three men met at the private garage in the lower basement of Fenrir. The town car was waiting, and soon they were on their way downtown. They drove in silence, and 20 minutes later the car stopped in front of a tall, sleek building.

Nick gave instructions to their driver, then they all exited the vehicle. They went inside the lobby, which looked like any luxury hotel in New York City, and headed toward the elevator. Grant took out a black metal card from his wallet, tapped it on the sensor, and pressed the button for the penthouse.

"What is this place?" Liam asked as they exited the elevator car. The small hallway led into a larger room which took up the entire top floor of the building.

It was obviously a high-end establishment, decorated in black and gold. In the middle was a large onyx-colored bar, and behind it, top shelf bottles of liquor lined the glass wall. There was no name at the entrance, nor any other type of marketing or promotional material anywhere that advertised its name. Yet, the place reeked of money. It wasn't just the decor that made it classy but also the well-dressed, beautiful men and women everywhere, from perched on the stainless-steel stools to draped over the couches and booths lining the sides. Even the bartenders and waitstaff looked like models.

"This is Luxe," Grant said.

"You're taking us drinking at a time like this?" Liam asked incredulously.

"Patience, Alpha," Nick said as his eyes scanned the place. He nudged Grant toward the far end of the bar.

With a nod, Grant led them across the room to approach a large figure hunched over the bar. Perhaps he felt eyes on him, as the figure swung around.

"Well, hello trouble." The man smiled at Grant, but it didn't reach his eyes.

"Hello, Sebastian," Grant greeted. "Alone for tonight?"

"Not for long." He rubbed his hand over his thick but neatly trimmed beard, and his gaze slid toward a blond in a skimpy silver dress across the bar. The blond peered at him from over her fruity drink, returning his heated look. "But before I move on to tonight's entertainment, tell me, where have you been? What happened to you?"

Grant smiled. "Something worse."

The man laughed. "Really?"

"Oh, yeah. Baby on the way, too."

"Well, shit." He gestured to the bartender. "A round of bourbon for my friends here. On me." As the bartender prepared the drinks, he turned back to Grant. "But we're not here to celebrate your doom, are we?"

Grant took the file from Nick and put it on the bar. "Sebastian Creed. CEO of Creed Security. You enlisted in the Marines as soon as you turned eighteen, went all the way to Spec Ops. Discharged honorably after ten years, then you started your own security firm. Hit it big when you got some military contracts, and now Creed Security is one of the biggest military and private security companies in the world."

Sebastian remained cool and collected, but his eyes glinted like hard steel. "You know when I take a shit, too?"

"I like to get to know my friends well, Sebastian," Grant said with a smirk.

"So do I," he said, taking a slow sip of his bourbon. "Mr. Grant Anderson, CEO of Fenrir Corp."

The Alpha didn't even blink. "You've been doing some research, too, I see."

"You think you can run a background check on me and I wouldn't find out? Your guys are pretty good, but mine are better." Sebastian Creed stood up, stretching to his full height. He was taller than Nick and Liam at about 6'5" tall. He probably outweighed them by fifty pounds, and his shoulders were broad and his arms massive. The fabric of his white shirt strained against his chest, and the sleeves were rolled up to the elbows, showing off the sleeve tattoo on his left forearm. "Now," he said calmly, "what do you want?"

Nick spoke first, his voice cool. "We want to hire your firm, Mr. Creed."

The giant kept his stance but swung his head toward Nick. "And you are?"

"Nick Vrost. Fenrir Corporation's Head of Security." Neither man held out his hand.

"And you?"

"I'm one of Grant's partners, Liam Henney." He held his hand out, which Sebastian shook with a firm grip.

"So this is business." Sebastian sat back down. "Let's talk. What can I do for you gentlemen?"

"We have a missing ... asset," Grant began as he sat next to Sebastian. "The asset was taken from us by force, and we need he—it back."

"So, standard corporate espionage stuff, huh?" Sebastian took a swig of his drink. "And you want me to retrieve your asset?"

"We will retrieve the asset. We're narrowing down its

location, but we already know that we'll need muscle to infiltrate the facility. Now, we've done research on your firm." Grant accepted the drink from the bartender and took a sip. "You're the best, and you're also discreet."

"Of course. Discretion is part of the game. But first you'll have to tell me what this asset is and why it's so important to you."

"No," Nick interjected. "It's on a need to know basis only. My team will take care of retrieval. You just need to make sure we can get in and out safely."

"Then we have no deal," Sebastian said coolly. "Have a good evening, gentlemen."

"I'll pay whatever you want. Double what you usually charge," Grant offered.

"See here, Grant." Sebastian looked at him straight in the eye. "My company is used to handling secrets. Classified stuff, even, so you can be sure your secret is safe with me. But I need to know exactly what I'm getting into."

"I've seen your record, Creed. Your company has run operations far more dangerous than what we're asking."

"The answer is still no."

"You'd turn away millions of dollars to do one small job, just because we won't tell you what it is we want you to retrieve?" Nick asked in an annoyed voice.

"Listen, Mr. Vrost, right?" Sebastian's eyes turned hard. "Money, I got. Lots of it. But you know what I can't replace with money, Mr. Vrost? The lives of good men and women. If I went in blind, I'd be risking the lives of my employees. Good, loyal people who've been to hell and back with me. And for what? The prototype for a fancy new gadget? A miracle pill that promises weight loss without the hard work? No. That's how people get hurt, and I don't do business with anyone who would treat my people like disposable toys. So, goodnight, gentlemen." He grabbed his glass and walked away.

"We'll find someone else," Nick said when Sebastian was out of earshot.

"There is no one else." Grant rubbed his hand down his face. "He's the best, you know that."

Liam watched the man retreat. If Grant thinks he's the best, then he might be the only one who can help them rescue Jade. "Grant, what's the harm in telling him the truth? At least part of the truth anyway?"

Grant frowned. "What do you mean?"

"Look, we just tell him Jade is a researcher in your R and D department and she's been kidnapped by a rival for the tech she's developed. It's kind of the truth," Liam reasoned. "Worst case scenario? We'll have to use some confusion potion if they see anything."

"We'll have to come up with some sort of plan to isolate his team from ours. Make sure they only tangle with the human forces."

"It'll be difficult." Nick scratched his chin. "But we could do it."

"Now, we have to convince Mr. Creed that the partial truth is enough," Grant said. "Something tells me he still won't agree."

Liam felt something in his gut, an instinct that told him what might work. "I have an idea. Let me take the lead." Grant nodded, and they walked over to Sebastian, who was now cozying up to the blond in one of the corner couches.

"Mr. Creed," Liam began.

Sebastian have them a languid look. "Please, call me Sebastian."

"Call me Liam, then," he continued. "May we speak alone, Sebastian?"

He whispered something to the blond and she nodded, then she stood up and left. "Okay, say what you need to say."

Liam looked at Grant and Nick. "We've talked it over, and we can tell you a little bit more about the asset. But not everything."

"All or nothing," he insisted. "And if you fucking lie to me, I'll know."

Liam sat next to him and fished out his phone. He opened the screen and pulled up the picture of Jade that Lara had sent. "The asset," he said, sliding it over to him.

Sebastian stared at the picture, his face inscrutable. "Oh, fuck me," he muttered under his breath, not knowing that Liam could hear him clearly with his enhanced senses.

"Well? Will you help us?"

Sebastian's face turned dark. "Fine. Let's talk, gentlemen."

CHAPTER TWENTY-TWO

A lynna sat behind her desk, put on her headphones, and switched on her computer. "Tell me what you have, guys." She was talking to her three hacker friends, who had helped them when Cady had been kidnapped. They were supposedly the best and didn't always work on the right side of the law, but they got things done quickly.

"Yes ... that's it." Alynna nodded. After a few seconds, a smile spread on her face. "Good girl! Jade, you are one clever girl!"

Lara shot to her feet. "What is it?"

"Jade was somehow able to keep her phone on her and leave it on," Alynna said.

"Were they able to track it?" Alex asked.

The Lycan nodded. "Yup, they're sending us her coordinates as soon as they finish. Now," she stood up, "let's pay a visit to Meredith."

The three of them took the Fenrir private elevators down to the sub-basement level. When they reached the bottom floor, the doors opened up to a small, narrow hallway. At the end was a burly Lycan guard who stood next to a metal door.

"Mrs. Westbrooke, Mr. Westbrooke," he greeted in a low, gruff voice.

"Hey there, Tank," Alynna greeted. "How's our guest?"

"Same as always."

"Good," Alynna said as she pressed her palm to the sensor by the door, making it slide open.

The room was sparse, with a twin bed in the corner, a desk with some reading material, and a chair bolted to the floor. There was another door in the corner, probably leading to the bathroom. It certainly wasn't the Ritz, but it was much less dreary than what Lara had imagined a Lycan prison would be like.

"Hey, Meredith,"Alynna greeted.

The young woman was lying in bed reading a magazine, her feet propped against the wall. There was a large electronic monitoring device wrapped around one of her ankles. "Hey, Alynna," she said. "Couldn't you get me something else aside from trashy celeb magazines? Or at least new ones? These are like two weeks old. I think some of these actors may have already divorced in this week's editions."

"Sorry, Meredith. You know we can't risk it." Alynna sat down in the chair.

"It's not like I can figure out an escape plan using Ryan Reynolds' photo," she grumbled. "Oh, you brought some friends along. What can I do for you?"

"So, I know you've been cooperating with us fully, but we need to ask you about something else."

Meredith huffed and swung her feet down. "Well, according to the punishment from the Lycan High Council, I'm bound to your clan for the next decade to do with as you please. So ask away."

"If I may say so, that's what you get for trying to break into an Alpha's secret lab."

"Yeah, yeah, whatevs. Now, what is it you wanted to ask me?"

"The Lycan scientist whose lab you broke into. Jade Cross. She's been kidnapped by the mages."

Meredith shot to her feet. "I told you! I don't know anything about mages! I swear!" She grabbed Alynna by the arms. Alex let out a growl and moved toward his wife, but Alynna put a hand up to stop him.

"I know, Meredith. You've been really cooperative," Alynna soothed, prying Meredith's hands off her. "But this can't be a coincidence. You break into her lab and now the mages kidnap her?"

"I haven't talked to anyone except you since you caught me," she said. "How would they know anything about that secret lab of yours?"

"Did you talk to anyone else while you were staking out the place? Did you already have buyers for whatever you wanted to steal?"

She shook her head. "No. I couldn't risk it, not without knowing what was in there. I was planning to take whatever I could and find buyers afterwards."

"How can we believe that?" Alynna asked, crossing her arms.

"I haven't lied to you about anything else!" She sat back down on the bed. "Dr. Cross ... is she ... do you know where they've taken her?"

Alynna nodded. "We do." She paused, looking at the woman's reaction. "We're going to go rescue her as soon as we figure out a plan."

"Let me help," Meredith said. "You know I'd be useful."

"I don't know ...."

"Look," she stood up and began to pace. "I've been trapped in here for days. I'm going crazy; I need to go out and be useful.

I'm bound to the New York clan for ten years of servitude. There's no place I can hide where you won't find me. Nowhere that I'd want to stay anyway, because there's no way I'm going to hole up in some cave somewhere without plumbing or WiFi. Plus, you have this." She pointed to the ankle monitor. "Mr. Vrost explained that this isn't an ordinary monitor. I'm well aware that you could blow my leg off from anywhere on the planet if you detonated it. Also," she looked at Lara, "I'm sure the witch would blow me off the face of the earth if I even touched a hair on her friend's head."

Alynna sighed. "I'll talk to Grant."

———

"This is crazy, right?" Alex asked as they were sitting inside an unmarked van currently speeding along the New Jersey Turnpike.

"You're turning into my brother." Alynna rolled her eyes. "Don't you trust me?"

"I do." Alex frowned. "It's her I don't trust." His eyes flickered to Meredith. The Lycan was sitting across from them, wearing a bored expression on her face. She was wearing the cat suit she'd been wearing when they had caught her, but no other weapons. "Don't need 'em," she had said. Meanwhile, the rest of the team was dressed in full combat gear, specially designed for the Lycans so they could take them off quickly in case they needed to shift into their wolf form.

Lara shook her head. This was really happening. Her thoughts drifted back to a few hours ago.

After Grant, Nick, and Liam had returned from their errand, they all met back at Fenrir. Alynna's hackers had found Jade's cellphone signal just in time before the battery died.

They had traced her to an abandoned warehouse somewhere on the border of Philadelphia and New Jersey.

"Not really original," Alynna had scoffed. "Maybe we should start going to all these abandoned warehouses and factories, and maybe we'll eventually find all the mage hidey-holes."

The Lycans had obviously poured a lot of their resources into defending themselves against the mages, because they already had plans in place for all kinds of scenarios, including kidnappings. They were able to use satellite images to pinpoint the exact location of the warehouse and found old blueprints of what it looked like inside. They had a few guesses of where they could be holding Jade, but they wouldn't know exactly until they got there. The most recent satellite photos, however, also showed the Lycans what they feared—the mages definitely had the place locked up tight and it was crawling with human guards.

Grant had explained that they had secured the services of some private security contractor to help them with the rescue. "Creed Security will be providing the manpower. Once we have our plan in place, Mr. Creed will be instructed on what we need done."

The plan was simple. Stake out the warehouse, try to figure out where Jade was, and get her out. Creed and his team would take the lead and disable as many of the human guards as they could, while Nick, Liam, Alynna, Alex, Lara, and Meredith would go and find Jade. They were not to harm the humans, nor shift or display their powers if they could help it.

They worked all night on the plan, catching a few naps here and there. A few times, Lara looked longingly at Liam as he lay on the couch or worked on the computer but knew she couldn't go to him. *No.* Jade was top priority now.

By morning they had a solid plan of action. Obviously, the

Lycans wanted to rescue Jade right away, but Creed had suggested they wait until nightfall.

And so now they were on their way to the warehouse. It was a three-hour drive, and they took two vans. Grant, Nick, and Dr. Faulkner, their resident Lycan medical doctor, were in one van, while Alex, Alynna, Liam, Lara, and Meredith were in the other. Nick and Grant were not happy about letting the Lycan thief come along but knew that they could use every bit of help they could get. Nick, however, warned Meredith that he had the trigger to her ankle monitor close by, to which the blond cheekily replied, "Noted. With thanks."

"So guys, remember," Alynna began. "No S-H-I-F-T-I-N-G if you can help it, okay?"

"Why are you spelling?' Alex asked.

"I'm practicing for the H-U-M-A-N-S," Alynna stated.

"I'm pretty sure all humans can spell," Meredith retorted.

Lara couldn't help but grin. Beside her, Liam cracked a smile, too, which only made her want to kiss him more. He'd been so tense since they got back. They all were. But seeing that smile on his face brought back memories of their time at the compound.

The van stopped, shaking Lara out of her thoughts.

"Looks like we're here," Liam said. The van's door opened, and they all filed out.

"This is the meet up point," Nick said as everyone gathered around him and Grant. "It's about a 20-minute hike behind that hill to the back of the warehouse," he explained. "Creed's team will move in first and take down any human guards. He had people scout ahead, and he says that there are approximately two dozen guys guarding the place."

"Do we know if there are any mages around?"

Nick shook his head. "We can't be sure. But we'll have to be careful not to shift around the humans. While Creed and his guys distract the guards, we sneak in and find Jade. You know the plan, right?"

Lara nodded. They were all paired up—Alex and Nick, Liam and Lara, and Alynna and Meredith—and they had assigned areas to look for Jade. Sebastian Creed had actually offered advice on where Jade was likely being held, based on how secure each area was. "All right, Creed's here. Let's go meet with them."

Lara straightened her back, trying to seem more confident. Dressed in dark combat gear and a tactical helmet, her face and form were well hidden. However, in front of the humans, she and the rest of the Lycan team had to look the part, so they didn't suspect anything was off.

Two more vans pulled up behind them. The front passenger door of the lead vehicle swung open, and a man stepped out. He was possibly one of the largest men Lara had ever seen, taller than any of the Lycans. His keen eyes scanned the area, as if looking for danger. His hand went up to his jaw, rubbing the thick, ruddy beard covering the lower part of his face. He was also dressed in full combat gear and heavy boots with various weapons strapped all over his body. Lara thought he could be handsome, if it wasn't for the fierce scowl on his face.

"Mr. Creed." Nick gave the man a curt nod.

"Mr. Vrost," he replied, his voice low. "Are we all here?"

"Yes."

Sebastian Creed looked at the Lycans, but if he thought there was anything off about them, he said nothing. "Fine. We'll try to keep out of each other's way." He turned to his team. There were about eight men assembling behind him, all dressed similarly.

"Wait, this is your team?" Grant asked. "There are two dozen guys in there, possibly more, and you brought ... eight guys?"

"Nine, including me," Sebastian huffed. "Trust me, my guys are the best. We can handle them."

"And no one gets hurt, right?"

Sebastian nodded and held up one of the guns from his holster. "These are special weapons; should knock them out quick once the rounds hit them." He put the gun back in his holster. "However, some of my guys are definitely carrying real ones. If shit goes down, I'm not taking any chances."

"Fine," Grant said, checking his watch. "Let's go."

The Lycan force hung back behind the cover of some trees as Sebastian's team went ahead.

Lara jumped in surprise as a hand slipped into hers but relaxed when she realized it was Liam's. In the dark, his eyes glowed like orbs of blue light.

"We'll get her back," Liam whispered.

"I know," Lara said. "We have to."

"Okay, we need silence now," Grant's voice crackled through the earpiece she was wearing. The Lycan team was using communicators, and Grant stayed behind to coordinate their efforts with the Creed Security team. Sebastian's guys also had communicators, but it would be too confusing to have everyone on the same frequency. He and Grant would be the main connection between the two teams, but if everything went well, there would be minimal need for the two teams to communicate.

"Creed's team is ready," Grant whispered. "Okay, sniper's in position ... and the guards are down! Go, go, go!"

Liam grabbed Lara's hand and tugged her along. They were about 20 yards away from the back entrance, and they quickly went in, side stepping the four guards lying on the ground. A few minutes later, shouts and screams came from the other side of the warehouse. The sound of boots thudding on the ground were like thunder, but it was a sign that most, if not all of the guards, had gone outside to see what the commotion was.

"We're in," Nick whispered, then began to point to where they would start looking.

Liam and Lara headed up the stairs. There was a room in the back of the old office that was built like a bank vault. It was one of the more secure rooms in the facility, and if Liam couldn't get it open, Lara would use her powers to blow down the door.

Lara suddenly stopped. Liam turned around and mouthed *Are you okay* to her, but she didn't know what to say. There was something strange about the place. There was a heaviness in the air, a weight in the atmosphere that didn't seem right. Taking a mental deep breath, she nodded and then pointed forward.

They walked carefully, quickly searching through all the rooms leading to the back room, just in case. Liam was turning his head, trying to see if he could pick up Jade's scent.

"Does anyone else feel like there's something strange here?" Meredith whispered through the comms. "I'm getting a serious case of the heebie-jeebies?"

"There's something not quite right here, guys," Alynna said.

A strange feeling blasted through Lara, but before she could chime in, she found herself facing the barrel of a gun. Her heart thudded against her chest, but on instinct she waved her hands, sending the man with the weapon flying across the wall. Behind her, Liam let out a growl and sprang in front of her, knocking down a second assailant.

"Liam!" she screamed. Through the comms, she heard the shouts and screams of her friends.

"They had more men hiding somewhere! They just popped

out of nowhere," Grant bellowed in her ear. "Fuck! Do what you can. Fight them off."

Loud growls, gnashing of teeth, and a howl sounded through the comms. More boots in the hallway. Behind her, Liam had overpowered the other man and cold cocked him with his own gun.

"Liam," she called. "You have to shift. They're coming!"

Three men marched into the hallway, and she waved her hand, pushing the first two backwards. They tumbled down the stairs, knocking the last guy down. However, he stood up and continued to march toward her. He raised his weapon and aimed at her.

A chill went through her. Then her temple started throbbing, and she felt like she had swallowed a large rock, the heaviness of it in her stomach weighed her down. It was blood magic. Those men ... their eyes were cold and inhuman.

A ripping sound and a growl came from behind as a dark blur lunged past her, knocking down the man coming at her. It was Liam's wolf, and he was scrabbling at the man. The guard was relentless, however, as if he didn't care about his own safety. Even with his weapon knocked down, he didn't seem to fear the giant beast. He clawed and kicked, even as the wolf pinned him down with its large paws. The man was bleeding from a large claw mark down his face, but he wouldn't stop moving.

"Liam!" she screamed. "Keep him down!"

She took a small vial from her pocket. It was a special knockout potion made by the witches in her coven. "Hold your breath," she told the wolf and then threw the bottle at the man's head. Blue smoke exploded as the glass shattered. Liam's wolf hopped off the man. The burly guard flailed for a few seconds, then his head rolled back and he closed his eyes.

"Thank God!" she cried out.

"Fuck, is everyone okay?" Grant's voice was strained through the comms.

"Liam and I are okay," Lara said. "I think I'm the only one who can talk right now, Grant."

"I'm here. Alynna and I are good; she's just getting dressed," Meredith choked out. "And next time, can we get a bigger bracelet for this fuckin' ankle monitor? I had to stop mid-shift or else I would have broken it and then we'd really see some fireworks!"

"Shit," Grant cursed. "Can you ... wait ... I need to get off our comms." In the background, she could hear Grant talking. "Yes, Sebastian? I know. Those bastards were prepared, hiding more men. I don't know where they came from. I haven't heard from everyone on my team yet, but as far as I know, they don't have her." Grant paused. "They're headed where? There's a basement? Dammit, Sebastian, stand down. Let my team get in there first! Fuck!" Then silence.

"Grant, we're good," Nick's voice popped in after a few seconds.

"Sebastian said he saw some of the guys go back inside. They're headed to a lower level basement, probably a new addition since it wasn't in the blueprints."

"She's down there!" Lara piped in.

"Yeah, that's the only logical explanation," Grant said. "Sebastian went in by himself, that bastard! Go and get him, get Jade, and we'll deal with it later."

Turning to Liam, she saw that he had changed back and re-dressed. "Lara ... I'm ...."

She lunged at him, wrapping her arms around his neck. "We'll talk later. Right now we have to go get Jade!"

As they ran down the stairs, more gunshots and shouts rang throughout the warehouse. Alex, Alynna, Meredith, and Nick had already regrouped on the ground floor.

"Follow me," Nick said as he ran toward the east side of the warehouse. They went down a long hallway and then a set of metal stairs that led to the basement level. Four armed men greeted them as they descended the stairs.

"Go in and find them!" Nick barked as he and Alex quickly changed, clothes ripping away as their wolves pounced on the guards.

Meredith, Alynna, Liam, and Lara ran through the door across from the stairs. It led to another hallway, and this time six guards were charging them.

"Bad guys sure love hallways!" Meredith quipped. She bent her knees and bowed low, like a spring waiting to be released. "You guys go," she shouted. She ran toward the men, her fists and legs flying as she took them down one by one, clearing a path for them to get through. They ran as fast as they could, and Lara waved her hand to blow away the last remaining door at the end.

Inside, four of Sebastian's men were surrounding two figures in the center of the room, their guns pointed toward the ten men approaching them.

"Take them down!" Sebastian's voice rang through the room. His men raised their guns, ready to fire. Just as Lara was about to scream, all ten of the remaining guards dropped to the floor. Sebastian's men looked at each other, confused.

Lara stumbled back, and Liam caught her before she fell. "Lara, what's wrong?" he asked.

"The blood magic ... it's just gone ...." Lara felt the heaviness of the entire place lift away, like a thick fog receding.

"Blood magic?"

She nodded. "Yes, I could feel it. These men ...." She let out a cry as she saw what was behind Sebastian's men. There was a small form crumpled on the ground.

Jade!

Tearing herself away from Liam, she hopped over the unconscious bad guys, past the four bewildered men, and straight to her friend.

"Jade ...." She knelt down, touching the other woman's face. Her eyes were closed, and a small bruise was healing on her cheek. A rattle off to the side caught her attention, and she saw the chains. Jade was chained to the floor by her wrists and ankles, probably as a precaution in case she shifted.

"Who the fuck would do this?" Sebastian threw one of the chains aside, the loud clanging making Lara jump in surprise. His eyes were hard like flint, and she could feel the anger rolling off him.

"Zac!" He called to one of his guys. "Go find a key. The rest of you, see if there are any tools around we can use to break these chains." The men dispersed quickly, eager to follow their boss' orders.

Lara pulled Jade's head onto her lap and brushed her hair away from her face. She was so still, and if it wasn't for her soft breathing, Lara would have thought worse. "You'll be okay, Jade. Don't worry, I'm here." Tears streamed down her cheeks. "Why isn't she waking up?"

Sebastian picked up a syringe nearby. "Drugged, I assume," he spat. "Jesus, how much did they put in her system?" There were about four other syringes scattered around them.

"Is she ...." Alynna gasped as she looked down at Jade.

Lara nodded weakly. "She's ... alive."

"I'll go ahead and get Dr. Faulkner!" Alynna tore out of the room.

"Boss!" Zac barreled toward them. He was a tall, lanky guy with a shaved head and a baby face. "I think I found 'em!" He raised his hand, jingling a set of keys hanging off a ring. He tossed it to Sebastian, who caught it effortlessly.

Making quick work of the locks, Sebastian released Jade

from the shackles and gently lifted her into his arms. Jade let out a faint moan, murmured something, and rolled her head against his chest.

"Hey, what are you doing?" Lara asked indignantly. She grabbed Sebastian by his arm and tried to pull at it, but the giant remained rooted to the spot, staring down at the tiny woman in his arms.

"Sweetheart," Liam soothed, as he gently pried her hands away. "She's fine. He's going to bring her to Dr. Faulkner."

Lara watched as Sebastian walked away with her best friend. Jade looked so much smaller and so fragile in his arms. Lara turned around and let Liam pull her close. His citrusy scent enveloped her, making her feel calm and safe.

"What the hell happened?" Grant's voice boomed throughout the room, but it wasn't through the speakers. The New York Alpha was standing by the doorway. Nick and Alex followed behind him, dressed in a fresh set of clothes.

"We were coming to get Sebastian and Jade." Liam cocked his head at the fallen bodies around them. "Then all of a sudden they all dropped like stones."

Grant leaned down next to one of the unconscious men and ripped his combat gear off. The Alpha lifted the man's shirt, revealing the same symbols that Marshal Aimes had carved on his chest.

"The blood magic controlling them, it's gone," Lara said soberly as she disentangled herself from Liam's arms. "It was here, surrounding them, then it just disappeared."

"And look who I found!" Meredith announced from the doorway. She dragged someone by the arm, a figure in a dark robe. Pushing him on his knees, she ripped off his hood.

"Filthy Lycans!" he spat. The man was completely bald, with sunken cheeks and a pale face. The whites of his eyes were tinged with red, and the pupils were dark pinpoints.

"A mage!" Lara gasped. "You found him?"

Meredith nodded. "There was a secret door off the side of the hallway. Found it when one of the guys tossed me aside. I kicked down the panel and found this asshole."

"Get your hands off me, you creature!" The mage struggled to get away from Meredith, and instead of pulling him back, she pushed him forward, sending him tumbling to his hands and knees.

"He was back there in a room with TV screens everywhere. They must have security cameras all over the place," Meredith explained. "When I came in, he was in some kind of trance, reciting some mumbo jumbo. He didn't even know I was in there."

"He was controlling them," Lara guessed. "That's probably how the spell works." She would have to tell Vivianne about this.

"And when you caught him, he lost control," Grant finished.

"Looks like we found our puppet master," Alex said as he grabbed the mage by the arm. The pale man screamed and tried to bite Alex, but the Lycan knocked him out with one sock to the jaw. He went limp. "I swear, I fucking hate mages."

Grant shook his head. "God, what a mess. Okay, let's all get checked out by the medical team. Dr. Cross should be on her way back to New York. I'll debrief with Sebastian, see if there's anyone who needs confusion potion. Hopefully not. If anything, the iron-clad NDA he signed should keep his mouth shut."

———

Dr. Faulkner examined Jade in the van. Lara refused to leave her side, and Liam was right beside her. Though the Lycan scientist remained unconscious, Dr. Faulkner said she seemed to be all right. "Her metabolism will burn away the drugs in a few hours. She shouldn't need the medivac chopper, but I'd like to keep her in The Enclave's Medical wing overnight."

"How could normal drugs work on her, Doctor?" Grant asked. "The mages had to use a special potion to knock me out when they tried to kidnap me."

"Well, Grant, despite her Lycan metabolism, she's not exactly very strong in her human form. I think they knocked her unconscious, judging from that bruise on her cheek." He shook his head. "Then they pumped her with drugs every hour or so. It's crude and takes a lot of effort and medication, but it worked. I think they put in a couple of extra doses when the attack started, but she should be up in a few hours."

"They chained her up, too," Lara said softly. The bruises on Jade's wrists and ankles had been red and angry when they got her out.

Dr. Faulkner sighed sadly. "Yes, hopefully those will fade soon." He eyed Sebastian Creed warily. The man was standing a few feet away from them, talking to Nick Vrost in hushed tones. "Did he see anything while you were in there? Suspect that Jade or any of you were anything other than normal humans?"

"I don't think so," Liam answered. "Why?"

"Hmmm," the older man said thoughtfully. "He was acting strange. Refusing to let Jade go. He nearly got into an argument with one of our security guys, but when I told him I was a doctor, he finally left her in my care."

"We'll keep a close eye on him, Dr. Faulkner," Grant assured him.

Nick, Grant, Alynna, and Alex stayed behind with Sebastian and his team for the cleanup and debrief. Liam and Lara rode with Dr. Faulkner and Jade in the van all the way back to The Enclave.

After settling her into the Medical wing, Dr. Faulkner

urged them to get some sleep. It was almost 5 o'clock in the morning by the time they were done. "There's nothing more you can do for her. Go and get some rest."

"I'll take her home," Liam said.

"But I want to be here when she wakes up," Lara protested. "She'll be alone, and she might be scared."

"I'll be here, dear, I promise," Dr. Faulkner assured her.

Too tired to protest, Lara allowed Liam to lead her out of the Medical building and to the waiting car. He gave the driver her address and slipped in the back seat with her, tucking her into his side as they drove back to midtown.

Lara must have drifted off because a few minutes later Liam was shaking her awake. "We're here," he whispered.

"Oh, right."

Liam stepped out of the car, swung over to her side and opened the door for her. "I'll walk you up."

"No," she said, shaking her head.

"Oh." He went quiet.

"Don't just walk me up, Liam." She stepped closer to him, looking into his eyes. "Stay with me."

CHAPTER TWENTY-THREE

"This is unacceptable!" Stefan raged at his companions. He pointed one bony finger at the figure in front of him, who flinched as the master mage hurled insults.

"Forgive me, Master Stefan!" The man held his hands up in surrender.

"Tell us again what happened, Finley," Daric said to the man.

"Master, we held the woman at the warehouse, as per instructions, keeping her sedated until she was ready for transport back here. She gave us no trouble."

"Then why did we send all our soldiers there?" Stefan raged. "It took us months to build up our army! Four dozen men gone!"

"Marcus said we needed them all," Finley cried. "In case the Lycans attacked. Which they did."

"Marcus was able to control all those men at the same time?" Vivianne asked.

"He was my most advanced student, after Daric," Stefan said.

"Still, how could they have overpowered our men?" Daric asked.

"They had help, Master Daric," Finley explained. "From some humans, all highly trained and well-armed."

"Better than our men?" Vivianne asked.

"Our soldiers are like a swarm of insects," Daric told Victoria. "We picked the strongest men, and under our control they have no fear or instinct for self-preservation. They will do what we tell them, but they have no independent thought. A small, well-prepared team could easily win against them, unless we had a literal swarm who could overpower them." He turned to Stefan. "I suspect Marcus wanted Grant Anderson and his Lycans to come to him."

"He said he wanted to crush the Lycans and show you how powerful he was, Master Stefan," Finley offered. "He told me that he was hoping the Lycans would try to take back their scientist, because he was going to kill them all with his army."

"Pure ego," Victoria spat.

"And it is his ego that caused us this loss!" Stefan shouted, sending the walls shaking. "Do we know where they have taken him?"

Finley shook his head.

"Probably to The Enclave or Fenrir," Daric guessed.

"We need to get rid of him, before he tells the Lycans everything!" He looked at Victoria. "How about our other mages? How is their training coming along?"

The redheaded witch gave a snort. "Not progressing as fast as we'd like. It's a shame we lost Marcus. Not all of our mages are adept at being puppeteers. We have one or two who might be good candidates."

"Accelerate their training!" he ordered, then turned to Daric. "And start finding us more men!"

"Yes, Master," Daric said with a bow.

CHAPTER TWENTY-FOUR

She was falling.

The air whipped around her, and gravity was pulling her down as she plummeted closer to Earth. But that wasn't what scared her or made her scream.

As she opened her eyes, she saw Liam underneath her. He was plummeting much faster, his hands reaching out to her, their fingers touching.

"Lara! Lara!"

Lara's eyes flew open, and she choked on a sob. Her body was covered in sweat, and she was sitting upright in bed. Liam's arms folded around her, drawing her close.

"Jesus, Lara, what's the matter?" he said, soothing her back with his hand. "You were screaming."

"I ... a bad dream. Nightmare," she managed to choke out.

"That's all it was, then, just a dream."

Lara bolted from the bed, freeing herself from Liam's grasp. She ran to the bathroom, closed the door behind her, and retched into the toilet. When her stomach was empty, she stood up and wiped her mouth with a towel. She turned on the tap, washing her hands with hot water, trying to ward the chill away. Looking up slowly, she looked at her reflection in the mirror.

Get a grip, Lara.

It was a dream. She was having some sort of PTSD episode because of seeing Jade chained up on the floor and fighting against those mage-controlled humans. *That was all, right?* She bit her lip and closed her eyes. Memories flooded back into her brain of Jonathan and the dreams. The truck hitting him. Blood.

A soft knock jolted her out of her thoughts. "Lara, sweetheart," Liam called. "I have some water here for you."

"I need a second," she called out weakly. Lara splashed water on her face, rubbed some moisturizer on her cheeks, and took a deep breath. It was all going to be all right. With one last final deep breath, she opened the door.

Liam stood in front her, a glass of water in his hand. "Are you okay?"

She nodded and took the glass from him. "Like I said, just a bad dream." She took a sip and handed him back the glass.

He gave her a smile. "I know something that will cheer you up, sweetheart."

"What?"

"Jade's awake."

———

"For the last time, Lara, I'm fine," Jade grumbled. Lara opened her mouth to speak, but the Lycan held a finger up. "And if you ask me again if I'm sure, I'm going to ... to ...." She looked around her. "Maim you with this neck pillow!" She hoisted the said pillow in the air, waving it around.

"Yeah, I think she's fine," Meredith quipped. She was lying on the couch in the corner, flicking through a gossip magazine.

"Is she supposed to be here?" Jade asked Lara in a low voice.

She was lying in the hospital bed inside her room at The Enclave's Medical wing, while Lara sat in the chair next to her.

"I can hear you," Meredith called out. "And yes, I'm here. Apparently, I'm going to stick to you 24/7 from now on."

"Meet your new bodyguard, Jade," Alynna said as she entered the room. "Meredith here has been assigned to guard you, at least while you're here in the lab. Once we work out some details, she'll also be escorting you to and from your apartment."

"For how long?" Jade whined.

"I'm sentenced to ten years of servitude to the New York clan to pay for my crimes." Meredith swung her long legs off the couch and walked up to the bed. "So you and I are gonna be good friends!" She put an arm around Jade, which the other Lycan shrugged off.

Alynna rolled her eyes. "Just until we know you're safe and no one's trying to take you."

"You get kidnapped *one* time," Jade said in an exasperated voice. Her eyes narrowed at Meredith. "You tried to steal my work."

"And your witch friend gave me a goose egg on the noggin', so I'd say we're even."

"C'mon, Meredith." Alynna took the blonde by the arm. "We need to sort out a couple of things before you start your new job."

"You mean, I get paid for this?"

"No." With that, the two women left.

Lara sighed and turned back to Jade. "I'm so glad you're okay, Jade." She looked down at her feet. "I'm sorry about the things I said. I don't think of you as just a Lycan, you know that, right? You're my best friend."

Jade's eyes softened, and she opened her arms. Lara eagerly embraced her friend.

"I know, Lara. We're good. Thanks for coming to rescue me."

"Well, it was a group effort. Now, do you want to talk about what happened?"

She gave a shrug. "I debriefed with the Alpha and Beta as soon as I woke up, since they didn't want me to forget any details. But to be honest, I don't remember much." Jade seemed to shrink into herself, hunching her shoulders. "I was walking home that night when I heard the vans braking behind me. These two guys grabbed me and I tried to fight them off but ...."

"It's okay honey; you're safe." Lara squeezed Jade's hand.

"Anyway ... they took my purse, but I actually had my phone in my pocket. So I put it in my bra, hoping they wouldn't find it."

"I knew you were smart!" Lara laughed.

Jade smirked at her. "I wouldn't stop struggling, though, and one of the guys ... he hit me across the face and I must have blacked out. From that point, everything gets spotty and ...." She took a deep breath. "I was in and out. Like, as soon as I showed any signs of waking up, they would pump me full of drugs. It was like swimming in molasses. I couldn't even lift my arms. They had me chained up, too."

"I know," Lara whispered.

"I was unconscious, but at some point I had a dream, a weird one." She shook her head. "Never mind, that's not important." She stared down at her hands.

Lara thought back to her own dream that morning. "No, Jade, tell me please." She took her friend's hands into hers.

"It wasn't a dream, as much as ... well at one point I suddenly felt ... safe. The visuals were muddy, but I could ... smell something familiar. It was like leather and musk ...." Her head suddenly popped up, and she gave a weak laugh. "This is silly, but I was reminded of my grandfather's study back in

England. You know, I hated it when my mom took me there, but that was the one place I felt happy. I would play in there for hours with my grandfather and loved the smell of his leather chair and the books."

"So you smelled old books?"

"No, silly. I mean, kind of ... I can't describe it. It was a scent, but more of a feeling." She straightened her shoulders. "Anyway, it's not important."

"Yes, what's important is you're safe," Lara said.

"And that we get back to work!"

"No, Jade." Lara stood up and crossed her arms. "You need rest!"

"And you need to grab my tablet from the lab. Call Milly and-"

"No."

"Oh c'mon, Lara. Please?"

Lara shook her head.

"Fine. But you have to talk to me and entertain me," Jade grumbled.

"Whatever you want." Lara sat beside her on the hospital bed.

"Tell me, when did you and Liam start sleeping together?"

Lara turned red. "We are not—"

"I can smell him on you."

"Motherfucker, I showered twice this morning!" She shot to her feet. "He said that ... hold on!" Her eyes grew wide. "Who told you?"

"You did," Jade said with a sly smile.

Lara collapsed on the bed next to her. "Shit."

"So, c'mon. Spill. I want the PG-rated details!"

Lara told her what had happened, from the time that Liam showed up at Rusty's to the disastrous dinner with the Morgans to Liam's arrival and the drive back to New York.

"Lara, I'm so happy for you!"

"What?"

"I mean, it's so obvious you guys like each other!" Jade exclaimed. "All those longing looks. Him chasing you around. Your jealousy whenever Alynna was around."

"I was not jealous!" Jade gave her a smirk. "Oh God, do you think she knew?" Lara buried her face in her hands.

"Probably."

"You're not helping! Besides, I didn't know you cared who I slept with."

"It's not that," Jade explained. "I'm hardly a romantic, but you know. It's nice. You two are nice together."

"Yeah, well," Lara shrugged, "I don't know what's gonna happen."

"You're not going to marry Weasel Wesley, are you?"

"Weasel Wesley." Lara laughed. "That's clever. But no. I don't think my dad would forgive me if I did."

"So, what's the harm in enjoying what you have with Liam?"

Lara turned away from Jade, not wanting her friend to see the worry on her face or the tears threatening to spill. What was she supposed to say? That she could actually harm Liam and she'd already seen him fall to his death? What a mess. Loving Liam could mean his death, but she was already falling so deep that leaving him now would rip her apart.

She wiped her tears discreetly and faced Jade with a big smile on her face. "You're right. Just ... enjoy the moment, right?"

CHAPTER TWENTY-FIVE

After spending the whole day with Jade, Lara decided to go home to her apartment and get some rest, then maybe call Vivianne and tell her what had happened. This was big, and the Witch Assembly would want to know about it. Liam had dropped her off at The Enclave that morning, but he couldn't stay as he had left Hugo alone for too long. The hotel staff was nice, and they offered to take care of the dog, but it was too cruel to just leave him with strangers. They didn't make plans for afterwards, though, so she just assumed that Liam would eventually call her or show up at her apartment.

"Good afternoon, Ms. Chatraine," the doorman greeted her.

"Oh, hi ... uhm ... Jim," she said back, looking at the young man's name tag.

"I'm new here, just started today, ma'am."

"Oh, right." She nodded and headed to the elevators.

"Ma'am, your fiancé is waiting for you upstairs," Jim called. "He arrived here a few minutes ago. I thought you wouldn't want to keep him waiting in the lobby, so I let him up."

"Fiancé?" Lara shook her head as she entered the elevator

car. Jim must have been mistaken. Maybe it was her neighbor's fiancé or something.

As the elevator began to move, a suspicion niggled at the back of her mind, scratching at her like an itch. When the doors opened, she finally realized what was going on.

"Wesley?" she asked as she saw the tall figure waiting at her floor.

"Lara." He turned to her slowly. "Where have you been?"

"Where have I been?" she echoed. "I was out. What are you doing here?"

"I was in the city," he explained. "I wanted to surprise you at Fenrir, but they said you weren't there. Actually, they said that they couldn't confirm if you were working there or not, and I tried to tell them who I was, but apparently these stuck up New Yorkers don't know anyone who's anyone outside their stupid little city," he sneered. "But no worries. I greased the wheels a little, and one of the security guys told me you didn't live far away. I came here, told your doorman who I was, and he let me up."

"You told him you were my fiancé?"

He nodded. "Of course."

Lara's jaw dropped in shock. She thought her mom was taking care of this. God, this was awkward. "Listen, Wesley, I-"

"I'm hungry. Let's go out to eat," he suggested.

"Wesley, no. You see-"

"I think I could get us a table at Peter Luger. Do you like steak?"

"I do, but Wesley-"

"On second thought, you should really watch what you eat. I know women want to look their best on their wedding day. Maybe we can get some salad instead."

"Wesley, listen to me!" she shouted.

"Lara, what's going on with you?" He put one hand on her shoulder.

She shrugged it off. "I don't know what you think you're doing here and what my mother told you, but I've already decided I wasn't going to marry you."

He laughed. "I know, my father told me that he and your mother talked. But I told him he must have been mistaken."

"No, he wasn't. I'm not interested in you, Wesley. I'm not going to marry you."

Wesley's face twisted in anger and confusion. "You can't be serious, Lara. You couldn't possibly do better than me."

"Oh shut up, Wesley. You're so full of yourself! Now please leave." Lara moved to get away from him, but he grabbed her by the arms and slammed her against the wall.

"No, you listen here, you little backwater witch!" Wesley's handsome face turned ugly, the anger and resentment rolling off him. "You won't find a warlock who's a better match than me. Now I know your family isn't as rich or as successful as ours, but I was willing to overlook that, since your bloodline is not only pristine but you're the only blessed witch of marrying age in this generation. The Morgans have never had a blessed witch in the family."

"Wesley, please, you're hurting me! Let me go."

"Not until you see reason! Can't you see how perfect we'd be together? How our children could become the most powerful-"

"I said stop!" Lara screamed. A gust of wind blew down the hallway but did nothing except ruffle Wesley's hair.

"You can't say no to me, Lara. You can't!"

Lara gasped as Wesley's eyes grew wide and his grip on her tightened. "You can't force me to marry you, asshole!"

"Just wait and see what I can do, you good for nothing witch!"

"What the fuck is going on here?"

Liam.

Wesley looked behind him. "Move along, buddy, this isn't your concern."

Lara used the distraction to lift her hands up and push Wesley away as hard as she could. He didn't expect it, and tumbled back, landing on his behind.

"You-"

"Shut up, Wesley!" she screamed at him. "Or you'll regret it!"

Liam stepped over Wesley and immediately went to her side. "What's going on here, Lara?"

"Wesley was just leaving," she insisted.

The warlock slowly stood up, wiping his hands on his trousers. "And who is this?"

"Get out of here!" With a wave of her hand, she sent another air current toward him, not strong enough to push him down, but enough to let him know the power she held.

"This isn't over," he said in a gravelly voice. "You'll get what's coming to you," he threatened as he went toward the elevator.

Liam gave Lara a confused look. "Lara, who was that and what's going-" His eyes moved to her arms, where hand-shaped bruises were beginning to form. "Sonofabitch!" He let out a growl and swung around to face Wesley's retreating back.

"No, Liam!" She grabbed at his arm. The power rolling off him was palpable. She could feel the wolf and the anger bubbling at the surface, threatening to break free. "Don't, please!" she cried.

"I'm going to kill you, asshole!" Liam's voice was inhuman.

"What the fuck?" Wesley turned around, slamming his palm on the hallway. "Lara, is this a ... Lycan? You let this dirty dog touch you? You spread your legs like a whore for this animal, but you turn me down?"

"You motherfucker!" Liam sprinted toward Wesley, moving with grace and speed. He grabbed him by the throat and slammed him against the wall.

"No, let him go! Liam!"

Wesley's face was turning blue, his arms and legs were flailing in the air. Lara didn't know what to do, so she sent a gust of wind toward Liam, forcing him to release Wesley. The warlock slumped back, and Liam staggered to stay on his feet.

"Fuck you, dog!" Wesley gasped, trying to get as much air into his lungs as possible.

"Shut up, Wesley, or I won't stop him next time."

The elevator dinged, and the doors slid open. Seeing her opportunity, she gave Wesley one last push toward the elevator. The doors closed just in time.

"Why did you let him go?" Liam snapped. He stalked toward her, trapping her against the door to her apartment.

"Because I didn't want you to do something you'd regret later on."

"Oh believe me, I wouldn't regret killing that bastard!"

"Liam, listen to yourself! Do you really want to take a life?"

"He hurt you!" He punched his fist into the wall next to her, leaving a dent on the surface.

Lara flinched in surprise. She could feel the wolf's rage, clawing at him, trying to get out. "Liam, stop!"

"I can't! Not until I know that bastard won't hurt you anymore!"

"He won't! I'll make sure! Now, please calm down."

"I can't," Liam's voice cracked. "Lara ... I ...."

Liam was going to lose control. The air crackled with his power, his wolf threatening to take over. Unsure of what to do, she grabbed the front of his shirt and pulled him down for a kiss.

Red.

Liam was seeing red. Crimson everywhere, like the blood he had spilled trying to protect Lara. His human side felt the anguish and guilt of harming someone. But his wolf relished in it, rejoiced in his ability to protect his mate. Mate? Jesus.

The moment he had arrived at Lara's apartment building, he knew something was wrong. First, the new doorman wouldn't let him in. He had explained he was Lara's boyfriend, and the young man gave him a strange look and told him that he was going to call the manager. It was a good thing the manager had seen him going up to Lara's place a couple of times and let him in.

As soon as he got to her floor, his wolf was at full attention. Something was definitely wrong. And as soon as he saw the bastard standing over Lara and touching her, he started seeing red. When he saw the bruises, he lost it. No one would ever hurt Lara and get away with it. It felt so good to wrap his hands around his neck, feel the life slowly drain out of him. His wolf howled in approval, but when Lara stopped him, the animal felt betrayed. The wolf was threatening to claw his way out of his skin, and he had struggled to keep control of his body.

But then Lara's sweet kiss distracted him. No, it just changed his bloodlust to pure lust. Desire shot through him, his body humming and yearning for her. His cock went rigid and he pressed it against her, seeking her hot core.

"Liam," she whispered as he dragged his lips down her jaw, her neck. Her pulse was strong, pounding in his ear, and he felt her melt against him when his mouth closed over it. He sucked on the soft skin of her neck, tasting her, as her scent and arousal grew stronger.

He wasn't sure how, but they made it into her apartment, and not a moment too soon. Pushing her against the wall, he grabbed at the neckline of her dress and ripped it down the middle. She let out a soft cry of shock, then a throaty moan as Liam pulled down the cups of her bra, freeing her breasts. Liam captured one pink pebbled tip, his tongue swirling around and sucking back. A hand moved lower, between her legs. Lara was already soaking wet, the fabric of her panties damp with her juices. He pulled her panties down and slipped two fingers inside her.

Lara let out another long moan as his fingers moved in and out of her. Liam captured her mouth again, his tongue wanting to taste hers. The kiss was urgent, rough, and needy, their teeth and tongues clashing. He twisted his wrist so the heel of his hand ground against her clit, making her hips buck against him. Her needy pussy sucked at his fingers, and he thrust in harder and faster, and his other hand grabbed at her breast, his fingers rolling the pebbled nipple. Soon, Lara's body wracked and shook as her orgasm poured over her. Her fingers thrust into his hair, grabbing at him and holding on.

Fuck, watching her cum on his hand was too much. Before she could even catch her breath, Liam pushed her against the wall.

"I need you now," he rasped as his fingers fumbled at his fly. Half a second later, his cock sprang free as he pushed his pants down. The need to mark her and claim her was overpowering. He was deep inside her in one thrust.

"Liam," she cried as her eyes glassed over.

"Fuck," he panted. Lifting her up, he wrapped her legs around his waist. "You're. Mine." He said the words as if he was marking her with each thrust. "Mine, you hear? I'll kill anyone who touches you."

She cried his name, over and over, as he moved in and out of her. Her cunt squeezed at him, milking him, giving him pleasure like he'd never felt before.

"Who do you belong to, Lara?"

"You," she gasped. "Only you."

"You're mine. You belong to me." He slammed into her, harder this time, but she took every inch of him. Her breasts smashed against his chest, her hard nipples scraping across the skin as they moved together. A low growl tore at his vocal chords, and he sank his teeth in her shoulder, hard enough to leave bite marks but not so hard to draw blood.

"Please," she moaned, her legs tightening around him.

"Let go, baby. Cum around me," he urged, changing the angle of his hips so that he hit her clit with each thrust.

She let out one last, loud cry as her back arched and her pussy squeezed tight around him. He couldn't control himself and shot his warm cum deep inside her. Slim arms wound around his neck, pulling his head down for a kiss. He continued to thrust, not wanting to stop, coaxing another quick orgasm from her body.

Liam felt his cock soften and slip out of her body. He slid her down to her feet slowly but kept her braced against the wall. His deep breathing slowed, evened, and he bent down to kiss her softly. The anger and darkness seemed to have subsided, the animal in him satisfied.

Lara rolled her head back, breathing heavily. Her face flush, lips swollen, pert breasts thrust out, and thighs slicked with his drying cum, she never looked sexier in his eyes. He wanted her again.

"Liam." She reached out to touch his cheek.

He took her soft hand and kissed it. "Are you okay? Did I hurt you."

She looked up at him shyly and shook her head. "I'm fine."

"I'm sorry, I don't know what got into me." He turned

around and rubbed his hand down his face. "Who the fuck was that man?"

"Shhh ... Liam," she soothed, running a hand down his back. She slipped her arms around his waist and pressed her cheek against his warm skin. "No one. No one you need to know."

"But he hurt you." The simmering rage began to boil over again.

Her arms tightened around him. "I'm yours, Liam. Only yours."

The words subdued the anger in him. He turned around and looked down at her beautiful face. Without another word, he lifted her in his arms and carried her to bed.

CHAPTER TWENTY-SIX

Jade stayed under observation for another twenty-four hours, but seeing as her Lycan abilities had basically healed her completely, there was no reason to keep her at the Medical Wing. Despite Lara's protests, Jade went to work immediately. It took her a day or two to get the lab up to speed again, but soon she had everything running the way she wanted. She immediately put all their resources into figuring out how the mages were using blood magic to control humans and also completing the power suppressing bracelet. It was a Friday afternoon, and Lara couldn't wait to get out of work. The time seemed to tick by slowly, and she gave the clock another impatient look, willing it to go faster.

"This is fascinating!" Jade declared as she perused the old books spread all over the table in her lab. "Plus, with what we know about how the mage controlled all those humans, it'll be easier to find out what we need. Hey, don't touch that!"

Meredith pulled her hand away from one of the leather-bound books. "I was just curious! I'm so bored in here! I can't even get any WiFi!"

Jade rolled her eyes. "These volumes are old and priceless!"

She tossed a glove at the other Lycan. "If you want to touch them, put these on. But I'd rather you not. I'm trying to catalogue them to make them easier to reference."

"So I can play with them?" Meredith's eyes glinted.

"You can help."

Lara shook her head. Meredith and Jade were complete opposites, with the latter being so brainy and serious and the former never taking anything seriously. At first they quarreled like siblings. Jade felt resentful at being under close guard, and Meredith took every chance to poke and needle the scientist. Yet, to give them some credit, the two were slowly getting along.

"Can we get any more information from our mage prisoner?" Jade asked Lara.

"You mean that guy who kidnapped you, kept you drugged, controlled three dozen humans, and attacked your friends?" Meredith said sweetly.

Okay, so maybe they weren't getting along that well, Lara thought to herself.

Jade ignored her words. "I would think he'd be able to tell us more about the process."

Lara shook her head. "According to Alynna, he's been silent as a stone. Refuses to talk to anyone."

"How about the humans there?"

"Apparently, they don't remember anything either. It's like their memories have been wiped away."

"Who were those guys anyway?" Meredith asked. "They all seemed well trained."

"Strange, right?" Lara said. "They're from all over. Special forces, Marines, Navy SEALs, private bodyguards."

Meredith gasped. "So the mages somehow kidnapped some of the best soldiers in the world and used their magic to control them? Man, these mages sound like dicks!"

Lara nodded. "That seems to be the case. Grant and Nick are working to make sure they all get back to where they need to be. Cady's working overtime to smooth things over with the human authorities and fabricating stories to explain what happened. It's a big mess." She did not envy her cousin right now.

"And the other humans? The Creed crew, I mean."

Lara shrugged. "I don't know. They don't seem to be suspicious about anything, so there's no need to make them take the confusion potion." She hated the stuff. Not only was it difficult to make, but it was also unstable. The Lycans who bought it from the witches thought it was expensive to obtain because the witches were spiteful, but that was far from the truth. Confusion potions were necessary to keep the humans in the dark about the existence of both witches and Lycans. One dose and it made memories unreliable. But in the wrong hands, human hands in particular, it was a dangerous potion.

"Maybe I can make sure, interview them and stuff ... I swear I'd pounce on any of those guys! At least they'd be taller than me in heels!" Meredith gave a lascivious smile. "Oh, that Sebastian Creed! He has to be single! Don't you think he was a tall drink of water on a hot day, Jade?" She elbowed the scientist.

Jade wrinkled her brow. "Who?"

The blond Lycan gave an exasperated sigh. "You know. Your knight in shining Kevlar. The guy who found you and freed you from your chains. Literally. Tell me, when he carried you off into the sunrise, could you tell if he was carrying a big gun in his pocket?"

Jade looked at Lara, a confused expression on her face. "Who is she talking about?"

"Who am I talking about?!" Meredith waved her hands in an exaggerated manner.

"Meredith," Lara warned. "Jade was drugged and unconscious until she woke up in the Medical Wing."

"Oh, man!" Meredith gave Jade a pitying look. "I'm so sorry." She shook her head. "I'm so sorry you missed the hotness that is Sebastian Creed."

"Hmm." Jade tapped her chin with her finger. "I need to check on something with Milly. I'll be back."

As soon as Jade left the inner lab, Lara turned to Meredith. "Why do you keep doing that?"

"Doing what?" The Lycan's face was blank.

"Goading her and prodding her like that! You need to leave her alone. She doesn't need any more reminders of what she went through!" Fury rose in her, but she kept her hands fisted at her sides.

"I'm giving her exactly what she needs," Meredith countered. "Can't you see how she's keeping everything inside? How it's hurting her? What she needs is to let it out before she ends up hurting herself or someone else."

Lara went slack-jawed. "What do you mean?"

Meredith tsked. "Ah, I forgot how dull your senses are." She shook her head. "Look, in polite Lycan society, they don't make observations like this out loud. But lucky for you, I wasn't raised in a polite society. Jade doesn't feel like other Lycans I've met."

"What do you mean?"

Meredith lowered her voice. "Her wolf ... it feels so ... repressed."

"Huh? What do you mean by repressed?"

"Well, when we're young, we're taught to control our inner wolf, master it, and most of all, keep it obedient to our human side. But you're never supposed to ignore it or try to inhibit it. But something about Jade ... I can't quite put my finger on it, but it's like she's walking around with this tightly capped bottle inside her. I'm just scared she'll explode one day."

"And you think this is because of her kidnapping?"

The Lycan shook her head. "Frankly, I don't know."

Lara went quiet. Shit, how could she miss the signs? God, she'd been walking around in a fog. A sex fog, an inner voice snickered.

Things with Liam had gotten hot and heavy. Or way past that. The sex was out of this world, and they spent each night tangled up in each other. And they weren't even limited to evenings. Yesterday, she returned from getting lunch for Jade and the other people in the lab when she saw Liam across the lobby in Fenrir. He gave her that handsome, wolfish smile of his and caught up to her as she was getting into the private elevator. As soon as he got in, he slammed his palm on the emergency brake and they finished what they had started weeks ago. He fucked her from behind, hard and fast, skirt around her waist, her body pressed up against the cold metal wall. They had finished in record speed, and by the time the security crew called them from the intercom, Liam was already zipping up his pants and she was fixing her makeup.

"Earth to Lara?" Meredith waved a hand in front of her face, shaking her out of her reverie.

"Yeah, uhm ... you're right." She straightened her shoulders. "I'll talk to Jade. Maybe she'll open up to me."

———

By the end of the work day, she still hadn't gotten through to Jade. The Lycan seemed determined to ignore her questions about what had happened. She let out a frustrated breath. She was an awful friend, letting Jade bear the pain alone while she was fooling around with Liam.

But what exactly were they doing? Just fooling around? She spent every free moment with Liam, not just in bed, but laughing and talking with him, too. That ache in her heart eased, but the fear in the pit of her stomach only grew. Jonathan. Falling.

She shook her head. No. Jonathan's death was a coincidence. Maybe in the catatonic daze she had been in, her mind had made it all up. A way to rationalize his death. Still, that didn't give her permission to fall in love with Liam. He was still an Alpha, and she was still a witch. Scandal from such a pairing aside, they also had a duty to their kind. She had to be practical, even if it felt like her soul was ripping apart. They would have to stop this now, before it was too late.

She tossed her bag on the kitchen counter as soon as she got home. A nice, hot bath should help relax her. Before she could run to the bathroom, however, her phone started ringing.

"Hello?" she answered.

"Lara, it's me."

"Liam," she greeted.

"Sweetheart, I'm sorry. I've been trying to reach you the whole day. I'm back in San Francisco."

"What?"

"Yeah, I couldn't stay away any longer. I'm so sorry I didn't tell you."

"It's fine," she said, trying to sound casual. Maybe this was what she needed. A break from him physically.

"So, I need a favor."

"Hmm?"

"I had to go quickly, and I had to leave Hugo behind at the hotel."

"Oh no!" Poor Hugo must have been going crazy, cooped up alone in Liam's suite. "What can I do? Do you want me to take care of him while you're gone?"

"Well ... sort of. I've chartered another jet; it's getting ready to leave."

"I'll make sure he's on it," she replied, thinking about how she would get the giant beast to the private airstrip.

"I want you to go with him. I mean, I want you to come here to San Francisco. Stay here with me. I don't want to be without you."

She should say no, that she'll be too busy working with Jade all weekend. "Sure." *Oh, fuck.*

"Great!" Liam's voice sounded bright. "I'll text you the details. I'll see you soon, sweetheart."

Crap.

CHAPTER TWENTY-SEVEN

She was falling again. The wind rushed around her, the ground was just beyond her vision.

"Lara!"

Liam's fingertips brushed against her. If only she could move faster, fall faster, she could touch him, grab his hand.

She tried to scream, but she couldn't open her mouth. The wind was too strong, and her vocal chords wouldn't work.

No! Liam!

But he fell faster, farther from her fingertips.

Lara woke up with a start, her breathing heavy. "Liam." Her throat was so dry, she could barely say his name. God, that awful dream once more. It brought chills to her.

No, this can't be happening again! She wracked her brain, trying to remember the dream in detail. It was so vivid and lifelike, but unlike Jonathan's dream, there weren't any details to tell her what would kill Liam. She stretched and sat up in bed, then wrapped her arms around her legs. Maybe it was just a dream. Yes, that was it. Just a dream.

Lara yawned, stretched again, and went to the bathroom to brush her teeth. She and Hugo had arrived in San Francisco the night before, not too late thanks to the time difference. A car had picked them both up but dropped her off at The Mark Hopkins Hotel in Nob Hill. There was a valet waiting for her as soon as she arrived, and she was whisked off to the top suite.

It was an amazing suite and had a fantastic view of San Francisco from the enclosed terrace. She was hoping she wouldn't have to wait too long for Liam, her body already thrumming with the need for his touch. Sure enough, when he arrived in the suite, she dragged him inside the suite so he could make love to her on the couch on the terrace.

After she was done freshening up, she put on the fluffy hotel bathrobe and went back out.

"Coffee and breakfast," Liam announced as he rolled the room service cart into the bedroom.

"Great! I'm starving!" she said. She was famished, and her stomach gurgled at the thought of food.

"I didn't know what you wanted," he said. "So I ordered one of everything."

The cart was heaped with all kinds of breakfast foods, from pancakes and bacon to delicate steamed dim sum.

"Good choice." She giggled as she grabbed a plate and piled the food onto her plate. "Oh God." She closed her eyes as she took a bite of the eggs Benedict. "This is amazing."

"Glad you approve," he said with humor in his voice. "Wow, you really are hungry."

"You wore me out," she said through a mouthful of bacon.

"If I recall, you were the one who woke me up in the middle of the night with your mouth."

She raised a brow at him. "Are you complaining?"

"Not at all, sweetheart."

Lara polished off most of the breakfast, though she didn't eat as much as she wanted to.

"Do you have to work today?" she asked.

He shook his head. "No. I was hoping you'd come and do some sightseeing with me."

"That sounds awesome. Now how about a shower before we go?" She gave him a cheeky grin before she stripped off her robe.

———

After breakfast and their ridiculously long shower, Liam and Lara got dressed and went down to the lobby. They drove around in his sporty little BMW with the top down, enjoying the unusually sunny San Francisco weather. Lara wanted to do all the touristy things, so they explored Fisherman's Wharf, walked the Golden Gate Bridge, and even rode the Cable Car. They went to lunch in the Mission District, and after a quick afternoon nap, they got ready for dinner in Little Italy. They sat in a corner booth of a lovely restaurant on Mason St.

"This is divine," Lara said as she took a bite of the veal scaloppini.

"I'm glad you like it," he said. Seeing Lara so happy and content put him in a good mood, and his inner wolf was very pleased. She looked especially gorgeous tonight with her golden red curls swept to one side and her makeup minimal. Since she didn't have a lot of time to pack for the trip, Liam had insisted on taking her shopping for a dress for tonight. The short purple dress was stunning on her, and the black stiletto heels made her legs look sexy. As he sipped his wine, he imagined pushing her down on the bed, getting between her legs, and having those spiky shoes dig into his back.

"Liam? Are you okay?" she asked. "What are you thinking of?"

He said nothing but gave her a heated look, his eyes dipping down to her luscious lips and then to her breasts. Her blush indicated she knew exactly what he was thinking of.

"Stop it," she said, glaring at him.

"What?" He gave her an innocent look. "I'm not doing anything."

"You know ... when you look at me like that ..."

"What?"

"You make me think of naughty things," she confessed.

"Just think of naughty things?" Underneath the table, he laid his hand on her thigh. Slowly, his hand inched up. Oh, he was going to do more than just make her think of naughty things.

————

The dream came faster this time. It was like a movie being rewound to the beginning. The action went backwards, going by too quickly for her to see. Then everything froze and started playing again.

They were standing in a large, circular room with tall windows. It was dawn, and the sun was peeking from behind the mountains. There was something wrong, though. Broken glass everywhere. And there was chaos all around. Shouting and screaming. Ripping and growling.

A figure in a black robe approached Liam from behind.

"No!" she tried to scream, but it was like she was just a member of the audience, unable to participate in the action.

The figure lunged at Liam. The Lycan didn't see him, and they struggled, then fell through one of the open windows.

The movie sped up again, and this time she was falling, too. Liam's face looking up to her, reaching out to her. Their fingers barely touching. The ground approaching way too fast, and then ....

Darkness. Empty. Cold.

Lara shot up from the bed, letting out a cry as she awoke from her dream.

"Sweetheart," Liam cooed. He was up, his arms hugging her to him. "Lara ... it was just a dream ...."

"I ... I ....," she choked. Was it just a dream? Her heart was thudding wildly, and as hard as she tried, she couldn't calm herself. She felt sick, her stomach tied up in knots.

Liam pulled her down, wrapping his long, lean body around her. "Try to get some sleep, sweetheart. It'll be better by morning."

Lara lay in his arms, staying as still as possible. When Liam's breathing finally evened, she relaxed a little bit. No, she wouldn't sleep tonight. She couldn't.

She lay awake for what seemed like hours, sometimes drifting into a shallow sleep but always waking up before the dreams took over. And by the time the clock on the bedside table told her it was morning, she was exhausted. Liam had remained wrapped around her all night, and she had to disentangle herself from his limbs so she could go to the bathroom.

God, she looked awful, she thought as she stared at herself in the mirror. There were dark bags under her eyes, and her skin was dull and lifeless.

The dream ... no, it couldn't be. But she couldn't deny it any longer. She was in love with Liam. Despite all her efforts, all the warnings, she had fallen head over heels in love with him. The dream last night was different. More vivid. Could she stop it from happening? Try to figure out the details and make sure he didn't go anywhere near that place where he would meet his doom? Or should she just run away now to keep him safe, even though it would rip her heart apart?

The solution to her problem came that same day. They were having brunch at the hotel when an older woman approached their table. She was attractive for sure, with long blonde hair and tightest dress Lara had ever seen.

"Alpha! How lovely to see you!"

Liam whipped his head around to see who was intruding on them. He put on his fiercest scowl. When his eyes landed on the woman, he jerked his hand away from Lara's.

"Belinda! How have you been?"

Lara could feel the older woman's eyes on her, and when she looked up, there was a faint glow in them. Lycan.

"I'm great! So," Belinda's eyes flickered over to Lara, "who's your ... companion?"

"This is Ms. Lara Chatraine," Liam said quickly. "Lara, this is Belinda Martin."

"How do you do?" Belinda's red-painted lips curled into a smile, and she extended her hand toward the witch.

"Nice to meet you." Lara gave her a smile just as sweet as they shook hands.

Belinda turned her gaze back to Liam. "How is your mother? I haven't seen her since we bumped into each other at the opera!"

"She's doing well," Liam answered, his voice tense.

She gave Lara a cursory glance. "Well then, I'll leave you to enjoy your meal." With one last predatory smile at Liam, the older woman walked away.

"So, is she ... your friend?" Lara asked cautiously.

"Er, my mother's friend. And a member of the clan."

"Oh." Lara took a sip of her coffee and looked away,

"Lara, listen," he began. "I need to tell you-"

"Can we go back to the room now?" she said in a terse voice.

"Lara, please." He took her hands in his and rubbed her palms.

She yanked her hands back. "I'm tired, and I'm getting a

headache. Why don't you finish your brunch? I'm going to go back." She stood up and left him staring at her.

Lara tightened her fists, mustering the courage to do what had to be done. She could hear Liam calling after her but ignored him. There was no way she was going to do this in the lobby of the hotel. She quickly stepped into the elevator, hitting the 'close' button even as Liam was running toward her.

She ran to the suite, flung the door open, and stalked toward the bedroom. After grabbing her small suitcase, she began to pack her things.

"Lara, what the hell was that about?"

The anger in Liam's voice was obvious, but she continued to put her things in the suitcase.

"And what the fuck are you doing?" Liam strode to her, grabbing her things and taking them out of the bag.

"Don't cuss at me!" she hissed and began to repack.

"Shit! Sorry!" He ran his fingers through his hair. "What's going on? Talk to me, please!"

Lara slammed the suitcase cover down. "Tell me Liam, why are we here? Is this where you bring all the girls you sleep with, when you're hiding them away from everyone?"

"What are you talking about?"

The idea had come to her in an instant. After Liam had jerked away from her when Belinda saw them, she knew this was her chance. *I'm sorry, Liam.* "That ... that woman! She knows your mother; she's part of your clan!"

"Yes, and so what?"

"Are you ashamed of me? Is that why you put me up here like some ... some ... dirty little secret?"

"No! I mean ...." He went quiet. "It's not what you think!"

"Well, then tell me! No, wait, never mind, I don't want to know!"

"Lara," he pleaded. "I can't ... I don't know ...."

Oh God. There was some truth to what she had said. Sure, she was the one who brought it up, but it still hurt. "I don't know either, Liam! I don't know what we're doing! I think it's time we faced the truth. This isn't going anywhere, and we should just end things before either of us gets hurt." Too late. "I'm going back to New York."

"No!" He grabbed her by the shoulders. "No, Lara. We can talk about this!"

She wrenched herself away from his grasp. "There is nothing to talk about!" Lara grabbed her suitcase and started for the door.

"Lara, don't go."

The sincerity in Liam's voice made her heart ache so bad. But she had to do this. For him.

"Goodbye, Liam."

———

Lara headed to the San Francisco Airport and took the first flight back to New York. Unfortunately, the only seat open was in First Class. It cost her an arm and a leg, but it was worth it. She wanted to get away from Liam as soon as possible.

"Would you like your meal now, Ms. Chatraine?" The friendly flight attendant was looking down at her, waiting for an answer.

"I don't ..." Her stomach gurgled in hunger. "I mean, yes, please ... uh ...."

"The name's Cheryl, Miss. Would you like the steak or the lobster?"

"Er, the lobster, I suppose."

The flight attendant nodded and walked back to the galley.

Lara relaxed into her comfy leather chair, glad that she had some privacy in her First Class seat. A few minutes later,

Cheryl returned holding a tray with her meal. Lara scarfed it down but waved away the wine she was offered. She wrinkled her nose. Ugh, the thought of alcohol made her nauseated.

"Excuse me." She stopped the flight attendant. "Uhm, actually I'd like the steak, too." Why not? She was paying for the flight out of pocket.

"Of course."

Pushing the tray away, Lara took a deep breath. Eating her feelings seemed to be working, or at least it distracted her from thoughts of Liam. The pain in her middle slashed at her. His handsome face swam into her consciousness, how he looked when she left that morning. Did this morning really happen? Sitting in the cabin of the plane, it seemed like a million years ago. Only the pain in her heart told her it was real. She told herself she was doing it for him. To keep him alive and away from the curse she carried.

"Ms. Chatraine?" Cheryl said as she stood beside her, tray in hand.

"Thank you, Cheryl." Well, might as well enjoy the steak.

CHAPTER TWENTY-EIGHT

The next day, Lara showed up to work bright and early. Sure, she looked like shit, since she hadn't sleep at all, but there were things to do. The mages hadn't retaliated yet, but they would strike back somehow. If they had the power to control humans, they were probably raising another army. Plus, who else could they control? The President? Other world leaders? On the grand scale of things, there were far more important matters than her broken heart.

"Good morning, witch," Meredith greeted, raising her cup. "Wow, you look awful!"

Lara wasn't in the mood this morning, so she waved her hand at the Lycan, sending the paper cup in her hand tumbling. The Lycan screamed as the hot liquid spread across her shirt, staining the white fabric like a milky brown abstract painting.

"I suppose I deserved that," the Lycan called as she pulled at her shirt, the fabric making sucking sounds. "Sonofa ... I'm gonna have to bring this to a professional!"

"Send me the bill." Lara smirked, then walked up the stairs to the inner lab, where she knew Jade was probably waiting for her.

"Oh good, you're here!" Jade said. "Milly didn't show up today, and Meredith is no help at all."

Lara frowned. Jade looked just about as good as she did—dark smudges under her eyes, her hair in disarray. "Did you stay up all night?"

"Too busy," Jade grumbled. She walked to the corner and took something off of the soldering table. "Here you go! Mark 32!"

"Thirty-two?" Lara asked in surprised tone. "What the hell, Jade? Weren't you working on Mark 15 the last time?"

"Yeah, I had to accelerate a bit."

"You worked on seventeen versions of the bracelet all night?"

"No, silly," Jade said flippantly. "I've been working on them all weekend."

"What? Didn't Meredith tell you to go home?" She moved closer and gave her hair a sniff. "When was the last time you showered?"

"I don't remember. And why would she? At least she didn't have to go back to her cell."

Lara slapped her palm on her face. "All right, let's get to work. But you're going home after this one last test."

Jade began to tell her about the improvements she had made on the bracelet. It all went over her head, of course, but she didn't need to understand the finer details. She just had to make sure it worked so they could use it on the mages.

"Well, let's test this baby out." She held her arm out and let Jade put the bracelet on her.

"After you." Jade pointed to the giant glass tube in the corner. They had constructed the special chamber for testing the bracelet. She stepped inside and closed the door behind her.

"All right," Jade put her safety glasses on, "the cameras are on ... go!"

Lara took a deep breath and concentrated on the pieces of paper at her feet. She spread her fingers, imagining the air currents around her, willing them to make the paper fly. Nothing. She tried again, concentrating harder, and squeezed her eyes shut. Still nothing. The power she usually felt coursing through her was still there, but it was like it wouldn't listen to her commands. The bracelet was dampening her powers, and no matter how hard she tried, she couldn't break free of its hold.

"Jade ..." She looked at her friend, who was peering at her from the other side of the glass. "I think you did it!"

The Lycan let out a small squeal, and for the first time since her kidnapping, Lara saw a real smile spread across her friend's face. "Oh my Lord! Really? You can't feel your power?"

"I feel the power—it's not gone—but I can't make it do what I want."

Jade opened the door to the chamber. "This is ... c'mon, let's keep testing!"

Lara stepped out of the chamber and began to wave her hands. Nothing. She tried to knock over a couple of the books on the shelves, but they wouldn't budge. Over and over, she tried to manipulate the air currents around her, but they wouldn't heed her call. It felt almost sad, like a friend who walked by and completely ignored you. But that was a good thing, in this case.

"You did it!" Lara embraced Jade. "You're a genius!"

Jade seemed surprised herself, her light green eyes growing wide behind her glasses. "I did ... oh my ... son of a sea biscuit!" She cocked her head to the side. "What's going on out there?" The look on Jade's face turned to that of annoyance, and then anger.

"What's wrong? Jade!" Lara bellowed after the scientist as she tore out of the inner lab. She ran after her, taking the steps to the main lab two at a time.

"What did you do?" Jade screamed at Meredith.

The other Lycan was standing next to one of the machines. Something inside it was whirling and making loud beeping sounds.

"Nothing, I swear!"

"What's happening?" Lara asked.

"It's overheating!" Jade pointed to the machine. "Someone must have left it on all night!"

"Who?"

"I don't know, but we need to get out of here!"

The machine shook, and the beeping sounds got louder and faster. Lara raised her hand, trying to push the machine as far away from them as possible, but nothing happened, even as she waved her hand frantically. "Fuck me! The bracelet!" She struggled to get it off her wrist, but it wouldn't budge.

"Get down!" Jade screamed right before the machine exploded.

The two Lycans dove toward the floor, away from the machine. Lara was standing farther away and dropped to the ground, but she was much slower than her shifter companions. A piece of metal hurtled toward her and ripped across her arm. Pain shot through her and the blood splattered against her face. She lay her head on the cool tile floor, breathing heavily to try and ease the pain. The emergency alarm blared above them, bringing pain to her ears as the ringing sound pierced the air.

A few minutes passed, and when there were no further explosions, they slowly got to their feet.

"Lara!" Jade cried out. "Are you okay?"

"I'm hurt! I have a-" Her eyes widened as she saw the cut on her arm. There was still blood on her skin, but the cut was healing right before her eyes. She quickly rubbed the blood on her jeans and put her arm behind her. "I mean, I'm okay!"

Jade let out a relieved breath. "Oh my Lord! I was worried that you ... I thought I smelled blood."

"Minor cut!" Lara explained. "Looks worse than it is."

"Let me see!"

Jade tried to take her arm, but she pulled away from her. "No! It's fine! Don't worry."

"I'm okay too, in case you were wondering!" Meredith called out to them. She stood up straight and shook the debris out of her blonde locks. With a sigh, she looked down at her stained shirt, which now sported a giant tear down the side. "I'm gonna need a new shirt."

Jade looked around the lab. "Let's call security and survey the damage."

Thankfully, the blast wasn't too big. It wasn't even strong enough to trigger the smoke alarms. However, the machine was blown to pieces, as well as the table and everything about three feet around it. But aside from that, the rest of the lab was unharmed, save for random bits of metal scattered around. It seemed the three of them jumped away just in time. If they were a foot or two closer, they would have been seriously injured, or worse.

"Dr. Cross!" A shout from the other side of the door called. "Open the door! The emergency alarm triggered a lock down!"

Jade ran to the door and slammed the button next to it. The panels slid open, and the emergency crew barged in, led by Nick Vrost. The Beta's ice blue eyes surveyed the damage. "What happened?" Jade quickly recounted the events.

"This machine, you think it was left on by accident?"

"Probably," Jade replied. "It's an ultrasonic cleaner. Milly's supposed to put everything in there that needs cleaning at the end of the day. She must have switched it on without setting the timer."

"She's been doing it since she started here," Lara said. "She does it every day. Why would she forget this one time?"

Nick's brows furrowed. "And where is your assistant?"

"She's not here yet."

The Beta's lips hardened into a grim line. "I'll have HR check on her. In the meantime, you'll have to evacuate the lab while we're doing a sweep. If you need anything, head to Cady's office."

"I'll need to grab a few things first," Jade said, before heading back to the inner lab.

"Lara." Nick turned his gaze on her, and he gave her a once over. "Are you okay? I smell blood on you."

"Y-yeah," she stammered. "I cut my hand. I'll be okay."

"Are you positive? I'm sure Jade wouldn't mind if you went home."

"I'll think about it."

Nick nodded and then turned back to his team, giving them instructions.

Lara needed to be alone. She looked at her arm again. This time, the skin was completely healed, as if nothing had happened. Shock and disbelief ran through her system. She'd seen this happen before. There was no denying it. She was pregnant, and Liam was the father. Her True Mate.

The day passed by in a daze. Jade and Lara both refused to go home and instead camped out in Cady's office. The scientist was currently on the couch, pouring through the old volumes from the New York coven library, and Lara was helping her mark pages and keep a catalogue of the important chapters. Meredith had stayed behind in the lab to help Nick and the rest of the security team make sure there were no other surprises.

Lara glanced at her cousin. Cady looked gorgeous as always, but she had the unearthly pregnant glow about her. She also looked like she was ready to pop at any moment. Cady was about eight months along or maybe more, she couldn't remember. Her large belly led her wherever she went, and she was constantly rubbing her lower back.

A warm feeling came over Lara, and she fought the urge to touch her own belly. How could it be so quick? A couple of days at the most. Her cheeks heated, thinking about that night Wesley was waiting outside her apartment. Watching Liam had been ... interesting. Again, he was showing those protective tendencies, and she couldn't help but react. She and Liam had been so hot for each other they hadn't bothered to use a condom. After that, it didn't seem to matter anymore anyway, and they continued to have unprotected sex. Not that it mattered after that first time.

She had missed it completely, but now that she knew it was there, she couldn't ignore it. The spark of life in her belly was small but strong. A child. A Lycan pup. Lara imagined a boy with Liam's blue eyes. Or maybe a girl with his smile. A stab of pain went through her, thinking of him.

A groan from Cady caught her attention. "Are you all right, Cady?" she asked.

"I'm fine," she sighed. "Just so ... tired."

"Why are you still here? Shouldn't you be at home resting? When are you due?"

"Any day now." The redhead gave her a weak smile. "I'm fine. I can't stay at home, I'll just go crazy, and there's nothing to worry about. This baby is going to be strong and healthy."

Lara felt that knot in her stomach. In nine months, she'd be in Cady's position. Did she have the strength to raise a baby alone? She would have to find it.

"Are you okay, Lara?" Cady's brows knitted together. "You seem pale."

"I'm fine, Cady, just shaken up."

There was a knock on the door. "Come in!" Cady called out.

Vivianne Chatraine breezed in. "Lara, Cady, Jade," she greeted each one of them. She walked over to Cady's desk and put an arm around her niece, placing a hand on her belly. "Cady, dear, why aren't you at home? You're so close to delivery, you should be near The Enclave Medical Wing."

"As I was telling Lara, I'm fine, Vivianne. Really. There's a lot of work to be done, and if I stay home, I'll just worry more."

The older witch gave her a smile. "Everything seems to be going well. I can't wait to see my grandniece or nephew."

"You and me both," Cady said wryly.

Vivianne walked over to the couch and sat next to Lara. "Darling, how are you? You seem pale? Have you been sleeping?"

"Just tired, Mother."

"There's something odd about you ...." Vivianne narrowed her eyes and tried to put an arm around her.

Lara tried to brush her mother off, but it was too late. As her mother's arm touched her shoulders, she felt the zing of power. The older woman's eyes widened, and her hand immediately went to Lara's flat belly. "Darling? Oh my! This is the best news!"

"What is it?" Jade asked as she lifted her head up from the book she was reading.

"Mother, please!"

"Darling, how far along?"

Not knowing what else to do, she got to her feet, batting her mother's hands away. "I'm not!"

"Not what?" Cady asked.

"Oh Lara, I'm so happy! I knew it!" Vivianne embraced Lara. "I knew it when he came to the compound."

"Who came to the compound?" Cady and Jade asked at the same time.

"Mother, don't—"

"Why, Liam Henney of course!" Vivianne said matter-of-factly. "And now Lara's going to have his baby. Another True Mate child!"

"What?" Jade jumped to her feet and grabbed Lara's arm. "Is it true?"

Before she could say anything, Cady let out a cry. "Oh my God, my water just broke!"

CHAPTER TWENTY-NINE

The news of the impending birth spread throughout the Fenrir offices. Lara immediately called Nick, and the Beta rushed to his wife's side. He carried her all the way down to the waiting car that whisked them back to the Enclave, where Dr. Faulkner's medical team was preparing the delivery room.

Lara was relieved that the excitement over Cady's baby had taken everyone's attention, even her mother's. Jade had been giving her strange looks, but she ignored her friend, not wanting to deal with this now. Someone from the security team called Jade, asking her to supervise the cleanup of the lab, so the Lycan scientist quickly left, but the look in her eyes said she was going to get an explanation, one way or another.

She collapsed on the couch in Cady's office. Her day couldn't possibly get any worse.

"Lara!" Alynna's head popped through the door.

"What is it? Is Cady okay?"

"She's fine! But your day is about to get more exciting! Meeting in the conference room. Now!"

Ugh, really?

Lara dragged herself to her feet and threw Cady's office door open. As she was leaving the office, she bumped into a solid wall. However, the familiar citrusy scent told her it wasn't a wall.

"Lara!" Liam caught her before she fell flat on her ass. "Finally! I was looking all over for you. Look, I'm so sorry. You're right, I was hiding you away, but it's not because I'm ashamed of you."

"Liam, please." Lara pulled away from him. She had to get away from him now. "What are you doing here?"

"I wasn't going to just let you go; you should know that by now," he growled.

"You should!" She pushed at him. "I'm not good for you!"

He caught her wrists and pulled him toward her. "Listen here, Lara-"

"Hey!" It was Alex Westbrooke. He was standing outside his office, arms crossed over his chest, leaning casually against the door. "Everything okay here?"

Liam dropped Lara's hands. "Yeah, we're good."

Alex gave Lara a concerned look, watching her intently as she slunk away from Liam. "I'm not asking *you*. Lara, are you all right?"

"Mind your own business, Westbrooke." Liam stepped toward the other Lycan.

"Oh yeah?" Alex stretched up to his full height, tipping his chin up. "Make me, Henney."

"Stop it!" Lara put her hands up and pushed the two men away from each other with her powers. They both stumbled back but quickly regained their balance. "C'mon, Alynna says we have a meeting now!"

She ran past them in a huff, pushing the conference door

open with such force it slammed against the wall. Several pairs of eyes swung over to her. "Sorry," she murmured before sitting in the empty chair between Jade and her mother.

Alex and Liam followed behind her, the tension between them palpable. Alynna rolled her eyes at her husband as he sat next to her, while Vivianne shot Lara a confused look. She ignored her mother.

"All right, we're all here," Grant began. He sat at the head of the table with Alynna on his right and Vivianne on his left. He turned to Liam. "I'm glad you're here, Liam. We could really use all the help we can get."

"Glad to be here." The San Francisco Alpha nodded. "Like I said, I want to take down those mages."

"Excellent. So sorry for the short notice, but we have some new developments. Alynna." He turned the floor over to his sister.

"Let's get this show on the road, folks." She cleared her throat. "This morning, there was an explosion in Jade's lab. We thought it was an accident, but upon further investigation we discovered it wasn't."

"How did you know it wasn't an accident?" Lara asked.

Alynna picked up her tablet and with a tap of the screen, the lights dimmed and the large monitor behind Grant pulsed to life. Milly's picture flashed on the screen. "Mildred Foster. She started working as Jade's assistant a few weeks ago, right after the previous assistant quit. She last clocked out at 9 p.m. last night, which was right around the time she left the ultrasonic cleaner on. Didn't show up to work this morning, and when HR went to her apartment ... well," Alynna took a deep breath, "I'm afraid she's dead."

Jade went pale. "What happened?"

Alynna shook her head. "We don't know yet, but we suspect

foul play. I went there myself and collected her phone and laptop. I had my friends hack into it." She tapped the tablet again, and a map popped up. "At first glance everything seemed clean, but they found messages and calls on her phone and email to one device. They tracked it all the way to the Adirondack Mountains." A different picture flashed on the screen. It was a large mansion built right into the side of the mountain.

"What are you saying?" Alex asked.

"Milly was a spy," Alynna said. "The mages got to her. She's not a witch or mage, as far as we can tell. I'm putting my money on either blackmail or plain old greed. Anyway, she's been feeding information to the mages. That's probably how they found out about what we were doing and about you." She looked at Jade. "I'm sorry."

The scientist went pale. "What do we do now?"

"Well, we think the mages are in that mansion. Although our prisoner hasn't been cooperative, when I showed him the picture, he practically peed his pants. He told us everything in return for protection. Apparently, he'd rather take his chances with us than with Stefan. He confirmed that the mansion is where Stefan and his cohorts are currently hiding out. He's also giving us some incredible intel about their defenses."

"Now," Grant spoke up. "This is our chance to strike back. Alynna, Alex, and Nick have been coming up with various plans in case we ever had such an opportunity."

"This is our best chance to really hit them hard," Alynna said. "And possibly capture Stefan and put an end to this."

"The bracelet!" Jade interjected. "We tested it before the explosion! It was working."

"Yes," Lara confirmed. "It definitely dampened my powers."

"Fantastic!" Alynna said in an excited voice. "Jade, I could kiss you! This changes things. I think I know which plan we should put into action. The bracelet will simplify things and put less risk on our people."

"Do we have enough people to put your plan into action?"

Alynna looked around the room. "With Nick gone, I'm not sure, but we could adjust."

"Grant," Liam spoke up. "I'll take Nick's place, whatever you need."

Lara's pulse ticked faster as she stared at the image of the mage stronghold. There was something about it that was bothering her.

"That would be awesome, Liam," Alynna said. "That will make things easier. Now, let's get the details ironed out."

As Alynna explained the plan, Lara tried to listen, but she couldn't concentrate. She had a gut feeling, and it wasn't a good one. She stared at the picture until her vision went blurry.

Oh God.

Her dream. The large circular room overlooking the mountains. Liam falling to his death.

A wave of nausea hit her, and she shot to her feet. She ran out of the conference room, barely making it to the bathroom.

After losing her breakfast in the toilet, she washed her mouth out and leaned her forehead on the cold tile wall. It was happening all over again. Jonathan. Now Liam. There had to be a way to stop it and save Liam.

She wiped her hand on her shirt and took a deep breath, preparing to face the others.

"Lara, darling, are you okay?" Vivianne was waiting for her outside the bathroom. "How bad is your morning sickness?"

"I'm fine, Mother. It's not ... I haven't." God, what was she supposed to say to her mother?

"Lara."

She froze. Turning around slowly, she faced Liam and his

electric blue eyes. His handsome face was etched with worry. "Are you all right?"

"Liam! She's fine; it's all normal you know." Vivianne swept past Lara to enfold him in a hug. "Oh, I can't tell you how happy I am."

Liam looked confused. When Vivianne let go, he finally spoke. "Normal for what?"

"A woman in her condition, of course!" Vivianne laughed, placing a hand on Lara's belly. "Oh. Wow. I never thought such power ... but of course it makes sense! A Lycan and witch as True Mates. This changes everything!"

"Lara?" Liam's face went white as a sheet.

Vivianne looked at Liam and then at Lara. "Oh dear. You didn't know?"

Liam shook his head slowly.

"I'm sorry ... Lara, darling, please forgive me! I didn't mean to ruin the surprise."

"It's okay, Mother," Lara whispered. "Please, can you give me and Liam some privacy?"

"Of course. I'll be back in the conference room."

Vivianne gave her a weak smile and left. Lara looked after her mother and waited for her to disappear around the corner before facing Liam.

"Did you know?" Liam's voice was cold and emotionless.

She couldn't lie. "I suspected. But I wasn't sure."

"And yet you left me? Let me think I was being selfish?!" Liam's face twisted in anger. "You knew you could give me pups, and you let me think ... I was ready to give up everything for you! I told my mother I didn't care about being Alpha and that I was in lo-"

"I don't want your pups!" she shouted. She knew what he was going to say, and she had to stop him from saying those words. So she thought of the only thing that could make him hate her. She lied to him, so she could save him.

A myriad of different emotions seemed to flash across Liam's face at lightning speed. Surprise, hurt, regret, anger, and then nothing. The last one was the worst for Lara. His eyes turned cold and unfeeling, his lips set into a tight line. "So," he spat. "I'm good enough to fuck, but not to be the father of your pure witch children?"

His words tore her to pieces. If he had ripped her beating heart out of her chest it would have hurt less.

"That's not ... Liam!" she cried out as he grabbed her by the shoulders and pushed her against the wall.

"Did you have fun slumming it with a dirty dog like me?" He leaned down close to her ear; his breath was hot. His legs nudged her knees apart, and he pressed his hips to hers. His desire was still apparent, despite his obvious hatred. "Is this what you want, Lara? What would you do to have it again, I wonder?"

Tears threatened to spill down her cheeks, but she swallowed them, along with the hurt. "Let go of me, Liam."

"I told you, sweetheart," he said the endearment sarcastically, "I'm never letting you go. This," he grabbed her stomach, "is mine. There's nowhere on Earth you can run from me."

"No!"

"I thought you didn't want pups? Oh, don't worry, I only want my heir. Once you've done your duty, you can go ahead and spread your legs for any man who comes along. I won't be around to service you. Maybe that Wesley-"

"Asshole!" God, how could he be so cruel? But this is what she wanted, right? For Liam to hate her. She wrenched free of his grasp. She would not cry in front of him.

"Liam? Lara?" Alynna called out from the conference room. "Everything all right?"

"We're good!" Lara responded, keeping her face away from the other Lycan.

"We need to get started on our plan. We leave tonight for the Adirondacks."

"Great," she answered, wiping the tears from the rim of her eyes. Taking a deep breath, she walked away from Liam and back into the conference room.

———

Liam stared at Lara as she walked away. *That cruel, cold-hearted bitch.*

His wolf was howling, scratching and clawing at him, wanting to be let out. It wasn't that it was angry. No. His wolf was in pain. Lara's rejection sent his inner wolf into a downward spiral, and he struggled to control both his wolf and his emotions.

Had Lara been playing him all along? What was her game? Why sleep with him in the first place if she knew she would get pregnant? The condoms. That's why she insisted. Except that one time. They were True Mates, after all.

Confusion. Hurt. Fury. His mind was in a jumble; his heart was threatening to break apart. And to think, he was ready to give up everything for her. His mother had been furious when he came home after Lara had left. Of course that big-mouthed Belinda had called her right away. He had never seen Akiko so angry, shouting at him about family and honor and duty. But he defied her, told her he was in love with Lara and he was going to pass along the Alpha title to Takeda's son.

He gave a bitter laugh. Well, joke's on him. Lara. Sweet, beautiful and gorgeous Lara. So kind and nurturing. But deep inside, she was as cold-blooded as a snake. Using him for fun, toying with his feelings. Rage burned through him. He was itching to let his wolf out and rip apart some mages. The wolf would welcome the fight, anything to relieve the pain burning a hole inside him. He swallowed down all of the emotions. *Don't worry wolf,* he said to his inner animal. *You'll get a chance to bleed something soon enough.*

CHAPTER THIRTY

The mountain mansion was an intimidating sight, even from a distance. It was monstrous, taking up about half the face of the cliff. To get to the front gate, one would have to hike about twenty miles through thick forest. The front side of the property was protected by an electric fence, plus various magical wards, while the back side was edged toward the cliff with a thousand-foot drop.

This is crazy, Lara thought, looking up at the looming structure. But the plan had to work. This might be their only chance for victory and to end it all. She pushed away the doubt and fear, along with her other feelings, and got read for the task ahead.

They prepared all day and all night. Lara stayed away from Liam as much as she could, not that it was hard. The Lycan obviously didn't want to be around her. Who could blame him after what she had said? He hated her, and that was the point. If he didn't love her anymore, then the curse wouldn't affect him. Liam would live and the price she paid would be worth it.

By evening time, they had the final plan in place. First, they would split up into two groups. One team would be comprised of their best fighters and fake a sneak attack on the front. They would disable the fence and distract the dozen or so men guarding the front. Then, they'd fool the mages into thinking they had caught the Lycans. Meanwhile, a smaller team would sneak in through the secret tunnel their mage prisoner, Marcus, had told them about. Finally, they would have to find Stefan and put the bracelet on him.

Grant was leading the front attack, with Vivianne assisting in disabling the magical wards placed by the mages. Alex, Meredith, and two of the Lycan security team members would be with him for their fake attack. Nick would stay behind in their command center at The Enclave. Cady had given birth to a healthy baby boy hours before, but he was reluctant to leave his wife and child. Since Liam had offered to take his place, the San Francisco Alpha was now in charge of the smaller team, which consisted of just Lara and Alynna. If he objected to being teamed with her or her participation at all, he didn't show it. A slash of pain went through her, thinking he didn't care about her, but she pushed it away. She was invulnerable anyway, thanks to the baby growing inside of her. And this was much more important.

Now here she was, waiting with Liam and Alynna on the east side of the mansion. It was still dark; dawn would arrive soon. Marcus had told them where to find the entrance to the secret tunnel but warned them about the magical wards placed on it. This was another reason why she had to go with the team. The mage had said it was the usual protection and warning spells, so Lara was confident she could disable them.

The three of them walked up the outer wall, which was covered with vines. Lara closed her eyes and opened her senses, trying to feel the magic around her. The rush of power came at her quick, making her stagger back.

"What's wrong?" Alynna whispered.

"I found the wards. Stand back," she said. The Lycans moved behind her, and Lara began to chant softly, placing her hands over the wall.

Undoing magical wards was not unlike disarming a bomb. Every warlock and witch did things differently, layering spells and magic over each other to try and trip up anyone who would try to undo their work. It took a lot of concentration, trying to unweave the different threads of magic over the door. However, once she got started, it was like she was in a deep trance. She'd done this before, but now the spells seemed brighter, more vivid in her mind's eye. She could see each one and every layer. Thankfully, though the spells were powerful, there weren't a lot of them. With the right words, she was able to disarm each one. One by one, the wards over the door began to disappear.

The effort took its toll on her, and she stumbled backwards. Liam caught her immediately.

"Are you okay?" he asked, looking down at her, his glowing blue eyes seemingly soft.

"I'm fine," she snapped and got to her feet. "The wards are gone." One last thing, according to Marcus. She brushed the vines aside to reveal a symbol scratched onto the wall. With the wave of her hand and the right words, the door revealed itself and opened.

"We're in," Liam whispered into his comms unit. Once they confirmed that there was a secret tunnel, the other team would begin their "attack."

Liam walked ahead with Alynna in the middle and Lara in the rear. Jade had worked all night creating three identical bracelets, and they carried one each. Whoever could get to Stefan first would try to get it around him. Of course, when the master mage found them, he was going to put up a fight, and Victoria and Daric would most likely be with him. Still, they had three chances to take him down, and that was three more than they'd had before.

The tunnel was dark and musty, and seemed to stretch on forever. Lara didn't have Lycan night vision, so she held onto Alynna's arm. When she felt Alynna stop, so did she. Opening her senses again, she tried to find more magical traps. "There's nothing protecting this end of the wall," she said softly. "We should be able to open it without any problems."

There was a scratching sound, then the door slid to the side, filling the dark tunnel with faint light. Liam brushed his hands on his pants. "Let's go."

They crept out of the tunnel, walking quietly. The tunnel led to a large, circular room. It was mostly empty, save for a few pieces of furniture and some sculptures. However, the entire wall was made of floor-to-ceiling picture windows, giving them a breathtaking view of the outside. Right now, it was almost dawn and from behind the mountains, the sun was peeking out, painting the clouds with shades of pink and purple.

The three of them walked across the floor to the single doorway that led out of the room. Angry voices came from the outside, faint at first, but as they came closer, the conversation became more distinct.

"Those foolish creatures!" a cruel voice bellowed. "How dare they! Thinking they could sneak up on us! And that Alpha, leading the attack like some hero!"

"It looks like we can win this, Master!" a female voice said. "By the time they get here, they will be too weak! We should kill them the first chance we get!"

"There's something not right about this, Master." It was a male voice. Whoever was out there was mere seconds away from crossing the threshold.

Liam looked at Alynna and Lara, then pointed to the wall. They all lined up, squeezing themselves against the concrete.

Lara's heart pounded in her chest. Her part in this was crucial. She had to distract them first, so Liam and Alynna could disable anyone protecting Stefan. Looking out the windows as the sun crept higher, she knew what to do.

"Get ready and close your eyes," she warned her companions.

Four figures walked into the room. The one leading them was tall and dressed in dark robes. Stefan was here. Lara recognized her aunt, Victoria, and Stefan's right hand man, Daric. The fourth figure, however, had the hood of his robes over his head, so she couldn't see his face.

"How much longer?" Stefan asked impatiently.

"Not too—" Daric froze, and then his head snapped back. Blazing blue-green eyes zeroed in on Lara. "You!"

Lara wasted no time calling up the wind from outside. She raised her arms, and the windows began to shake.

"Get down!" Daric shouted as the sound of broken glass filled the air.

One by one, the windows shattered, sending shards of sharp glass everywhere. Lara let out a cry. She had never pushed her power this much, and it seemed to have no limits now. Her hands gave out a faint glow, and the wind continued to swirl around them, howling like a banshee.

"Now!" Liam yelled as he and Alynna sprang into action. There would be no shifting for them, as their wolves wouldn't have the dexterity to put the bracelet on Stefan.

Lara saw Daric get up, and she immediately sent a strong gust of wind his way to knock him back. His large body slammed against the wall. The warlock groaned in pain and struggled to get up. She sent another blast of wind his way, knocking his head back. Daric's large body slid down the wall and his eyes rolled back before the lids closed. In a split second, she made a decision. Grabbing the bracelet from her pocket, she wrapped it around Daric's wrist. Hopefully, either Liam or Alynna would get the chance to cuff theirs on Stefan, but at least for now, the warlock would be incapacitated.

Liam stalked over to Victoria, who stood in front of her master. She began to hurl bottles of potions at him, which he easily evaded. When she ran out of potions, she lunged for Liam, sending them both to the ground.

Lara looked over at Stefan, who stood in the middle of the room, ready to strike. This was her chance. She walked toward him, raising her hand, ready to knock him out. A shout made her freeze in her steps.

"Stop!" a voice bellowed. "Or the Lycan bitch dies!"

Lara whipped her head around. The other mage! Whoever he was, he had been the wild card. They didn't think there would be another person guarding Stefan, and they weren't prepared.

The hooded man had Alynna in a headlock, his arm wrapped around her neck like a vice. "Think you can shift faster than I can snap your pretty neck, Lycan? Why don't we try to find out."

"No!" Liam and Lara shouted at the same time.

"Stand down, filthy dogs," the figure said.

Lara felt the goosebumps rise all over her arms. That voice.

"Tsk, tsk. Too bad for you, Lara. You chose the wrong team." The man used his free arm to pull his robe back.

Her throat went dry, and she choked out his name. "Wesley."

"That's right, you stuck up little witch!" Wesley roared. "When your mother sent out feelers that you were ready for marriage, I jumped on the chance! I wanted to prove my loyalty to Master Stefan by fathering the next Fontaine witches and warlocks and then handing them over to be turned into mages."

Lara gasped. "You monster!"

Wesley laughed. "Couldn't you just have accepted my proposal? Then we wouldn't be in this mess!" His grip on Alynna tightened, making her gasp and her eyes water.

"Let her go!" Liam said. He had subdued Victoria, gripping her arms behind her.

Stefan laughed and walked over to Wesley. "Excellent job, my protégé." He looked down at Alynna. "Ah, so this is her? The spawn of Michael Anderson? Hmmm ... doesn't seem so special to me," he cackled, tracing a long, bony finger down Alynna's cheek. She tried to wrench away, but Wesley held her in place. He turned to Liam. "Alpha, I don't think you have the stomach to kill Victoria."

"Try me!" Liam said, pushing Victoria down to her knees. She screamed in pain, letting out a string of expletives.

They were in a standoff. Lara looked around. *Think. Think.* Her eyes were drawn back to Alynna, who was staring at her. The Lycan was looking at her, mouthing words. What was she saying? Her lips were forming ... numbers. One, two, three. Over and over again. Alynna was signaling her! She gave a slight nod, indicating she understood. Alynna blinked and counted with her mouth slowly.

One. Two. Three.

On three, Alynna let out a sharp yell as she planted her feet flat on the floor and pushed up at Wesley, while Lara raised her hand and sent a loud gust of wind their way. Wesley and Alynna tumbled over, and Liam released Victoria to shift into his wolf form. The wolf erupted from his skin and landed on all four paws with a loud thud. Alynna and Wesley were still struggling on the ground, but as soon as he got the chance, Liam's wolf swiped a large paw at Wesley, batting him away and leaving bloody marks across his back.

"No!" Stefan shrieked. "Victoria! We must leave!"

"Master!" Victoria cried as she got up and grabbed onto

Stefan. She looked at Daric, who was still unconscious. "What about Daric?"

"Leave him!" he said. "He was weak enough to get captured. Let him pay for his mistakes."

Lara screamed. "No!"

But it was too late. Victoria and Stefan vanished into thin air.

Liam shifted back into his human form and helped Alynna up. The look of concern he gave the other Lycan shot a stab of jealousy through Lara. No, she mustn't think of that. Alynna was alive, even though Stefan and Victoria got away.

"Alynna!" Alex shouted as he entered the room. He quickly went to his wife's side, pulled her into his arms, and lowered his mouth down to capture hers in a desperate kiss. They pulled away from each other, and Alex looked deep into his wife's eyes, touched her face, and murmured soft words to her. Lara looked away from the tender moment, not sure how she could take more of this.

Grant, Meredith, Vivianne, and the rest of the Lycan team quickly followed from behind Alex. While it looked like they were worse for wear, at least they were all alive.

"What happened?" Grant asked as he tossed Liam a pair of pants.

"Stefan and Victoria got away," Liam explained as he put on the trousers.

"Daric!" She suddenly remembered the warlock. Her eyes moved over to Daric, who was still unconscious. *Good.*

"Is that ...." Grant looked at Lara with an amazed expression.

"We couldn't get the bracelet on Stefan, but I put mine on him," Lara explained.

Grant signaled to his team, and two of them grabbed the

unconscious warlock. "Take him away and put him in the secure room in the basement of Fenrir."

"Looks like I'm going to be evicted," Meredith quipped.

"Or you have a new roommate," Grant retorted. Meredith quickly shut her mouth and busied herself with helping the other Lycans take Daric away.

"Everyone else okay?" Grant asked. "What happened?"

"We got through the tunnel. And then-" Lara stopped short. Her blood froze all of a sudden, and she realized why.

Wesley stood up quickly, swaying from side to side like a drunk man. With a savage snarl, he lunged at Liam, whose back was to the warlock.

"Liam!" she screamed to warn him, but it was too late. And just like in her dream, they struggled and then staggered toward the open windows.

Lara ran as fast as her legs could carry her, but she was too late. The two men tumbled out of the window. The last thing she heard was Alynna's scream as the force propelled her forward, and without a single thought, she dove right out of the window.

She was falling fast. Liam was so far away from her, his body plunging toward the Earth. He was too far away for her. Suddenly, a burst of power shot through her and she felt the wind currents push her down faster until she reached Liam. Their fingers were touching, and she grasped his arm, pulling him up until she embraced him. Another surge of power rushed through her, and this time, she forced the currents upwards, pushing against them. She felt the power tapping out, but it was enough to slow them down as they approached the ground. They were still about ten feet away when the wind currents died and they landed on the rocky dirt with a loud thud.

The bright oranges and blues of the sunrise were the last thing she remembered before everything turned black.

CHAPTER THIRTY-ONE

Consciousness came slowly to Lara. First, she became aware of the steadiness of her breath, her blood pumping through her veins. She was alive. Next was the feeling of soft sheets on her skin and warmth. A sweet, flowery smell brought her awake, made her open her eyes.

She'd know that perfume anywhere. Glancing to her side, she saw Vivianne, fast asleep on the chair next to her bed, a blanket over her. "Mother," she rasped out.

"Lara!" Vivianne's eyes flew open. "You're awake."

"What happened?" She shook her head. Then it came rushing back to her. Liam. Falling. Going after him. "How long was I out?" She looked outside and saw the sun was setting. The buildings and the view of the Hudson River told her she was probably in the Medical Wing of The Enclave.

"Darling, you scared me half to death!" Her mother pulled her into a tight hug. "I thought ..." Her voice hitched, and tears flowed down her pale cheeks. "When you jumped, I thought for sure I had lost you! But then I could still feel you. I knew you had survived the fall somehow. We all searched for you, and we found you and Liam on the ground. He was passed out as well."

"Liam!" She cried. "Is he okay?"

Vivianne nodded. "He's fine. You saved his life."

Her mother's words rattled in her brain, and she burst into tears. Vivianne embraced her again, comforting her as her body was racked with sobs.

"It's all right, darling," Vivianne soothed, rubbing her hands down her daughter's back. "I felt the burst of power while you tried to save him, through our blood bond. Just like I knew you were still alive."

"Mother, I don't know how I did it." Lara shook her head. She'd been using her magic for a decade, yet she'd never felt this kind of power. "No, wait." Her hands went to her belly. "I think ... I don't know how, but I think the baby ... he ... she ... I could feel my power growing."

Her mother's eyes lit up. "Darling, your baby must have somehow magnified your powers! A True Mate child, possibly both a Lycan and witch? This is monumental!" Vivianne's excitement quickly faded when she saw the forlorn look on Lara's face. "There's something you're not telling me. Why did Liam sound surprised that you were True Mates? Darling, you must have felt it! Why didn't you tell him right away?"

Lara's face crumpled, and a fresh wave of tears flowed down her cheeks. "Mother ... it was ... awful," she choked between sobs. "Jonathan ... the curse."

Vivianne listened to her daughter recount the whole story about how she had discovered Liam was her True Mate weeks ago and how she had tried to stop herself from falling in love with him. And when the dreams got stronger and she couldn't stop herself, how she did what she could to make Liam hate her. "The words I said, I can never take them back," she sobbed. "He despises me and threatened to take away our child!"

"Darling." Vivianne looked at her daughter sadly. "Surely this can be fixed."

Lara shook her head. "It can't. You didn't see his face, Mother. Didn't hear the words he used. Liam will never forgive me and ...," she let out a sigh, "maybe it's for the best."

"But you saved him! It's done, you broke the curse!"

"But what if it's not?" Lara asked. "Are you sure? What if another dream comes and I'm not there to stop it?"

"Darling," Vivianne began. "In your dream with Jonathan, you saw him die right? But in the dream with Liam, did he die?"

Lara thought for a moment, then shook her head.

"Maybe you were meant to save him."

"It doesn't matter." Lara turned away from Vivianne and wrapped her hands around her folded legs. "He'll never understand, and he'll never forgive me for saying those words." The look on Liam's face when she had said she didn't want his pups ... it was like she had murdered their child right then and there. She deserved all his cruel words.

"Darling ...."

"Please, Mother," she said, her voice shaky from crying. "I just want to go home."

Vivianne gave a resigned sigh. "I'll call your father. He's already on his way. I'm sure he wouldn't mind making the trip back right away."

CHAPTER THIRTY-TWO

Liam shifted on the hospital bed. No matter which way he lay down, he couldn't find a position that didn't make him uncomfortable. He glanced at the clock. It had been hours since the Lycan nurse had come in and checked on him last. He had been disoriented, not sure where he was. The nurse had explained that they had brought him in, unconscious from a fall. He had a concussion and a few broken ribs, but she didn't have any other details.

He could feel his body knitting itself together quickly, thanks to his accelerated Lycan healing, but he didn't have the strength to get up and try to find some real answers. When the nurse left, he had fallen back asleep, only to wake hours later. When he looked out the window, it was already dark. With a sigh, he leaned back on the bed and closed his eyes. What he could remember seemed like a dream. The sensation of falling. Lara's scent. And hitting the ground hard.

"Jeeze, Henney, you look like hell."

Liam's eyes shot open. He swung his gaze over to the doorway where Alex Westbrooke was standing.

"Yeah, well you look like shit, too." Liam rubbed his face.

His body was still sore, but his ribs weren't broken anymore. "Oh wait, that's how you look every day," he shot back as he tried to get up.

Alex gave him a dirty look, and then his mouth turned up into a grin. He walked over to the bed and helped Liam sit up.

"Thanks," Liam said wryly.

Alex went quiet. "No man, thank you. And I'm sorry. About, you know," he gave Liam a sheepish grin, "those other times I acted like an asshole."

"Wow, I must have hit my head real hard because Alex Westbrooke is apologizing to me."

"Oh, shut up," Alex snapped. He took a breath. "Look man, I know things haven't been easy between us. But Alynna told me everything, how you got that warlock off her and saved her life."

"Well, to be honest, I think Alynna's fairly capable of saving her own life," Liam confessed. "But if it's going to make you stop acting like a dick around me, then you're welcome." He held out his hand toward the other Lycan.

Alex shook it. "All in the past, right?"

"Hey! Look who's here!" Alynna burst into the room, pushing a big stroller through the door. "Mika! You haven't met Uncle Liam yet," she cooed to her baby. She stopped the stroller by his bed and picked up a small bundle. "Here you go. Say hi, baby!"

Liam smiled at the baby Alynna was holding up to his side. The perfect little girl with a mop of dark hair and green eyes smiled at him. "She's beautiful," Liam said softly. He suddenly remembered Lara, and hurt stabbed at his heart. He looked at Alex and Alynna with envy, knowing he would never have this. That cold-hearted bitch has probably already taken the first chance to get rid of his pup.

"Liam, what's wrong?" Alynna asked with a frown. She

handed the baby to Alex, who was eager to cuddle his daughter. She sat next to him on the bed, a concerned look on her face.

"Yeah, I'm just ... you know. Healing is a bitch." He winced. "Now will someone tell me what happened?"

Alynna opened her mouth to speak, but was interrupted by a knock.

"Come in," he called in an annoyed voice.

The door opened slowly, and Vivianne Chatraine walked in. "Alpha," she said. "I hope I'm not interrupting? I'd like to speak with you, if you're feeling better."

Alynna got to her feet. "It's fine." She took Mika from Alex and put the baby back in the stroller. "We were going to go see Aunty Cady and little Zach anyway. It's so convenient that everyone we need to visit is in the same place," she joked. "Get well soon, Liam. We'll visit again." Alex put his arm around his wife as they left Liam's room and flashed him a genuine smile before they left.

Liam swung his legs over the side of the bed, planting his feet on the cold floor. "Hello, Vivianne," he greeted. "You'll forgive me if I have a hard time getting up."

She rushed to his side and put a hand on his shoulder. "Oh goodness, no, don't even worry about it."

He gave her a grateful smile and then relaxed his body. "What can I do for you?"

"It's about Lara."

Liam's blood froze in his veins, and he felt the pressure building behind his eyes. "No."

"But-"

"I said no," Liam said, his voice sharp like steel. "I don't want to talk about her. I don't even want to hear her name." Out of respect for Vivianne, he held his tongue, even though he was tempted to tell her what he really thought of her daughter.

"Alpha," she said, straightening her back, as if she were

mustering the courage to defy him. "Don't you remember? Lara saved you. She jumped out of that window to save your life."

Liam's head snapped up in surprise, shock registering on his face. "What?"

"It's true. They probably haven't told you what happened, but you can confirm it with Grant or Alynna or anyone who was there that day. Everyone thought Wesley was dead, but he got up and attacked you. The two of you fell out the window, and Lara went after you."

"Out of a window?"

Vivianne nodded. "And she saved you. At least, she was able to slow both of you down before the fall became fatal."

"Is she-" He stopped himself. No, he didn't care about her anymore.

"Yes." Vivianne gave a weak smile. "Children of True Mates protect their mothers, after all. Though in this case, he or she also protected their father."

Liam's head was spinning, and he was thankful he was already sitting down. "I don't understand."

Vivianne sighed. "This is Lara's story to tell, but I'm afraid both of you are too stubborn, so I'm going to have to take matters into my own hands." She took a deep breath. "Lara believes she's cursed."

"What?"

"Well, actually, maybe she was. I'm not sure. Blessed witches like her have an immense gift, but nature doesn't give gifts so easily. There's always a price to pay." Vivianne hesitated for a moment, then continued. "When she was eighteen, Lara fell in love with a man named Jonathan."

"I don't see the point in telling me this." Visions of Lara happy and smiling in the arms of another man filled his head. A stab of jealously went through him. He pushed it away, unwilling to feel anything for that woman.

"Shush, Alpha," she admonished. "Let me finish, and I promise I'll leave you alone and never bother you again. Then you can decide for yourself what to do."

"Fine," he grumbled.

"Thank you. Now, one day, he told her he loved her. Moments after that, he was struck by a truck as he was crossing the street. He died in front of Lara."

Liam's jaw ticked, but he said nothing.

Vivianne continued. "Lara confessed to me that she'd been dreaming of his death, before it even happened. She said everything in her dream came true. Down to the last detail—from the road where they were standing to the color of the truck. She was hurt and confused, unsure of what was going on. And I had to tell her."

"Tell her what?"

"Other blessed witches had the same experience. All of them fell in love, dreamed of the death of their lovers, and then the dreams came true. And for Lara, it happened again." Vivianne looked up at him, her eyes deep pools of green. "Liam, she's been dreaming of your death. Of you falling."

Liam's heart leaped to his throat. He shook his head. The bad dreams she'd been having. She hadn't wanted to tell him what they were and now he knew why. "No. It can't be."

"She'd fallen in love with you and was afraid that you'd die too, like Jonathan. So she did what she thought was best. To save you, she had to hurt you and make sure you didn't fall in love with her."

His head was spinning, and the bile rising from his stomach burned his throat. "Fuck. No," he cried in anguish. Why didn't Lara say something when she was having those bad dreams? She could have told him.

"She loves you, Liam. She said those things because she thought she was protecting you."

"Godammit!" He pounded his fist onto the bed. "The things I said ... Vivianne, she'll never forgive me."

"It's true, she was hurt by your words," Vivianne said. "But I don't think all is lost. Besides, you have a child on the way."

The baby. His wolf was going crazy at the revelation, growling and scratching at him. Lara loved him. His pup was growing inside her. He looked up at Vivianne. "I want her back."

Vivianne gave him the brightest smile. "Good."

CHAPTER THIRTY-THREE

"Are you okay, baby?" Graham asked his daughter.

"Huh?" Lara said absentmindedly.

"You've been staring out of that window for hours. Who are you waiting for?"

"No one. I'm fine." What was she doing? God, she was a mess. She hadn't even been home for forty-eight hours, and she'd already gone mental.

Graham had arrived in New York not long after her mother had called him. He was happy to make the drive back right away since he hated the city so much. As soon as Lara had seen him, she collapsed in his embrace and bawled her eyes out. Her dad's presence and his bear hugs always made everything better, at least for a little while. She had told him everything, of course. Frankly, she'd been scared to tell her father she was pregnant, afraid he'd be angry and disappointed. What father wanted to hear that anyway? But she should have given her dad more credit. All he did was hug her closer and tighter. And tell her everything was going to be okay. No questions about the father or any other comments. He just packed her up in the car and drove her away. Vivianne had stayed in New York for another night, saying she had some business to attend to, but she was back the very next day.

"I'm going to sit outside," she said, getting up from the couch. Some fresh air would help clear her mind.

She walked out to the back porch and sat down on the wicker couch, staring out into the woods. This was a terrible idea, she realized because this only reminded her of Liam. Actually, being home reminded her of Liam. She thought about going back to New York, but her apartment would undoubtedly bring back memories of the Lycan as well. It's not like she could do anything about it. The child in her belly would tie her to Liam forever. Liam would, of course, follow up on his threat, but what could she do? A child needed a father. Plus, as a Lycan, he or she would definitely need help from Liam. Maybe after some time away from each other, Liam and Lara could at least put the hate and ugliness aside and do what was best for the baby.

The sound of a vehicle pulling up to their driveway pulled her from her thoughts. Her parents hadn't said they were expecting company. She didn't really feel like meeting people right now.

A bark and large paws hitting the ground startled Lara. "What the—Hugo!" she cried as the beast barreled into her. The dog leaped up on the couch and began licking her face. "Down boy! Oh, my!" He settled next to her, taking up most of the couch, his giant block head on her lap. Hugo seemed appeased when Lara began to scratch his head.

"He missed you a lot."

She really shouldn't have been surprised. It's not like a dog could travel across the country on its own. "What are you doing here?"

Liam was standing in the doorway from the kitchen, looking devastatingly handsome in a pair of dark jeans and a blue shirt that clung to his muscular arms and shoulders. She turned away, concentrating on Hugo instead.

"We need to talk."

Lara stood up, and Hugo let out a whine, obviously unhappy at the loss of his new favorite head scratcher. "There's nothing to talk about." She turned away from him, wrapping her arms around herself.

"You jumped off a cliff to save my life. Why?"

She shrugged. "I don't know. It was an impulsive move. I'm not a monster, you know. I wasn't going to let you die if I could save you."

Liam stepped closer to her, close enough that his scent invaded her senses. God, why couldn't he just stay away? When he put a hand on her shoulder, she shrugged it off.

"Just go away, Liam!" she cried. "I don't want to see you. Send your lawyers after me, I don't care. Just leave me alone."

"Never," he said, his voice edgy. "Lara, I'm sorry for what I said. I was wrong to say those things."

The memory of his words still brought pain to her gut. But it was her own fault.

"Lara, I lo-"

"Shut up!" she shouted, whirling around to face him. She gave him a hard shove, but Liam remained immovable. Her eyes grew wide when he saw the expression on her face. "Don't! Don't say those words!"

Liam gently placed his hands on her shoulders, a relieved look on his face. "You do care about me," he said softly. "Otherwise, you wouldn't have tried to stop me from saying I-"

"No!" She slapped her hand over his mouth. Realization hit her. "Wait. You know? About the curse?"

He nodded.

"Who told ... Mother!"

"Yes, darling?" Vivianne's head popped in through the doorway.

Her head swung over to her mother. "You told him about Jonathan!"

"I had to."

"Why?"

"Because you're being stubborn! Both of you!" Vivianne said in an exasperated tone. "And I'm doing what's best for my grandchild." She looked behind her. "Your father is coming out here, by the way."

She gave herself a mental head slap. *Oh, fuck me.*

Vivianne moved aside and let Graham through, then followed behind him. The burly warlock walked up to Liam and sized him up, looking at him from head to toe. The scowl on her father's face told Lara that he knew about Liam.

Without a word, Graham turned around and began to walk back into the house.

"Daddy, where are you going?"

"I'm going to get my shotgun."

"Daddy!"

"It needs cleaning!" he said gruffly as the door slammed behind him.

"He's kidding," Vivianne said, patting Liam on the shoulder. "It doesn't need cleaning; he keeps it pristine. By the way, Alpha, your room is ready and I even bought a bed, a water dish, and some food for Hugo." She patted the dog on the head, then left.

"What's going on here?" Lara asked.

"Your mother invited me to stay."

"What?"

"She asked me to come, and I offered to help around the compound."

Lara's head was spinning. "I don't believe this."

He gave her a cheeky grin. "I told you, you'd never get away from me." He took her hand, and Lara fought the urge to pull it back.

No, she couldn't. Shouldn't. "Liam, I don't know. What if ..." There was no guarantee she still wasn't cursed. If she began dreaming about Liam's death again, then it would be her own damn fault.

"Everything will be okay, Lara. I believe in this." He kissed her hand. "I believe in us and that what we have is more powerful than some curse. And I'm going to stay right next to you until you believe it, too."

Tears burned at her throat. She didn't know what to say. "I ... I have to go." Pulling her hand away from him, she went inside the house.

CHAPTER THIRTY-FOUR

For the third straight day in a row, Lara watched Liam as he worked outside under the heat of the summer sun. He had been working with her father since he arrived, helping him around the compound.

Every day he would get up early to follow her dad, doing chores and making repairs for the other families that lived on the compound, with Lara accompanying them. The other day, he helped fix the fence around Estella Rodriguez's home (much to the delight of the wily old witch, who unashamedly stared at Liam's ass each time he bent down). And yesterday he worked on the broken-down playground in the middle of the compound. There had been fewer children each year, so it was just left in a state of disrepair. In the three years, however, a few babies had been born and would soon need a place to play. Liam and Graham fixed the broken swings and replaced the rusted-out slides while the youngsters played with Hugo. When everything was done, the children looked up at Liam like he was their hero.

Most of the witches and warlocks who saw him walking around the compound gave him curious glances but said nothing. Of course, Lara was pretty sure that by now everyone knew exactly who he was. Witch covens weren't unlike other neighborhoods in suburban America. Gossip pretty much spread like wildfire.

Three days he'd been here. Still, she didn't know what the heck was going on. They would get up, do work around the compound, go home, and then have dinner together. Afterwards, her parents would retire to their bedrooms. So did Lara and Liam but separately in their own rooms. He would bid her goodnight and then disappear into the guest room, with Hugo in tow.

To say that she was confused was an understatement. What was he trying to do? Today, for example, he was helping Graham replace the steps on the back porch. Poor Hugo's paw had fallen through one of the boards as he was running up, which revealed that the boards were rotting. Liam had taken his shirt off while he worked, and sweat soon covered his back. She had felt her mouth go dry, watching the way his muscled back contracted and stretched as he carried the rotted floorboards away.

"Are you ever going to talk to him?"

Lara whipped her head around. Vivianne walked into the kitchen, a basket of herbs in the crook of her arm.

"I do talk to him."

"I don't think 'pass the salt' counts as talking," Vivianne said wryly.

"What do you want me to do, Mother?" she asked, putting her hands up.

Vivianne walked over to her, crossed her arms over her chest, and looked her straight in the eye. "Well, why do you think he's here?"

"Damned if I know." Lara shrugged. "I've been trying to ignore him."

"Yet you go with him whenever he's out and about."

"I'm going with Dad. I want to spend time with my father, but Liam's always following him around. What the heck does he think he's doing?"

"I think he's trying to gain your father's respect," Vivianne said. "Wants to show him that he's worthy of his daughter."

Lara remained silent.

"My, my." Vivianne fanned herself with her hand as she looked out the window. "I think the temperature just went up ten degrees in here."

"Mother!"

"Oh pshaw!" Vivianne's green eyes sparkled, and she waved her fingers at Liam through the window. "I don't know how you waited weeks before getting all over that."

Lara put her face in her hands.

"It reminds me of the first time I saw your father without his shirt on ..."

"Lalalalala," Lara put her fingers in her ears, "I can't hear you."

Vivianne let out a rich laugh. "C'mon, darling, I'm just looking. Can't blame a woman for admiring the goods."

"Kill me now, please!"

"I didn't know I raised such a prude," Vivianne joked.

"It was probably thanks to all those times I walked in on you and Dad," Lara deadpanned.

The older witch gave her a wicked smile. "Did you and Liam make use of the kitchen table while we were away? You know, your father made it the perfect height for—"

"Argh!" Lara put her hands up. "I'm going to see if they need my help. I can't talk to you when you're like this." This was getting out of hand. She was going to put a stop to this here and now.

Vivianne's laugh rang out, the sound traveling to the back porch as Lara opened the door.

Graham turned his head toward her. "What's going on with your mother?"

Lara muttered something under her breath about horny old ladies.

"What was that?" Graham asked.

"Nothing, Daddy." She sighed. "Liam, can I talk to you?"

Liam flashed her a smile. "Can it wait? We're a little busy," he said, waving his hands at the steps. Graham was bent down, lining up the fresh boards.

"It's okay, son," Graham said. "I'll be fine. I need to take a break anyway and see what my wife is up to." He stood and stretched his back. Walking up to the porch, he gave Lara a kiss on the cheek before disappearing into the kitchen.

Liam wiped his brow with his arm. "All right, let's talk." He stood up straight to his full height and looked up at her on the porch.

Lara stared at the wide expanse of his chest like a drooling idiot. When he gave a polite cough, her eyes quickly moved up to his grinning face. "Not like that!"

He crossed his arms over his chest, making the muscles ripple deliciously. "Like what?"

"Argh!" She let out an exasperated shout, grabbed the T-shirt hanging on the railing, and tossed it at his stupid face. "Here. Put this on."

With another cheeky grin, he put the shirt on. Slowly.

Lara gave an inward groan.

"There," he said as his head popped up through the shirt's neck hole. "Better?"

It was the white shirt from the last time he was here chopping wood. When they had first had sex.

"Ugh, it's fine." She waved her hand, trying the remove the image of them in her head.

"Now, what did you want to talk about?"

"Liam, I—" A giggle from the kitchen made her stop short. It was followed by a throaty, masculine laugh. "Uh! Mother!" She shook her head, carefully hopped down from the porch, and grabbed his arm. "Let's go." She stalked into the woods behind her house, with Liam in tow.

As soon as they were far enough away from the house, she turned to him. "Liam, this isn't going to work. You're going to have to leave sooner or later."

"Says who?"

"Oh, for God's sake, you're an Alpha. You have your clan to think about."

"My clan will be fine," Liam said. "And I don't have to be Alpha."

"What?" she asked. "You can't not be Alpha!"

"Sweetheart, I told you." He moved closer to her, taking her hand in his. "I don't care about being Alpha. Not if it means I can't be with you and our child."

"Liam ..." She shook her head and turned away from him. "I can't do this. I can't be selfish."

"Lara, listen to me." He spun her back around to face him. "Have you had any more dreams about me?"

She shook her head. "No, I haven't."

"See? There's no more curse!"

"How can you know that?"

"I can't, but there's one way to know for sure." Before she could say anything, he pulled her to him, locking her arms down with his. "I love you, Lara."

She opened her mouth to protest, but he quickly silenced it with his lips. Lara struggled, wiggling against him, but Liam's arms were like a vise. She sighed against his lips, her body melted against him, and she relaxed. He smiled against her, and his tongue parted her mouth before deepening their kiss.

A warm, comforting feeling spread through her. It wasn't just desire but also a strangely soothing sensation, coming from deep within her and her belly. With a gasp, she pulled away from him, her hands going to her stomach.

Liam grinned down at her, his blue eyes filled with wonder and love.

"Did you feel that too?" she asked.

He nodded. "Was it ..." He looked at her stomach.

"I think so."

His hand hovered over her flat belly. "May I?"

She nodded. He got on one knee in front of her. She then took his hand and put it on her tummy. "There's not much there, I'm afraid," she said with a little laugh.

Liam's eyes widened, and he shook his head. "Oh no, Lara. There's everything in here."

Tears formed in her eyes at his words. "Liam," she gasped. "I love you, too."

His arms wound around her waist, then he put his cheek against her stomach. She ruffled her fingers through his hair and closed her eyes, enjoying the moment.

She felt his lips moving against her, which made her giggle. "What are you doing?" she asked.

Liam looked up at her, his cheek still pressed to her abdomen. "Talking to our baby."

Our baby. The words made her feel warm all over. "And what are you saying?"

"I'm asking her if now is the right time to propose to her mother. I'm already down on one knee, after all."

Lara gasped, as tears spilled over her cheeks. With a deep breath, she spoke again. "A-A-And what did she say?"

"I think she said it's a good time." Liam looked up at her and held his open palm out. A sparkling diamond ring lay flat on his palm. "Lara Chatraine, will you marry me?"

"Liam, yes. I will marry you." She pulled him up to his feet, then he slipped the ring on her finger. "I love you, Liam."

"I love you, too, Lara." He leaned down and kissed her. Suddenly, he pulled back. "Wait. I don't have to change my name, do I?"

She smacked him on the chest before pulling him down for a kiss.

CHAPTER THIRTY-FIVE

Graham and Vivianne greeted the news of their engagement with much happiness and relief.

"I'm very happy for you, son," Graham said as he shook Liam's hand. "For both of you." He looked at his daughter, and for the first time ever, Lara saw a glimmering of tears in his eyes, which he quickly brushed away with a swipe of his hand.

Vivianne, on the other hand, was unabashed about the tears flowing down her cheeks. "Darling ... this is the most wonderful news!" She hugged them both tightly.

Liam and Lara stayed at the compound the rest of the week. They spent their days working around the compound with Graham, playing and running with Hugo, or helping her mother with the herb garden. Liam cooked for them twice, showing off his skills in the kitchen. Nights were spent wrapped around each other, making love and lying in each other's arms, talking about the future.

Finally, they said their goodbyes to Graham and Vivianne for now, packed up Hugo, and drove back to New York City.

Lara wanted to delay having to face the rest of the Lycans, but Liam wanted to tell everyone right away.

"Another True Mate pairing?" Grant said, an astonished look on his face. They had invited everyone to dinner at Muccino's downtown. The restaurant, which was an off-shoot of Frankie's family's original restaurant in New Jersey, was in its opening week. They all sat at the chef's table behind the kitchen, where they could see Dante Muccino and his kitchen crew in action and still have some privacy.

"I'm not surprised," Frankie said, smiling warmly at her husband.

"Pay up, losers!" Alynna said, stretching out her hand. Alex, Nick, Cady, and Jade all fished out bills from their wallets and slapped them on her palm.

Lara looked at the group. "You bet against us?"

"No, silly," Alynna rolled her eyes. "We all knew you guys were sneaking around. But I got the closest date to when you'd both pull your heads out of your asses and actually figure out you were in love."

"I'd have won if I actually had money to bet." Meredith pouted, then stuffed her face with an artichoke parmesan crostini. She closed her eyes and let out a moan. "Oh my God," she turned to Frankie, "Lupa, your brother's single, right? Does he like blondes who love to eat and sport really rockin' ankle jewelry?"

Lara shook her head mentally, still puzzled at how the Lycan somehow got an invitation and permission to leave Fenrir. She looked at Jade and took a guess how.

"So, what's next?" Cady asked. "Are you planning a big wedding? You know who could help you plan—"

Alex, Nick, and Grant collectively groaned.

Lara laughed. "I think we're good, but you'll have to tell Callista thank you if she offers." She had heard all the stories about Grant's very ... *helpful* mother, who apparently was the queen of all Lycan weddings. "Besides, we've talked about it." She looked at Liam, who smiled back at her. "We're not going to have a big wedding. A private ceremony at the justice of the peace, maybe."

"But you'll have a party, right?" Alynna asked.

"Of course," Liam said. "We'll probably have one here in New York after the ceremony and another one in San Francisco."

"Awesome!" Meredith raised her glass. "And you know what that means, right?"

Lara cocked her head. "What?"

"Bachelorette party!" Meredith whooped. "How about Vegas?"

CHAPTER THIRTY-SIX

A kiko greeted the news of Lara and Liam being True Mates with some apprehension, of course. Lara was very anxious over Akiko's chilly behavior toward her at the start, but Liam explained that his mother was raised in a different culture and different time and did not show her emotions to new people so easily. He assured her that Akiko approved of her.

She didn't understand it at first, but Lara got the surprise of her life a few days after they arrived in San Francisco. The clan had gathered at Gracie Manor and Lara was formally introduced to the clan. A few of them, particularly the ones who knew Alfred and Maeve Williams, expressed their anger over the fact that their future Lupa was not Lycan and a witch, to boot. Akiko suddenly silenced their protests. The older Lycan declared that Lara was one of the most qualified people she knew to replace her as Lupa. She praised Lara's kindness, her nurturing heart, and her loyalty to Liam, proven by how she jumped off a cliff to save his life. Akiko said she was proud to call Lara her daughter and Lupa.

Lara was shocked. She didn't even realize Akiko knew about

what had happened during their attack on the mages. She glanced over at Akiko, who was looking defiant as she addressed the clan, telling them that whoever didn't approve of Lara was free to leave. When she stared back at a stunned Lara, her face remained stoic, but her eyes were shining with pride. Liam's face, on the other hand, said, "I told you so."

And so Lara had very little doubts after that and the wedding proceeded as planned. Two weeks after he proposed, Liam and Lara got the wedding they had hoped for, and much more. They were married by a judge in the woods behind the Chatraine house with only Graham, Vivianne, and Akiko attending as guests, plus two witches from the coven to act as witnesses.

After the quick ceremony, they all drove back to New York City for the party. The rest of the coven, the New York Lycans, the San Francisco Lycans, and all their other guests were already waiting for them at The Conservatory at the New York Botanical Gardens. The Victorian-style glass conservatory was decorated with fairy lights, white and pink paper lanterns, cherry blossoms, dahlias, and hydrangeas. The couple walked in hand-in-hand. Lara was dressed in a long, off-the-shoulder white gown with her hair swept to one side and small flowers at the nape of her neck, while Liam wore khaki pants, a gray vest, a white shirt, and a skinny black tie. All the guests were waiting for them at the entrance to the conservatory, cheering them on as they arrived. Even Hugo, wearing a bow tie around his neck, was there, barking and woofing happily.

"I love weddings!" Alynna said as she grabbed a champagne flute from a passing waiter. "Especially the free booze!" Liam had gone to dance with his mother and left his bride in the care of Alynna and Alex.

"Slow down, baby doll," Alex said, taking the champagne

flute from her hand. "Do you remember the last time you were drinking at a wedding?"

"Didn't you start a conga line and make it wind around the Waldorf Astoria lobby?" Lara reminded her.

"Yeah!" Alynna grabbed the glass back from her husband. Then she poked a finger at his chest. "And then what happened afterwards?"

"I got lucky in the janitor's closet," he said with a goofy smile. He grabbed two more champagne flutes from another waiter and handed one to his wife. They clinked glasses, cheered Lara and Liam, then downed the bubbly in one gulp. "Excuse us, Lupa," Alex said with a wink. "We need to get this party started." The couple walked away hand-in-hand, laughing and giggling.

"Is everything okay?" Liam asked as he approached his bride from behind, cupping a warm hand over her belly. "How are my girls?"

Lara laughed. "You really think it's a girl?"

"Or boy." He kissed her cheek. "It doesn't matter really. But seeing as the baby obviously has some magical powers, it's probably a girl, right?"

"Probably," she teased. "Or it might be a Lycan boy."

"Or both?"

"Possibly," Lara thought. "You know, Lycans once had the ability to use magic. Or so we're told."

"Maybe our child will be the first one to find that power again."

Lara shivered, and he pulled her closer to his body. "I know what you're thinking. Our child will definitely change things. But I promise I'll protect you. Both of you." He spun her around to face him. "No one will take you away from me."

"I believe you," she said, getting on her tiptoes and pressing her mouth to his. Liam wrapped his arms around her waist and lifted her up off her feet.

"Woohoo!" A shrill holler made them pull apart and turn toward the source of the sound.

Meredith grinned at the newlyweds, her face mere inches from theirs. "Save it for the honeymoon, newlyweds! We're here to par-tay! Hey, have you guys seen Jade? It's like she disappeared or something!"

"C'mon, Mer, Alynna's starting a conga line." Enzo Morretti, Frankie Anderson's human half-brother, popped up from behind Meredith. With a wave to Liam and Lara, he took the blonde Lycan's hand and pulled her away to join the growing dance line.

Liam groaned. "I didn't know those two knew each other. Or that we even invited Meredith. How did she manage to get out of Fenrir?"

"Well, Alynna's been giving her points for good behavior. She says she's been saving them up to go to the wedding. She's not allowed to drink anymore, though," Lara's face broke into a cryptic smile.

"And Enzo?"

"Well, that's the reason why she's not allowed near alcohol. They met at my bachelorette party and have been getting along like a house on fire since then. Hey!" Liam gave a scowl, and she soothed him, rubbing her palm on his arm. "I promise there were no male strippers, okay?"

"Fine," Liam said. "You're my wife, after all, for now and always." He kissed her again, then pulled away. "But are you ever going to tell me what happened at the bachelorette party?"

"Some other time," Lara said with a laugh. "But for now, we have a conga line to join!" She pulled Liam to the dance floor, laughing as he caught her by the waist and spun her around for one last kiss.

———

Pssst ... turn the page to find out what happened at the bachelorette party!
It's actually a preview of **Book 5: Taming the Beast**

Get it now at select online retailers!

Want to read some **bonus** scenes from this book, featuring Lara and Liam's **dirty, hot, and explicit** adventures? Sign up for my newsletter now! You'll get access to ALL the bonus materials from all my books and THREE free ebooks!

Head to this website to subscribe: http://aliciamontgomeryauthor.com/mailing-list/

I love hearing from readers! If you ever want to tell me what you think, send me a note at alicia@aliciamontgomeryauthor.com

PREVIEW FOR TAMING THE BEAST

BOOK 5 OF THE TRUE MATES SERIES

The Bachelorette Party, one week ago...

"I can't believe you talked me into this," Jade said with a frown. She was not happy. The dress she was wearing was too tight, the thong panties were riding up her behind, and the heels were too high. Oh, why did she let Meredith do this to her?

Meredith rolled her eyes. "You're here. Get over it." She gave Lycan a once over. "And you look hot."

"Meredith! Jade?" Lara said as she came up behind them. "Uhm, wow!"

"I know, right?" Meredith gushed. "You're welcome." The blonde gave an exaggerated bow.

"It's just that...I've been asking you for months to let me give you a makeover!" Lara pouted. "And now I miss it!"

"Well, you were a little busy," Jade retorted. "How is Liam?"

The witch blushed. "You know I had to...spend some time convincing him to let me have this bachelorette party."

"Don't be jealous, Lara," Meredith said. "I had to twist her arm to let me put her in that dress and put some makeup on her. Et voila! My masterpiece."

The Lycan scientist was wearing peach lace bustier dress that pushed up her breasts without being vulgar. While the lace went below her knees, the underskirt stopped about halfway, giving a teasing view of her thighs, while the sky-high heels not only added height to her petite frame but also elongated her legs. She wore minimal makeup, just enough to emphasize her thick brows and pouty lips, while her hair was styled in sexy waves down her back.

Lara looked like she still couldn't believe her eyes. "Jade, you look gorgeous. You've been hiding this all this time?"

The scientist gave her outfit another pained look. "Yeah, well, don't expect me to wear this every day now. I only did it because it was a special occasion."

"How did you convince her, exactly?" Lara asked Meredith.

"I promised her I would stop singing that song that doesn't end if she'd let me give her a makeover," Meredith explained.

"And then how did you get out of Fenrir?"

"Oh Lara, don't you know? They let me out now if I'm good!" Meredith had broken into Fenrir Corporation's offices when she was caught and detained by the New York Lycans. They gave her a choice: be shipped off to the Lycan Siberian prison or stay in New York and serve the clan. As a Lone Wolf, Meredith had no clan to call her own anyway. So, instead of living out the next ten years in the wastelands of Siberia, she decided that servitude to the New York clan was a better option. Currently, she was helping protect Jade, who had been the target of a kidnapping attempt by their enemies.

"But you're still wearing your ankle monitor, right?"

The blonde Lycan stuck a foot out. The ankle monitor was there, but tonight, it was decorated with sparkly Disney Princess-themed stickers. "Yeah, I can't do anything about that. And I can only go out if Jade needs protection and no one else can take her. So, I decided she needed protection on the way to this boutique on 5th Avenue and the makeup store."

"I don't know why I let you do this," Jade grumbled. As she attempted to walk, she nearly stumbled and had to grab onto Meredith. "It's impossible to walk in these things!"

"Oh shush, you're a woman, you'll figure it out."

"Ladies," Frankie Anderson came up to them, dressed in a cute, vintage-style blue dress and matching heels. As she looked Jade over, her mismatched blue-and-green eyes sparkled. "Oh wow, Dr. Cross? You look great!"

"Thank you, Lupa," she replied, using the traditional honorific for the wives of Lycan Alphas. Frankie was married to New York's Alpha, Grant Anderson, but she was also an Alpha in her own right to the New Jersey clan.

"Yes, well, Alynna and I are already at our table," she said warmly. "Let's go."

Frankie led them to a VIP table cordoned off in the corner, where her sister-in-law, Alynna Westbrooke, was already waiting for them.

"There's the beautiful bride!" Alynna waved happily at Lara, and immediately put a tiara on the other woman's head and draped a sash that said "Bachelorette" across one shoulder. "Let's get this party started!"

"I think someone's already started the party," Meredith said, making a drinking motion with her hands.

"Hey! I'm a new mom, and this is my first time out in months!" She took a swig of red wine. "Woohoo!"

"How many have you had?" Lara asked, shaking her head.

"Two!"

"Two glasses?"

"Two bottles!" She grinned. "Lycan metabolism, you know!

I need just that much to get me happy. But I'll burn it off in an hour or two when I have to go back to the ol' ball and chain!"

The rest of women settled down, and a handsome Lycan waiter brought them more drinks (including non-alcoholic ones for Frankie and Lara) and snacks. It was early yet, so Blood Moon wasn't very crowded.

"Here you go, ladies!" Alynna moved over to the other couch and sat between Jade and Meredith. She passed them both shot glasses filled with a clear gold liquid. "I'm afraid with these two knocked up," she motioned to Lara and Frankie, "it's up to us to try and bankrupt Blood Moon tonight. Don't worry, though, I hear the owner's loaded!" The club was a well-known hotspot, at least for Lycans.

Jade gave the glass a delicate sniff. "What is it?"

"Oh my God, this is top shelf tequila!" Meredith exclaimed. "Oh, we're gonna get smashed tonight!"

"Put those metabolisms to good use ladies!" Alynna raised her glass in the air.

"I don't think-"

"Oh, come on, Jade," Meredith placed the glass to the other Lycan's lips. "Live a little."

"This smells vile," Jade wrinkled her nose.

"You've never had tequila before?" Meredith asked incredulously.

The brunette shook her head.

"Oh, you're in for a treat." She gave Alynna a wink. "Ok, here's what you do. First, put some salt on the back of your hand, grab one of those lime wedges..."

Jade's nose wrinkled as she followed Meredith's instructions.

"...And then you lick, shoot, and suck!" Meredith demonstrated with a flair, spitting the lime wedge over the couch.

"Eww!" Lara gagged.

"C'mon, you try, Jade!" Meredith urged her on and refilled her own shot glass. "Let's do it all together now." She nodded at Alynna. "Ok now...lick...shoot...suck!"

Jade did as she was told and winced as the liquid burned a path down her throat. She nearly threw up, but suddenly, the warmth pooling in her belly felt good. The sourness of the lime was a good way to end the shot, too.

"All right!" Meredith cheered her on. "How was that?"

"That was actually...pleasant," Jade remarked.

"Let's do another one!" Alynna raised the bottle.

They did two more shots, and Jade simply shook her head when Alynna tried to pour her another one. "I think...I'm gonna pace myself." The warm, pleasant feeling in her stomach felt nice, but something told her she should probably slow down. Surely, people didn't do more than three shots of tequila in a row, right?

"Well, hello, ladies." A tall, handsome man with broad shoulders and chocolate brown eyes approached their table. "Have room for one more?"

"Get lost, loser," Meredith snapped. "This is a private party."

"Aww," the man looked at Frankie. "I don't get points for being related to the owner's wife?"

"She's right, Enzo," Frankie smirked. "This is a private party. And you are a loser."

Enzo put his hands over his heart. "Ouch, such words from my own sister!"

"Wait!" Meredith exclaimed. "You're her brother? But you're a..."

"Handsome young man?" Enzo finished. "Such charming and smooth guy?"

"I was gonna say jackass," Meredith retorted. "And human."

"I like her," Enzo said to Frankie, who shook her head and laughed.

"Meredith, this is my half-brother, Enzo Moretti," Frankie introduced. "Don't worry about being nice to him. I can confirm, he *is* a jackass."

"Nice to meet you, Meredith," Enzo flashed her his best smile.

She gave him a raised brow. "Same here."

Enzo turned his attention to the rest of the party. "Hey, Alynna, Lara...who's this...Dr. Cross!" Another smile spread across his face. "Is that you? You clean up nice!"

The look he gave her made Jade blush from head to toe, and Meredith gave him a slap on the head.

"Ow! Are we in that stage of our relationship already?' Enzo said, rubbing his head. "'Cuz I was hoping you'd take me out to dinner first before we started the spanking."

"Enzo, what are you doing here?" Frankie asked.

"It's Tuesday night, sis, my night off, so thought I'd check out this place," he said. "I'm also meeting up with some buddies, so I'll see you ladies later." With a smile and a wink, he walked off towards the bar.

"I think it's time we're headed out too," Frankie declared as she stood up.

"Awww, Frankie," Alynna protested as she took a shot of tequila. "Noooo...."

"C'mon, now." Her sister-in-law took her by the arm. "We've got husbands and you have a kid waiting for you at home. No more drinking. I don't want to bring you home stinking like a sailor!"

"Fine," she pouted. "Enjoy the rest of the night ladies. Just order whatever you want, on us!" She grabbed her purse and followed Frankie towards the exit. "And don't do anything I wouldn't do!" With a final wave, both women left the club.

"Now that our chaperones are gone," Meredith began. "Let's talk about where we're going next. I know this great strip club-"

"No strippers!" Lara protested.

"Why not?" Meredith asked. "Aren't pregnant women supposed to be horny all the time? I bet some hot, gyrating male bodies and six-pack abs are what your hormones need right now! Don't you have urges?"

"I don't need strippers," Lara said smugly. "I get my urges satisfied plenty. Four times before I came here."

Meredith groaned. "Fuck me. No, I mean it," she put her hands on her face. "It's been way too long since I've had sex." She turned to Jade. "How about you, Jade? When was the last time you..." She looked meaningfully at Jade's crotch. "Got your grass mowed?"

"Meredith," Lara warned.

"What?" The blonde Lycan looked at her, then turned back to Jade. "C'mon, Jade, spill!" She took another shot of tequila.

Jade blushed a bright red. "That's none of your business!"

"Don't evade my question!" Meredith slurred. "Has it been that long? I promise not to laugh. Your dry spell can't possibly be longer than mine."

"I don't think so," Jade said, looking at her shoes.

"Try me, Jade."

"Well, uhm, twenty-four years."

"That's not—HOLY CRAP!" Meredith's eyes widened. "You're a vir-"

Jade slapped a hand over the other woman's mouth. "Shush!"

Meredith looked from Jade to Lara, who also seemed shocked at the revelation.

"Jade," Lara began. "I didn't know. I mean, you never talked about it, but..."

It seemed impossible, but Jade turned even redder. "I'm just...it's not...you see..." She dropped her hands to her lap. "I'm not a weirdo who's saving herself for marriage or anything," she said defensively. "I've just...never had a chance! And I gave it the good ol' college try."

"Wait, weren't you like, fifteen when you went to college?" Lara asked.

"Fourteen, and it was an academy for gifted youngsters," she corrected. "And I let Jeremy Goldsmith get to second base...er, maybe one point five base? What's under the shirt, over the bra?"

Meredith rolled her eyes and Lara clamped her hand over the other woman's mouth so she wouldn't hurt Jade's feelings.

Jade sighed. "Look, it's not like I want to stay a virgin. I've put some thought into it and I'm ready. I even started birth control, just in case. I just need to...find the right person."

"What have you been doing?" Meredith asked. "Tinder? Online dating? Going to bars?"

The scientist looked at her with wide eyes and shrugged.

"Oh my God! Nothing? How are you supposed to meet guys?"

"I haven't figured that part out yet," Jade retorted.

"What are you looking for in a boyfriend, then?" Lara asked.

"Other than a penis, I haven't really thought about it yet."

Jade's bluntness sent both Lara and Meredith sputtering their drinks.

"Holy crap! Jade, you whore!" Meredith said as she cleaned up the tequila she spit out all over the table. "I knew you had it in you!"

"Jade, honey." Lara put her hand on top of the other woman's. "You can't mean that! I mean, you don't want to just... lose it to some random guy, do you?"

"I've decided that I'm just not cut out for a boyfriend or

relationships," Jade declared. "I'm too busy with my work. I don't want distractions."

"Then why did you say you're ready?" Lara inquired.

"I just want to give sex a try, and get it over with and see what the fuss is all about. Like an experiment."

Meredith looked at Jade with a raised brow. "Well, that escalated quickly."

"C'mon now, Jade," Lara said. "Is that really what you want?"

"Why would I want a boyfriend anyway?" Jade said in an exasperated voice. "Emotions and feelings are way too messy. I don't like it. I prefer real things, like facts and hard evidence."

"You said hard," Meredith snorted.

Jade shot her a warning look and continued. "Tell me, how am I supposed to act when I don't know what to expect?"

"Honey, that's not what life and love are about. It's not science."

"Have another shot, Jade," Meredith handed her a glass. "Maybe you'll start making more sense."

Jade threw back the golden liquid. "Besides, you never know who you'll meet on these dates! I mean, what if we meet for dinner and he chews with his mouth open or breathes too loudly? Or what if he's the type of person who licks the cream off the cookie, then puts it back in the package?"

"You're right Jade." Lara rolled her eyes. "Anyone who does has got to be a monster."

"I'm being serious!"

"What do you care, though?" Meredith pushed another shot at her. "As long as he licks your cream?"

Jade took the shot glass, contemplating the amber liquid. "I want to know what I'm getting into before I get into it! Is that too much to ask?" She knocked the shot back. The burning was actually starting to feel good now. "Argh. Never mind, I don't want to talk about this anymore."

"Aww Jade, I'm sorry for making fun of you." Meredith rubbed the other Lycan's arm. "Maybe we can help you find someone to pop your cherry! Let's start with the guys you know."

Jade sighed, grabbed the bottle from Meredith, and then poured herself another shot. How many was that now? Her thoughts were getting fuzzy.

"No one?" Meredith asked incredulously. Her eyes drifted over to Enzo Moretti, who was at the bar, talking with Sean the bartender and a bunch of other guys. "There's one! Enzo Moretti."

"Ew, no," Jade took the shot. "He's a man whore. Who knows what he's carrying."

"Jade, you're a Lycan, you can't get STDs," Meredith pointed out.

"Jade likes his twin more!" Lara giggled.

"I do not!" Jade protested loudly.

"He has a twin?" Meredith's eyes grew wider.

"Yup," Lara said, popping the p. "He's the total opposite of Enzo, though. Smart. Likes to read. Works with computers."

"Oh, so he's a male version of you!" Meredith said to Jade. "Boring!"

"What?" Jade asked. "He's not boring!"

"Yes, he is. You were yawning while you two were dancing at the Alpha's wedding," Lara pointed out.

"Oh, hell no," Meredith shook her head. "You want someone who's exciting. And experienced."

"What about Gabriel from Marketing?" Lara suggested. "He's cute and French, plus he's been flirting with you in the cafeteria for weeks!"

"Ooh, sounds promising!"

"We both work here and I don't want it to get awkward," Jade countered. "Besides, I like the lemon curd muffins at the cafeteria. I'd have to stop going there if things went south with him."

Meredith shook her head. "Really? Lemon curd muffins are more important than your lady muffin?"

"I'll buy you some next time, and then tell me what you think is more important." She pouted. "I should probably face facts here. Who would want to have sex with me?"

"Jade!" Lara admonished.

"Oh shut up, biatch," Meredith said.

"No, you shut up," she said. "That's easy for you guys to say." She motioned to Meredith. "Look. At. You. You're tall, blonde, and gorgeous, plus you've got legs 'till Connecticut! " Then she shot a look at Lara. "And don't you even start with me! You're marrying that sex-on-on-a-stick Alpha who gets all growly and protective whenever he's around you."

Meredith sighed. "You are so completely fuckable, Jade, trust me. You'll find someone. Let's keep going down your list."

"What list?" Enzo said as he popped up behind Meredith.

"Jesus Christ on a cracker! Are you sure you're not Lycan?" Meredith exclaimed. "No one gets the drop on me!"

He flashed her a smile and then a wink. "Pretty sure, babe. But I heard I'm built like one where it counts."

Jade giggled.

"Hey, pretty doctor." Enzo slid into the booth next to her. "How are you? You look real nice."

"Where's Matt?" she asked.

"Ouch. Really? You want hanger steak when you can have filet mignon?"

"That doesn't make sense," Jade slurred. "You're twins. You have exactly the same DNA. Don't you know that monozygotic twins develop from the same fertilized egg and—"

"Have another one, Jade," Meredith shoved a shot glass at her.

"Whoah, there," Enzo frowned at Jade, his voice turning serious. "Jade, are you ok? What's wrong? This doesn't seem like you."

Meredith opened her mouth, but Jade shot her a warning look. "I'm fiiiiiiinnnne, Enzo, really I am." She drank the shot. "I promise, this is my last shot of tequila!" She shook her head. "Wow, I feel...great!"

"Sounds like the tequila talking," Meredith stage-whispered to Lara.

Jade sighed. "I just wanna have some fun!"

Enzo took the shot glass away from her. "If you want to have real fun, Jade, you don't need alcohol." He stood up and took her hand. "I'll show you how."

————

Sebastian Creed slunk back into the booth, taking a slow sip of his bourbon. As the gorgeous waitress stopped by for the umpteenth time, he waved her away before she could ask him if he wanted anything again.

Oh, he knew what exactly what she was offering, and part of him was tempted. The young, blonde waitress was leggy, tall, and had a mouth that looked like she could suck the chrome off a bumper. He could probably have her quitting her shift early for an evening romp with him at the hotel across the street. But, the other part of him was just not cooperating. Not anymore. Not since her.

He narrowed his eyes, looking around him. Blood Moon. Not the strangest name for a club, but still, not the type of place she would frequent. And yes, he knew her habits. Where she went to get her coffee, the supermarket where she shopped, even the Chinese takeout place she stopped at on Wednesdays. Once, he had already been waiting inside the small, greasy little takeout place, standing in the corner, his hoodie covering his head. She entered, gave her name the old man who worked the cash register, and got her bag of food before walking out without a care in the world. All the while, he had been standing there, waiting for a glimpse of her pretty little face and a whiff of her perfume that reminded him of cherries and vanilla. She never even left the 10-mile radius from her apartment to her workplace.

Jade Cross. Dr. Jade Cross, as he'd learned. Dr. Cross worked in the R and D department at one of Fenrir's food subsidiaries. That was about as far as his soft background check on her went. Her records had a big gap, but he realized that was probably because she had moved to England when she was twelve years old. She came back to America after she finished her two PhDs at the age of twenty, and then went to work for Fenrir right away. Still, he couldn't imagine why she was kidnapped and kept in such a way. The memory of her chained down still made his blood boil. He wanted her safe, and he couldn't feel at ease knowing that anything could happen to her. Yeah, that was it. That's why he kept following her around.

Fucking hell, what's wrong with me? His hand gripped the glass so tight, he thought it would break. This wasn't him. Never in his life had he actually stalked a woman. He felt like a fucking creeper. Yes, it definitely wasn't him doing this. It was the—

"Are you sure I can't get you anything else?" Tall, blonde, and leggy asked as she stopped at his booth again. She leaned down so far he could see the edge of a nipple over her low-cut blouse.

"I have all I need here." He gestured to the bottle of bourbon. "But," he said as he slipped two, one-hundred dollar bills into her palm. "That's for you. Now, come back here when I call for the bill, and not earlier than that, OK? There'll be more where that came from."

The waitress' eyes grew wide at the generous tip. "Uhm, yes...sure sir, whatever you say!" She hopped away, a giddy look on her face.

Sebastian took another drink. *Where the heck was she?* Just a second ago, she was sitting in the booth with her girlfriends. Now, the booth was empty, except for one of the women, whom he recognized from the night of the rescue. The redhead was not what he'd expect from a member of Fenrir's security team, but he knew better than to judge a book by its cover.

His fingers curled tight into his palms. Just before she disappeared, he saw that young, arrogant prick slide into the booth next to her, putting his arm over the back of the booth. Imagining that kid's hands all over Jade was driving him insane, especially since Sebastian had yet to touch her since that night.

Christ Almighty, he had gone crazy. Crazy for some chick. And they hadn't even spoken to each other.

He pushed the glass away from him, his keen eyes sweeping over the crowd, looking for her. A few minutes passed and he still couldn't find her, and *something* in him was itching. Scratching.

Calm down. She didn't leave yet.

"How do you know?" he muttered under his breath. Really? He was talking to it now? He shook his head.

A loud whoop caught his attention and he saw the tall, blonde one - another one of Fenrir's security team, though he could tell that this one actually had some combat training - on top of the bar. She reached down and pulled something up.

Jade.

Sebastian recognized the slinky peach dress, watching with envy at the way it touched her body. Jade usually dressed conservatively, always in long-sleeved shirts and pants or long skirts. Tonight, though, when she walked into Blood Moon, he almost didn't recognize her. Gone were the glasses that were usually perched on her tiny, pert nose. She didn't really need any makeup on her perfect, peaches-and-cream skin, but she wore just enough to enhance her already gorgeous features. Her long hair hung around her shoulders in waves, covering her back. He wondered what it would be like to thrust his fingers through the soft locks and wrap it around her hands while he—

Oh fuck, now she was dancing on top of the bar. He saw Grant's sister order a bottle of tequila, along with the wine she had already drunk. They were probably celebrating, a bachelorette party, based on the tiara and sash on the redhead. As Jade danced to the beat of the music, his eyes trailed up from her delicate ankles, up slim legs, over the delectable swell of her hips that nipped into a tiny waist, and to the curves of her breasts. Her soft tits weren't overly large, just right, and he imagined his hands could cover them entirely. Fucking hell, his dick was so hard, his zipper was practically imprinting on it. Despite his best efforts, he couldn't turn away, and his gaze continued up the path to her neck and to her face.

That goddamn pretty face that got him into this mess in the first place. She was even more beautiful than in that picture Liam Henney had shown him. And when he saw her lying on the dirty floor of that warehouse, rage burned through him and he wanted to kill something. Jade had looked so fragile and beautiful, despite the healing bruise on her jaw.

Finally, the song ended, and Jade hopped off the bar with her friend. The strobe lights in the dim room blinded him for a moment, and he lost her again. Tamping down the urge to look for her, he poured himself some more bourbon, watching as the golden brown liquid spill out of the bottle and into his glass.

Maybe he should call the waitress over. She was just his

type, not that he had one, exactly. If he did, it certainly wasn't brainy little geniuses with juicy, blowjob lips. It had been weeks since he had his dick stroked, and the waitress would be a much easier catch than the women at Luxe. She'd appreciate the attention from a man like him, and she probably wouldn't be too clingy. But the thought of sleeping with any other women left a bad taste in his mouth.

The mental clock in his head ticked the minutes away. His head shot up and he scanned the room again. Jade wasn't anywhere in the room and it had been too long since he saw her last. Looking towards their table, he saw the redhead, the blonde, and that cocky kid, but not Jade. The redhead stood up, waving her hands and looking around them.

A bad feeling in his gut hit him instantly. Jade was gone, he could feel it. He shot to his feet, slapped a couple of bills on the table, and quickly slid out of the booth. He remained calm, years of training teaching him that in emergency situations, he had to keep his head on straight or risk losing it. His heartbeat slowed, and his breathing evened. *Think.*

Sebastian wasn't sure where it was leading him, but he followed that feeling in his gut. He slipped towards the back exit, which led to the dimly-lit alleyway behind Blood Moon. Opening the door slowly, he sharpened his ears, listening for any strange sounds as he quietly slipped out.

"You're so beautiful, baby," a voice said. "And so sexy."

There was a soft groan. "No, don't...I'm not feeling well... can we go back to my friends, please?"

He had never heard her voice, but something told him that was her.

"C'mon, baby, don't be like that," the male voice replied. "Just one kiss..."

White hot fury filled his veins and Sebastian stalked

towards where the voices were coming from. His vision sharpened as he approached them.

The man had one hand braced against the wall, his body leaning forward. He was blocking Sebastian's view, but he didn't need to see her to know she was there. The scent of her perfume was unmistakeable.

"What are you doing?" he asked, trying to keep his voice even.

"Nothing that concerns you, buddy," the man said, turning his head to face him, the features on his face obscured by shadows. "The lady and me were just looking for some privacy. Move along, now."

"Are you sure she wants to be alone with you, *buddy*?" He shot back. "I don't think she's sober enough to be making decisions like that."

The other man turned around, leaving Jade behind him. He swayed slightly as he stretched up to full height, though he was still at least half a foot shorter than Sebastian's 6′5′ frame. "Look," the man said. "Why don't you just be a bro, and leave us alone." He fished his wallet clumsily from his pocket, opening it to take out some bills. "Now, how much will it take to-"

"I suggest you choose your next words carefully," Sebastian warned, crossing his arms over his chest.

"Aw, c'mon—"

"Hey! What's going on here!" a voice from behind shouted.

"Jade!" a female voice cried out, followed by the clacking of heels across the concrete.

While he was distracted by the newcomers, Sebastian took the man's wallet out of his hand. Of course, the man was so drunk and probably high, he could hardly protest.

"Let me repeat my question. What the fuck is going on here?" It was the cocky bastard that was cozying up to Jade earlier. The young man was almost as tall as him, but built on the slim side. Deep brown eyes narrowed at Sebastian. "Who are you?"

"The name's Sebastian Creed," he said, then took out a plastic card from the other man's wallet. "And this is...Mr. David Ronson. 235 West 75th Street, Apartment 4B." He gave the other man a feral smile. "Mr. Ronson was taking your friend out for some fresh air and I think he got a little carried away."

David's face paled and he slunk back. "Hey, it was all a bit of fun. And she wanted it—"

"Remember what I told you about choosing your words carefully, David?"

"Y-y-yes," he choked out. "I mean...shit...fuck this shit! She's not worth the trouble anyway," David shook his head, and looked over toward's Jade's direction.

"Don't look at her," Sebastian said, his voice scarily even. "Don't think about her, don't even dream about her. Got that?" Sebastian flashed him an angry look.

"Jesus!" David jumped back, his face twisting in fear. "What's wrong with your...never mind! I knew that new stuff I got from my dealer was shit! It's making me see things!" He rubbed at his eyes and blinked several times.

"Go," Sebastian commanded. "And never show your face here again."

David backed away slowly, and then turned around, picking up his pace as he disappeared down the alley.

Sebastian watched him leave, calmed himself, and then turned around. The redhead and the young man were helping Jade up, as she had slunk down to the ground. Her eyes were half closed, and she was tripping over the ridiculously high heels.

"I'm fine," she muttered. "Just fine." She blinked several times.

"Jade, you're not fine!" The redhead shook her head, pulling at her friend's arms. "If it wasn't for..." She swung her gaze over to Sebastian. Green eyes widened in recognition. "Mr. Creed! What are you doing here?"

"I, uh," he cleared his throat. "I was inside the club and I saw your friend go outside with that man," he quickly explained.

"You guys know this man, Lara?" the tall guy said.

"Yeah, he's...uh..." Lara stammered.

"I'm a contractor with Fenrir," Sebastian said. "I've worked alongside Miss..."

"Chatraine," the redhead said. "Lara Chatraine."

"Yes, sorry, we didn't have time for an introduction that night."

"Yes, we are all quite busy with work," Lara said.

"I'm Enzo. Enzo Moretti," the younger man held out his hand. "Thanks, man. If you hadn't thought to come out here, who knows what would have happened."

"She and that guy were dancing and then they just disappeared," Lara explained as she wrapped one of Jade's arms over shoulders. "Sorry, she's never been drunk."

"I'm not drunk!" Jade slurred, her head popping up. She blinked a few times at Sebastian. "Hey..." Luminous light green eyes peered at him. "Who are you?" she asked, disentangling herself from Lara. Jade slowly lumbered towards him. "Do I know you?"

Her voice was sexy and low, with a slight English accent that he found irresistible. It sent blood straight to his cock, and Sebastian was glad the alley was dim. "We haven't been formally introduced yet, darlin'," he drawled.

"Too bad. Because you are...hot," she said, poking her finger at his chest. "Like, ridiculously hot. And you make me feel all tingly. And you smell good, too. Say," she said, tracing her fingers along his left forearm. "How far do those tattoos go?"

Her touch sent tingles over his skin. He didn't think his dick could possibly get harder, but he was proven wrong.

"Uhm, Jade," Lara warned.

"And you are hot, too!" She turned to Enzo, who was standing behind her.

Enzo gave an amused smile. "Oh yeah?"

Sebastian's eyes narrowed at the younger man, his fists tightening.

"And you're always flirting with me," Jade giggled. "You do it on purpose, to make me blush. But, I think your twin brother is hotter if that makes sense. But you," she swung back to Sebastian. "You are one sexy son of a biscuit and I want to--"

"Jade!" Lara grabbed her friend and slapped a palm over her mouth. "I think it's time you went home. Before you say anything you'll regret in the morning."

"I'll take her home," Sebastian offered.

"Are you crazy? I'm not letting my friend go home with a stranger!"

"I meant I would take her to her apartment, of course," Sebastian said. "And I'm hardly stranger."

"But you don't know where she lives."

Sebastian bit his tongue before he could answer, *Yes, I do.*

"And you won't know how to take care of her, either." Lara let out a long sigh. "I'm going to call my fiancé and have him pick us up. We'll stay with her tonight. Enzo, take care of her for a minute. And where is Meredith? If we lost her, Grant will have—" She stopped short as her eyes flickered towards Sebastian. "Uhm, I'm gonna make that call now," she said, taking her phone out of her purse and turning around as she spoke softly into the receiver.

"C'mon, Jade," Enzo said, putting an arm around the petite woman, and guiding her towards the door that led back into Blood Moon.

"Enzooooo..." she blinked at him and then giggled. "Filet mignon. Your DNA is the same as filet mignon," she hiccuped.

Enzo rolled his eyes. "No more tequila for you, young lady."

"But it's sooooo good. That's why I finished the bottle!"

"She finished the whole bottle?" Sebastian roared at the other man. "How is she not dead?"

"Uhm, good genetics?" Enzo offered. "C'mon, Jade, let's go back inside and find Meredith. Maybe get you some water."

Sebastian frowned as he watched the other man take Jade away. Enzo was way too close to her, and it sent an unfamiliar, tight feeling into his chest, like a fist squeezing around his heart.

"Mr. Creed," Lara caught his attention. "Thank you again for your help."

"Nothing to it, I was just at the right place, at the right time."

"Yes, lucky us, then," she narrowed her eyes at him. "Well, I guess I'll see you around." She turned to walk away.

"Will she be ok?"

Lara gave a small laugh. "She'll sleep it off. My fiancé's on the way, and I'll stay with her tonight so she's not alone,"

"She's got good friends," Sebastian remarked. "Especially considering what happened to her."

"Indeed," Lara shrugged and walked away. He detected a hint of hesitation in her voice. Or was she hiding something else?

"Wait," he called and Lara stopped in her tracks. "I know something's going on here." There was the gut feeling again, and he was listening to it this time.

A gust of wind blew through the alley, ruffling Lara's hair. "I don't know what you're talking about."

"Since this began...all of this...it's been fishy. And I'm going to get to the bottom of it. I always find the truth."

Lara huffed and turned around. "Really, now, Mr. Creed?"

She crossed her arms over her chest. "Tell me, do you like your life now? The way it is? The reality you live in?"

He shrugged.

"Because, if you do and you don't want things to change, I'm warning you now: Stay away from Jade. Stop trying to look what's beneath the surface." There was a chill in her voice and another gust of wind blew his way. "If you knew the truth, then your world will never be the same."

Taming the Beast is OUT NOW
Get it at select online retailers!

Connect with Alicia Montgomery:
Official Website
Facebook
Twitter
Email